Talk about the weather

The Home's governing council was not elected by popular vote, but appointed by computers programmed to seek
out those who had the right combination of leadership, intelligence, and ability. It did not search only the databases
of those who wanted the jobs, but those of everyone, so
that the best and the brightest could be appointed to the
council for long terms. Michael 177 had been the Mayor
for more than a decade.

"First item," he said, "is the outbreak of juvenile vandalism. Incidents have increased in the last month."

"It's spring," said Jane 158. She was a dour woman,
which meant that something had gone wrong in the
birthing process.

"Nonsense," said Michael 177. "That is meaningless on
The Home. We have no regular seasons, there is no alteration in the light levels from one season to the next, the
magnetic field is not changed, and our growing cycles
have been established to reflect a continual harvest, not the
growing seasons controlled by weather."

"Our biology is not that far removed from that of our
brothers and sisters on Earth," said Jane 158.

"We have, over the course of the flight of *The Home,*
changed that biology so that when we arrive at The New
Home, we will be better suited for that planet. I say again,
nonsense. Simple solution," said Michael 177. "Test the
food and make sure that chemical levels are appropriate.
We might want to add something for the gym classes . . ."

"Bodes well for t

"Fans of first-end   ldle's
book . . . and will eagerly await the next book in the
series."—*Midwest Book Review*

THE EXPLORATION CHRONICLES:
BOOK TWO

Ace titles by Kevin D. Randle

SIGNALS
STARSHIP

THE EXPLORATION CHRONICLES

STARSHIP

KEVIN D. RANDLE

ACE BOOKS, NEW YORK

This is a work of fiction. Names, characters, places, and incidents either are the product of the author's imagination or are used fictitiously, and any resemblance to actual persons, living or dead, business establishments, events, or locales is entirely coincidental.

THE EXPLORATON CHRONICLES: STARSHIP

An Ace Book / published by arrangement with
the author

PRINTING HISTORY
Ace mass-market edition / January 2004

Copyright © 2004 by Kevin D. Randle.
Cover art by Danilo Ducak.
Cover design by Judith Murello.
Interior text design by Julie Rogers.

For information address: The Berkley Publishing Group,
a division of Penguin Group (USA) Inc.,
375 Hudson Street, New York, New York 10014.

ISBN: 0-441-01128-4

ACE®
Ace Books are published by The Berkley Publishing Group,
a division of Penguin Group (USA), Inc.,
375 Hudson Street, New York, New York 10014.
ACE and the "A" design
are trademarks belonging to Penguin Group (USA) Inc.

PRINTED IN THE UNITED STATES OF AMERICA

10 9 8 7 6 5 4 3 2 1

PROLOGUE

SHIP'S YEAR ONE

LIEUTENANT COLONEL THOMAS HACKETT, A fairly young man who had already spent two years in deep space, had been on the team that had turned the alien ship, and now lived on Mars, was not unhappy with his new assignment. After those years in space, with little or no gravity, with eternal ship lighting that could become annoying but was not so bright that it was overwhelming, Hackett was comfortable on Mars. It felt more like home than did the standard one-gee environment of a sun-bright New Mexico.

Now he sat at an oversize desk that held two computer inputs, both voice and key, a stack of disks that contained all the information of a standard, Earth-based library, and three monitors, including the one that hung on the wall and was called, for obvious reasons, a flat-screen. Opposite him, on a large, plastic wall made of the same building material that had been used all over Mars, was an exploded view of Starship *Alpha*. He didn't like the name, but no one had ever suggested anything else that covered the point.

Enterprise, which was suggested periodically by the fans of an old Earth-created television series, just didn't sound right to him. Yes, there was a tradition to go with it, including a history that embraced the old United States Navy, but humanity's first steps into the galaxy should be on board a ship with a dramatic name. Something that told the story, as Starship *Alpha* did, without a tradition that found its roots in television fantasy.

Hackett had volunteered for the mission, to a star system that was only twenty or so light-years away, but his request had been denied. He was needed on Mars, as the commander, or liaison officer, or the CEO of the operation. He was too important to this first mission to be allowed to fly away on it. General George Greenstein had promised to let him go, later, on one of the follow-up missions. Hackett had to be content with that.

Of course, the mission to that star, so close when speaking galatically, was quite far when they had yet to figure out how to travel faster than light. Yes, the aliens could do it, but they had not shared the technology with the inhabitants of Earth. To take all of humanity's eggs from the single basket of Earth, the generation ships had been designed. Traveling at a fraction of light-speed, they would take, literally, generations to reach their destination. Those who boarded the ship in orbit above Mars would not live to see the destination. Their grandchildren would not live to see the destination. In fact, probability suggested that there would be a catastrophic failure at some point, and no one on the ship would be alive when they reached the destination.

Sarah Bakker, the young astronomer who had discovered the signal that led to the discovery of the alien ship, tapped at Hackett's door, then stuck her head in. Space travel hadn't disagreed with her any more than it had with Hackett, and, like him, she enjoyed living on Mars. That she was in charge of the scientific end of the Galaxy Exploration Team that was launching the mission didn't hurt.

"They're about to light the fire," she said.

Hackett chuckled and shook his head. Light the fire was another throwback to old Earth traditions, when the rockets had been mostly of a chemical nature and some of the earliest experiments involved a man with a match.

"You going to watch it here or in the lounge?"

"Who all is in the lounge?"

Bakker shrugged. "Some of the technicians, two or three scientists, but not Russell. I think he went in search of a drink."

"Good for him."

"So you going down there?"

Hackett stood up, and said, "Why not? Oh, did they ever decide on a name?"

"Official or unofficial?" asked Bakker.

"Unofficial, of course. If they have an unofficial name, that's going to end up as the one they use."

"They're calling it *The Home* because that's what it's going to be for the rest of their lives."

"I sometimes can't get my mind around that concept. Locking yourself in a spaceship for the rest of your life. It's almost as bad as being in jail."

Bakker looked at him curiously. "I thought you wanted to go on this mission?"

"I did. I do. But I'm just saying that it's permanent confinement with no chance to change your mind."

"Well, I guess you could for a couple of years after launch. I mean, they do have shuttles, and they certainly could bring someone back to Mars if he or she decided to drop out. Besides, the thing is nearly twenty miles long and what—five—wide. It's not like you'd be locked in an eight-by-ten cell."

"With all the amenities of home," added Hackett.

They left his office, a room that was larger than eight-by-ten, walked along a brightly lighted corridor until they reached the lounge, a room fifty feet long and thirty wide. Nearly all of one wall was covered with a flat-screen. The picture on it was split, for the moment, into four areas showing the flight deck of *The Home,* the interior of the ship, where several hundred people sat watching the ceremonies just as people around the Solar System watched, a view from what had been designated as the leading end of the ship, and, finally, a view taken from a satellite that showed all of the ship as it continued in its orbit of Mars.

As they entered, one of the technicians looked at them, and said, "They're about to fire the engines to break orbit. Ten minutes, maybe less."

Hackett looked at the long table pushed against one wall. It held all kinds of food, from fruits and vegetables that had been grown in the Martian soil to beef raised on Mars, which had come from Earth as little more than frozen cells. There were breads and rolls and even chocolate, which was so expensive that only government agencies could afford it.

Opposite the food was a huge window that looked out on the reddish Martian landscape. In the distance was another habitat dome that rose nearly one hundred feet high. It was quite broad across the base, to resist the winds that sometimes blew with hurricane force.

Hackett grabbed a roll and bit into it without bothering to butter it or smear it with grape jelly. He leaned back against the rear wall and watched as the ship began its generations-long journey.

The whole production was anticlimactic. The rocket burn was visible, but there was no rapid acceleration as there was when a chemical rocket lifted from the ground. There were no impressive displays of billowing smoke, no bursts of fire that lighted the sky. Just a hint of brightness at what was considered the rear of the ship but no feeling of acceleration. The ship didn't suddenly become smaller as it gained altitude or distance. There was no noticeable change in attitude.

After several minutes the view on one of the screens changed slightly, but only because the orbital dynamics had changed the perspective.

But none of that mattered. The Mayor of the city that

had been constructed on the ship moved until he was centered on the crowd. He stood there, a tall, reed-thin man with jet-black hair and a slightly Asian cast to his face. He leaned forward, toward the microphone that had been installed, not because it was needed but because tradition demanded it.

He said, with only a slight hint of irony in his voice, "We begin our journey."

Hackett grunted and leaned close to Bakker. "That's it. That's the momentous speech. A historic event has just taken place, and the best this guy can do is, 'The journey begins.'?"

Bakker smiled, "Well, it's not as if they're going to be out of touch any time soon. We'll be able to talk to them for years to come."

Hackett finished his roll, grabbed a small bar of chocolate, and said, "I'm going back to my office."

"You want some company?" asked Bakker.

"Sure. Let the technicians have at the food and take the afternoon off. Our mission is completed. We got the first ship off without a hitch."

"Well, that's not quite true."

"Then in the immortal words of the Mayor . . . the journey begins."

"That's not exactly what he said."

"So who cares?"

CHAPTER ONE

YEAR TWO TWO SEVEN

[1]

JASON 215 (MEANING HE WAS BORN 215 YEARS after the launch) was a young man, a child really, who was less than thrilled with his days in school. He was thin, but then so were all his classmates. He had short-cropped, dark hair, as did his fellows, bright blue eyes, and sharp, pointed features that had a slightly Asian cast. Looking around the classroom, it could be suggested that he was related to all the other students, though some of those relations were on the order of third and fourth cousins, if not more distant.

Jason 215 sat in front of the electronic teacher, which was a fancy name for the computer flat-screen, a technology that was two centuries out-of-date, and tried to pay attention. He knew the information was important, but he couldn't keep his mind focused. He didn't want to hear the story of the launch again, nor was he interested in seeing pictures of *The Home* as it had looked when launched from Martian orbit two centuries earlier. He'd been hearing about this since he was born, and the story didn't excite him anymore.

The flesh-and-blood teacher, a young, short woman named Jessica 192, was walking among the students, checking their flat-screens. She looked as if she might be their older sister, her facial features, hair, and eyes matching theirs. If there was a difference, it was that she was just a little shorter than normal.

Her job, as the flesh-and-blood teacher, was little more than glorified baby-sitting because each student had his or her own educational program designed to take the student forward as rapidly as possible. She was there to prevent the students from playing games that were not authorized, view records that would be studied later, and keep their education on track with as few distractions as possible. And she would answer specific questions if they were deemed relevant by the educational computer and needed a verbal response.

When she stopped near him, Jason 215 looked up, and asked, "Why must I see this again?"

Jessica 192 crouched near him so that her eyes were level with his, as she had been taught to do, and asked, "Are you not interested in our history?"

"Yes, but I've seen all this before. I already know it by rote."

"Are you questioning the wisdom of the educational computer?" she asked, her voice containing just a hint of annoyance.

"No, but I know this already."

She smiled slightly, and said, "The computers know what each of us must study, and since this is the lesson for today, I think the computer thinks you need to have a review. Besides, don't you find history fascinating?"

"No. It's boring."

Jessica 192, surprised by the response, asked, "How can

you say it's boring? History is filled with our ancestors, with heroes and bravery. It is our most exciting subject."

"It's boring," said Jason 215 stubbornly. "I don't like history."

"Maybe you'd like to tell the Captain that," said Jessica 192 sternly.

Jason 215 felt a sudden coldness and wondered if he wasn't going to be sick. Lowering his voice, some of the defiance gone, he said, "No. I simply meant this was boring because I already know it."

Jessica 192 said, patiently, "Why don't you just study this until the next lesson? It won't be that long. Then maybe there will be something that doesn't bore you."

"Okay," he replied, and turned his attention back to the screen, where there was a picture of *The Home* as it had looked as it passed Jupiter on its journey out of the Solar System.

Against the colorful backdrop of the yellowish Jupiter, the giant red spot shrunken to little more than an inflamed pimple, *The Home* looked gigantic. The main living pod, nearly twenty miles long and five in diameter, was a huge black smudge with little surface detail visible, even in the bright glow of the planet.

Surrounding *The Home,* connected to it by umbilical tubes called access tunnels, were the specialization pods that included additional farms, the navigational pod, a weapons pod, maintenance and storage, the cryonics, special crews' quarters, and some research and development pods. And, finally, most important, the shuttle pods. It looked as if *The Home* was surrounded by nearly two dozen small satellites floating along with it.

But that picture was over two hundred years old, and *The Home* had accelerated far beyond the Solar System, leaving Jupiter behind as it flew on, toward the stars. *The Home* was designed to move the human race from the cradle of its creation into the galaxy so that destruction of Earth, or the sun, would not mean the end of humanity.

Jason 215 listened as the breathless narrator told him of the approach of an alien ship, one that could have meant the end of life on Earth. The narrator talked of a brave few who had met the aliens at the very edge of the Solar System and how they had driven the aliens away. And, finally, he heard, once again, about the decision by the bravest of the Earth's leaders to design starships filled with colonists.

That's what Jason 215 was. A colonist, heading to a new planet, in a new star system, where they could claim a new life. Humanity would be able to survive any disaster on Earth or in the Solar System. Humanity would not disappear as had the dinosaurs or hundreds of thousands of other species. Its survival was ensured.

A picture of the first Captain filled the screen, looking like exactly what he was—an old man whose clothes were two hundred years out of date, whose head had been shaved bald, and who had the fleshy appearance of someone who overate because there had been so much excess food.

The Captain's name was Jonathan Rogers, a man who, it was said, could trace his family back to something called Europe and whose great-great-great-times-ten-grandfather had once been a king. Jason 215 didn't believe anyone had ever been a king. It was only so much hype designed to keep the residents of *The Home* in line and make the Captain look and sound, well, captainly.

The lesson ended as the narrator said, "We must all do our part to preserve *The Home*. It is our duty to obey the laws, listen to the Captain and the Mayor, and to prepare for the day when we will reach our destination. It is our duty to be the best residents we can be and to all work toward the goal of human survival."

The image on the screen faded, replaced by a single red word. RECESS.

[2]

JASON 215 LEFT THE CLASSROOM AND WALKED out into the main part of *The Home*. Overhead, in the distance, if he squinted, were other structures and even a small lake filled with fish. Centered in this main section, though Jason 215 didn't understand the physics, was a bright ball that glowed yellow like the sun of the solar system. It all gave the impression that he was outside, in cultivated fields, but, in reality, it was just another part of *The Home*. Artificial gravity and a slight spin kept the water in the lake and the people opposite him on their side of *The Home*.

Cynthia 216 and Thomas 215 walked up to him. Both were about the same height, though Cynthia 216 was slightly taller. Both had brown hair, Cynthia 216's longer than Thomas 215's. They were thin, almost skinny, with pale skin, light eyes, and a look like they were brother and sister though they were not.

"What did the teacher want?" asked Thomas 215.

"Thought that I wasn't paying attention to the lesson. Told me that I'd have to go see the Captain if I didn't change my attitude."

"I don't know anyone who has ever had to see the Captain," said Cynthia 216.

Jason 215 nodded, and said, "I sometimes wonder if there is a Captain. Maybe it's like all those Roman gods we had to learn about. Just a lot of garbage to scare us."

Cynthia 216 suddenly looked frightened, and said, quietly, "You better not let the teacher hear you, or you *will* get to see the Captain. Then you'll know the truth and I bet you won't like it when you do."

Jason 215 grinned broadly, filled with false bravado. "I'm not afraid of the Captain. He's never around here anyway."

Pamela 215 walked up then. She was a little shorter than the others, and her skin was a shade darker, but her facial features, eye color, and hair color, matched theirs. She looked like she might be a cousin rather than a sister.

"Private talks are not allowed," she warned.

"We weren't having a private talk. We were simply talking," said Jason 215.

"Private talks breed discontent," Pamela 215 said, nodding wisely, as if she had thought of it herself

Thomas 215 said, "We were talking about the Captain and his job."

"Very difficult," said Pamela 215. "We must respect him for all he does for us."

Jason 215 noticed that she was merely repeating some of the lessons they'd all had in recent days. It was as if she had embraced the idea so thoroughly that it had become her own. Jason 215 wished he could do that, but he always seemed to have questions that made it difficult for him. He'd learned that some questions were not meant to be asked, so he sometimes sat quietly wondering while the others absorbed the information, repeating it religiously. They never seemed to question anything they were told by the teachers.

Jason 215, now taking a different tack, said, "Yes. The Captain deserves our respect. He is doing a very hard job, and we all should thank him."

Pamela 215 looked at him suspiciously. She glanced at the others, then turned, looking back over her shoulder at a group of other children playing with a large red ball that seemed to float through the air.

"I'm telling that you didn't want to play with me," said Pamela 215, then whirled, running toward the group that had the ball.

"So," said Thomas 215, nodding wisely, "you're not afraid of the Captain."

Now Jason 215 grinned, and said, "Because he would never come down here just to yell at me."

[3]

AFTER SCHOOL JASON 215 WALKED HOME, having forgotten about Pamela 215's threat to tell. He wandered through Central Park, past the fruit trees standing in long rows like soldiers on parade, past the vegetable gardens that looked more chaotic, like the results of a battle, and out onto a grassland where cattle grazed. Jason 215, having never seen a full-grown Earth cow, didn't know that these were genetically engineered beasts that were about a quarter the size of a normal cow, that they produced more milk and fattened faster than a normal cow, and matured more quickly. The cows provided meat for those who needed it, or rather wanted it, though most people were vegetarians who ate the processed crackers that came from the food factory pod. Meat was reserved for special occasions and for those whose jobs demanded more protein.

He reached the residential area. There were a number of private apartments that faced the park and had views of the green belt. Set back were openings onto streets, alleys really, that held the doors of more apartments. As people progressed in their jobs, as they received promotions, they moved closer to the apartments at the front of the residential area. Until, when they were at the top of their professions, as they neared the end of their lives, they had the opportunity to live in the front apartments with their views of the green belts.

He walked down the alley, toward his own apartment. The light filtered in not only from the end but from all around him. Over him, growing up the sides of *The Home* like ivy or moss, were more apartments. There were lights on fully now, during what was considered the day, but later at night they would dim, as if the sun had set. Jason 215 didn't completely understand the light-and-dark cycle, but then he had never lived on Earth or even in a planetary system, where day and night were governed by the orbits of planets.

He came to his front door. It looked like all the others except for the number on it. At one time it had been painted a different color, but now, on orders from the main steering committee, all doors were painted the same color. It gave the area a look of uniformity rather than the disordered appearance that had marked the residential areas in past generations.

He touched the panel next to his door so that it could read his thumbprint, and it opened quietly, with only a slight bong to alert anyone inside that the door had opened.

He knew that both his mother and father would be at work and wouldn't return for an hour or more.

He walked into the computer alcove and sat down. He sat staring at the dark screen for several minutes, trying to figure out what he wanted to do. This was "free time," so he could play games, read books, watch videos, or wander the virtual library looking for things of interest. Today he didn't know what he wanted to do, or to read, or to see. Nothing had fired his imagination.

He heard the door bong and turned. His mother, Janet 189, his father, Randolph 185, and his teacher, Jessica 192, walked through the door together. He looked at his parents, who looked almost as if they were twins; his mother was a female version of his father. Both were tall, thin, with brown hair, blue eyes, and sharp but fine features. They looked something like the neighbors, who looked like everyone else on *The Home,* only with slight variations. Jessica 192 could have been a daughter, or maybe a sister to them.

"Jason, you're home," said his mother.

"Yes."

"I thought there was baseball after school."

"I didn't feel like playing," he said.

"You're not sick, are you?"

"No, Mom. I just wanted to come home."

His father spoke for the first time. "A lot of people went to a lot of effort so that you could play some baseball after school. You have a duty to them, and you have a duty to your teammates. You don't want to let them down."

There wasn't a response to that, so Jason 215 made none. He sat at the computer, looking at his parents, then at his teacher, wondering what was going on.

The teacher said, "If we might sit down?"

Janet 189 touched her forehead, and said, "Where are my manners? Please, make yourself comfortable. Our house is your house."

When the adults had found places to sit, his father said, "Jason, why don't you join us in here? What we're talking about concerns you, too."

For the first time Jason 215 began to worry. The only time he was ever invited to join in adult conversation was when he had gotten into trouble, like the time he and William 214 and Patrick 212 had been found in one of the farming pods. They had sneaked in because someone had said there were giant animals there, but they had seen only vegetables. They ate some tomatoes and uprooted a couple of brussel sprout plants. They hadn't eaten very much, but it had been the act of taking without asking that had bothered everyone. He and his friends found themselves in the Med Center, explaining to the doctors why they had committed the acts of vandalism. He remembered little about it, except that he had been overwhelmed by guilt.

As he sat down, his father said, "We've been talking with your teacher here, and she said that you haven't been paying attention in class. Is that true?"

"No."

"Are you suggesting that your teacher is lying about this?" his father asked, surprised.

Jason 215 realized too late that the question was one of those that couldn't be answered. Whatever he said was going to be wrong. He was going to get into trouble. In fact, he was already in trouble. He decided to try to explain.

"I told her I was bored."

"Like when you didn't go play baseball this afternoon?" asked his mother.

"No. My lesson was about the history of *The Home*. I already know that."

"You already know everything there is to know about it," asked his father unkindly.

"Well, no, but I did know this lesson."

"Maybe there was something new in it," said his mother. "Something that you didn't see because you weren't paying attention."

He suddenly felt defiant. He suddenly felt that he was being picked on because he was smart and sometimes figured out things before they were taught to him. He sometimes asked questions that made the teacher angry and once this had earned him a trip to the administrator to explain why he was being a smart aleck, which resulted in another trip to the Med Center. Now it was happening again, and he'd done nothing wrong.

So, rather than remaining silent because that was the best strategy, he said, "How do we know that what the teacher is telling us is true?"

Randolph 185 looked shocked, and the color seemed to drain from Janet 189's face. Jessica 192 just grinned, and asked, "Is that what you think? That we're making up the lessons that we teach you? That the information isn't true?"

Jason 215 realized that he had gone too far in voicing his private concern. He had never said anything to anyone because he suspected the reaction would be bad. Now he was seeing it. They were all surprised. They were all staring at him, and he could see that they were angry with him.

But, still defiant, he said, "I looked at some of the history files, and they don't agree with what you've been telling us in class."

Jessica 192 leaned forward, her elbows on her knees, and said, "You must realize that we have drawn that information from all the sources that are available to us. Sometimes the men and women who created the original files had what we call a political agenda. That means they wanted certain information circulated because it was beneficial to them. It might make their lives a little better, it might gain them a little fame, it might move them ahead in their quest for a better position . . ."

"You mean they lied?" asked Jason 215.

"No. Lie isn't quite the right term. But you have to learn how things were before *The Home* was created and sent into deep space. Residents competing with one another rather than working together for the greater good. Residents who wanted to have a bigger apartment, one with four or five rooms, all to themselves, might, for example, shade the truth so that it benefited them. They wanted to have more food than their neighbor, who might not have enough. They wanted more clothes and even their own private car, so they were less than honest."

"Car?" asked Jason 215 confused.

"Yes, car. It was a personal conveyance designed to take a resident from one location to another rapidly. A terrible waste of resources. Some residents owned, for their own use, two or three cars, while others had no car at all."

Randolph 185 asked, "You understand?"

Jason 215 wanted to shake his head because he really didn't understand, but he knew better. Rather than risk a lecture and a trip to the Med Center, he said, "Yes."

Jessica 192 said, "When you live on a planet, the resources are more plentiful. You can't imagine the space on a planet. So these residents wasted them in personal struggles to become the richest, the most famous, and the most admired person on the planet. They cared nothing for their fellow residents. And, to reach that goal, they sometimes wrote things or produced things that were less than accurate. But for us to understand history, we have kept all that information in the library files so that we can see how bad things once were."

"So it's not true?"

"Well, Jason, this is one of the reasons that some files are not available to students. You don't know enough to understand how these things work. When you're older, you'll be able to read all the files, but only as you grow. Then you'll be able to understand the truth as it is, rather than how some residents would like it to be."

Jason nodded, but he realized that his question hadn't really been answered. The teacher had told him that some of the information in their library wasn't accurate, but that didn't mean that everything the teacher said, or that appeared on his flat-screen, was accurate. They had provided him with no way to verify the information.

"Do you understand, Jason?" asked Jessica 192.

He nodded but said nothing.

"Well, then, I think we're through here," she said evenly. "Why don't you run along. Maybe the baseball game is still going on."

Jason 215 knew a good thing when he heard it. He stood up and walked over to the flat-screen, logged off, and headed for the front door. His parents were in an animated conversation with Jessica 192. He heard her say, "There's nothing to worry about here. Some of our brighter students think of the strangest things. Gives us fits."

"What can we do?"

"Monitor his computer time. Explain things to him when he asks questions. And I think we have a counseling program that will help remove some of these thoughts."

[4]

ROBERT 209 WAS LARGE FOR HIS AGE. HE WAS bigger than his fellows, had lighter skin and round, blue eyes. He had a shock of brown hair that was unruly, and, no matter how often he combed it, he could not get it to lie down properly.

Robert 209 was not an intelligent boy. He had trouble learning to read, had trouble with basic math, and had no desire to learn the history and geography of a planet that he would never see. He hated school, hated the teacher, hated the flat-screen, and hated all the students who were smaller and brighter. They made him look like a stupid brute, and, because of that, he became a stupid brute who could get along only with those bigger and older than he and bullied those who were younger and smaller.

All this meant that he skipped as much school as he could, though he was fooling no one. His password was not logged into the computer, and his flat-screen remained idle. The scores on his aptitude tests showed that he was not progressing as fast as his contemporaries, and though the flat-screen and the individual educational programs meant that he would stay with those his own age, they could see that he was still studying the lessons they had mastered a year or two years earlier. Naturally, they all made fun of him because he was such a stupid brute. Had the society allowed it, he would have dropped out of school and found some low-paying job to fill his days, but even the menial tasks that were still performed with human labor required an advanced education. It wasn't enough to dump the garbage, it had to be dumped in a specific way with consideration to the impact the components of the garbage would make in specific environments.

At the edge of the park named for some long dead Earth hero, was a group of smaller children. Robert 209 watched them play for a moment, some kind of game that involved lots of running, yelling, and a big yellow ball that had to be thrown and caught. Robert 209 couldn't figure out the rules or if there were any real rules, but he knew how to end the game.

He walked over slowly, waited until the ball was thrown at a small girl, and then bumped her aside with his hip. He grabbed the ball and held it over his head as the girl fell to her hands and knees. He then looked from face to face of the smaller children now surrounding him.

When no one moved, he demanded, "Well, don't you want your ball?"

"You're not supposed to be here," said the girl who had been bumped aside.

"Yeah, well I am. Babies want their ball?"

Jason 215 walked toward Robert 209, and said, "Yes, we'd like our ball."

"Then why don't you try to take it?"

Pamela 215, who had been standing at the edge of the group said, "I'll get the teacher."

"Yeah. You get the teacher. You too scared to get the ball yourself?"

Thomas 215 said, "It doesn't matter. Recess is about over anyway."

"Then I'll just keep the ball."

"You do and I'll tell the teacher and you'll be in very bad trouble."

There was a quiet bong in the distance, and the children looked in that direction.

"Class is about to start," said Pamela 215.

"Please," said Thomas 215, "can we have our ball back?

Robert 209 looked from face to face disappointed. He had wanted them to chase him, or jump up at the ball, but they hadn't done any of that. It was as if they didn't care that he had taken the ball and ruined the game. They showed no emotion, and he had wanted to see some tears, or, at the very least, a little fear on their faces. Instead, they stood around and tried to talk to him. Finally, he tossed the ball at one of the girls as hard as he could. It hit her in the stomach, knocking her down. She sat there and stared at him as if she couldn't understand what he had done or why he had done it. She wasn't hurt.

"Take your damned ball," said Robert 209. He turned and walked away from the park.

[5]

JASON 215 AND HIS FRIENDS, CYNTHIA 216 and Thomas 215, left the park and walked across the grass toward the classroom door. As they neared it, Cynthia asked, "Why does he act like that?"

"I think he was dropped on his head when he was young," said Thomas 215. "He's brain-damaged."

"Then they should operate," said Jason 215. "He is not a proper resident."

Thomas 215 looked at his friend, and asked, "When did you decide that?"

Jason thought back to his meeting with his parents and his teacher. They had talked about a lot of things, including what it meant to be a good resident. The situation was different on *The Home* because everything was limited. Every action had a consequence that impacted on the lives of the other residents. Because of that, everyone had to be conscious of what they had did and how they did it. A loud noise, for example, while funny to those who made it, might be disturbing to other residents. Older residents had a low tolerance for loud noise because the physiology of the ear had changed with age. Or, in the past, it had meant some kind of problem that could lead to injury and death. Loud noises frightened because of what they once meant. A considerate resident did not produce such noises as a joke.

And sometimes the chemical balance of a resident's brain could shift, requiring medication to improve life and bring thought back to the norm. Jason 215 didn't mention to his friends that he was required to take two yellow pills daily and one green one with his lunch. Of course, he didn't understand that the pills were altering his body's chemistry.

And he didn't bother to mention the additional counseling sessions at the Med Center. These discussions, completed with the help of powerful hypnotics, helped him understand why *The Home* had been organized the way it was, and why the residents had to be so tolerant of others' feelings.

To his friend he said, "I didn't just decide that. It's the way it has always been."

They reached the door, and, as they did, Jason 215 turned and looked back. Robert 209 was standing near a large fruit tree covered with oranges. The crop would soon be harvested and added to the nutritional content of the evening meals. But Robert 209 was reaching up, pulling oranges from the tree, and throwing them across the park, or at the trunks of other trees so they exploded into a spray of fruit juice and pulp. It was vandalism for the sake of destroying something. He shook his head in disgust.

The teacher, Jessica 192, appeared in the doorway, and said, "Hurry in, Jason. We don't want to keep the others waiting."

He pointed. "What about Robert?"

The teacher looked, sucked in her breath, and turned her attention to Jason 215. "Don't worry about him. He'll be looked after."

"Will he get some extra medicine?"

"Well, I don't know. Sometimes that's all we need. A little extra medicine."

"He took our ball."

"Did he give it back?"

"Yes."

"Well, then nothing was hurt. Everyone had fun, didn't they?"

"Until he took our ball."

Jessica 192 knelt near him and looked into his eyes. "Sometimes people do selfish things. Sometimes they forget to be good residents. We have to remind them so they can be better residents."

Jason 215 nodded.

"Now get to your flat-screen. I think you're going to enjoy the next hour."

Jason walked over to his desk and sat down. He tilted the screen slightly and touched the mouse button. The screen burst into color that swirled, danced, and finally coalesced into a picture of children standing around an adult. The adult looked strange because he was thicker, fatter, than anyone Jason 215 had ever seen. He held a huge green object that had a moist red center filled with black-and-white seeds. He was eating from it by leaning his face into the red pulp. When he straightened, the juices were running down his chin and staining his shirt. Although the children had lifted their hands as if to ask for some of the watermelon, which was clearly too large for the fat man to eat, he just stood there, ignoring them. He seemed to be saying, "I have mine, and you don't get any of it."

That image was replaced by another that looked as if it came from inside *The Home*. A woman who was short and thin with straight dark hair had a much smaller melon but she was cutting it into even smaller pieces so that she could share it with the children around her. Everyone seemed to be happy; all were sitting on the grass, eating their small pieces of melon.

There were no spoken words and no narration. The point was made with the happy faces of the children, the music that seemed to enhance one picture and detract from the other, and in the look of the two adults. One was fat, with little hair on a very shiny head. He refused to share.

And the other was thin, like all the residents in *The Home*. She helped her fellows.

The message was not subtle for an adult, but Jason 215 was not an adult. He just saw two stories and realized that Robert 209 was the fat man because he took the ball. He had been mean and he hadn't been a good resident and that was why he was outside, by himself, when the rest of them were inside, learning.

[6]

WHEN SCHOOL ENDED, JASON 215 JOINED HIS friends Cynthia 216 and Thomas 215. They walked over to the park, but Robert 209 was not there, and all evidence of his act had been removed. There were no bits of orange on the ground or wet smudges on the trunks of any of the trees. Someone had cleaned it all up, and the park looked as it did when they had been there during recess. Neat and pristine and ready for use by the residents.

"What do you think will happen to him?" asked Cynthia 216.

"Rehabilitation," said Thomas 215.

"What's that mean?"

Jason 215 thought about that because he began to suspect that he had been rehabilitated. It was the price he had paid for complaining about his lessons and asking questions that shouldn't have been asked. It was counseling and extra medication, and though he didn't know what was wrong with that, he suspected that something might be. It troubled him briefly, but then he forgot all about it and turned his attention to his friends.

"Just means they talk to him," said Jason 215. "It means that he'll be told why we don't waste food."

Cynthia 216 looked at him confused because she hadn't seen Robert 209 throwing oranges at trees. She said, "We all know that it is wrong to waste food. We have to be very careful with our food because we only have so much available."

Thomas 215 nodded obediently. "Our resources are finite. Not like those on a planet."

"Well, I'm sure that Robert will understand," said Jason 215. "They'll make him better."

"Maybe we should go visit him," said Cynthia 216. "He is sick."

"I'll bet we'll see him tomorrow," said Thomas 215. "I'll bet he'll apologize for taking our ball."

"Yes," agreed Jason 215. But he wasn't sure that he believed that.

[7]

SECURITY, DRESSED IN DARK-COLORED UNI-forms and carrying stun clubs, had neatly surrounded Robert 209 as he plucked the oranges from the trees. He hadn't even realized that they had approached him until one of the security residents grabbed his hand so that he couldn't throw the last orange. He'd jerked forward, trying to free himself, but was held tight. When Robert 209 saw the other three security residents, he stopped struggling.

One of them, wearing a helmet of molded black plastic, shin guards that might have been worn by a baseball catcher, thick gloves on his hands, and even goggles to keep foreign objects out of his eyes, stepped directly in front of Robert 209, and asked, "Just what are you doing?"

Robert 209 dropped the orange he was holding, and said, "Nothing."

"You are wasting food," accused the man.

Robert 209 knew that he had no response for that. He stood quietly, glancing at each of the security residents.

"Guess you'll have to come along with us."

"I have to go to school."

"Looks as if school has started without you. Come along, and there won't be any trouble."

The security residents surrounded Robert 209 and led him across the park, past the modified baseball diamond, past the small lake that held several varieties of fast-growing, genetically altered fish, under a canopy of trees that were doing their part to put oxygen back into the atmosphere of *The Home.* They came to a gravel path, crossed it, and entered the administration area. The buildings had a front that looked to be made of massive stone, like the courthouses built on Earth two or three hundred, or one thousand years earlier, but that was simply decoration. Stone buildings would be impossible to build on a ship in space. Though once the stone had been boosted into orbit, the problem with excess weight would have been eliminated but not the problem of mass.

The security residents and Robert 209 walked through a door and stopped, each holding the palm of his hand over a small scanner that detected the microchip implanted there. Entry to the building was impossible without a chip and a scan.

"I think I would rather go home now," said Robert 209. He was beginning to get scared.

"It's a little late for that."

"I only threw two oranges," said Robert 209. "The other boys threw some, too. I can tell you who they were. We all threw the oranges."

"The evidence will be reviewed in the judge's chambers."

"But I don't want to see the judge."

They walked up a short flight of wide stairs, past a statue of Justice complete with her scales and blindfold. They turned down a short, brightly lighted corridor, past doors leading into offices. One opened into the law library, which looked as if it contained row upon row of legal texts. But they were only decoration to conceal the plain bulkheads. The library was on disk. Every legal decision was there, every precedent, every law and every interpretation of that law up until the launch. After that, the library had been updated by shielded, direct beam communications. But now, the distance between *The Home* and Earth was making it very out-of-date.

They came to a set of double doors that guarded one of the courtrooms. One of the security residents opened the door, and the others forced Robert 209 inside. Sitting at the far end, behind a massive desk raised two or three feet off the floor was the judge, James 163. He was an older man, with gray hair, facial wrinkles, and a look of real annoyance.

One of the security residents walked to the rail that separated the entrance from the bench, and said, "Richard 190, Your Honor. Juvenile misbehavior."

James 163 looked at the flat-screen in front of him. It contained the vital statistics of Robert 209, called up when the scanner had read his implant.

"Is that all?"

"No, sir. He told us that he had thrown two oranges but that other boys had thrown them, too."

James 163 looked down at Robert 209 for a moment, then asked, "Is this true?"

Although telling the truth would have helped him now, he stuck with his lie. "I only threw two. Jason 215 and Thomas 215 also threw oranges."

James 163 asked, "What segment?"

Richard 190 gave the judge a number, then a time of apprehension. The judge then scanned the security disk, watched Robert 209 take the ball from the smaller children, push them around, and finally, in anger, throw the ball at the girl. As the children left, Robert 209 began to throw oranges.

"We can add lying, assault, general misbehavior, and intimidation to the list."

"I didn't do any of that," whined Robert 209.

James 163 touched a button and the wall in back of him disappeared into a large display showing Robert 209 alone, throwing oranges. The judge reversed the display, then stopped and started it at the point where Robert 209 joined the group of other children. He let it play on to the very end without a word or comment.

The display darkened as the security residents slipped up and apprehended Robert 209. The judge, in a reasonable voice, asked, "Would you care to change your statement?"

"This is a frame."

"Unfortunately, no. You feel no remorse for lying to these residents, lying to this court, and for the wanton destruction of food, not to mention your attitude toward your fellow residents and students?"

"You're just picking on me."

James 163 shook his head sadly. "You will receive psychological rehabilitation, sixty hours of community service, and one year's probation. Any recurrence will be met with much harsher punishment. Do you understand?"

Robert 209 knew that now was not the time for a smart mouth. He said, almost contritely, "Yes, sir."

[8]

EVERYONE HAD EVENING CHORES BECAUSE there was so much that had to be done that no one wanted to do. Everyone wanted to be the Captain, or to be a member of the Flight Crew but no one wanted to stir the muck in the main recycling pools, even if that only meant pushing a button and monitoring the results on a flat-screen for an hour. And while many of the tasks could be done robotically, it was believed that working together on the menial tasks built a bond among the residents. Everyone had to do some of the dirty work so everyone felt a kinship for his and her fellow residents.

After dinner in the communal dining room, Jason 215 and his friends began the task of cleaning up, moving the stack of plates toward the dishwasher, the glasses to the side, and the silverware into the bins for their cleaning. The discarded food was gathered into small cans to be carried into the recycling pits so that it could be used in another form.

Jason 215, however, didn't want to stay behind and clean. He wanted to run the alleys, chasing his friends and playing games. He stood at one end of the long, narrow communal room and watched as others his age swarmed around trying to separate the spoons from the forks, the plates from the glasses, and the green vegetables from the crackers and bread and thought about the fun that they could be having. It had been a while since he had thought about fun, and he didn't realize that the length of time between his visits to the Med Center and his feelings of resentment, no matter how mild they might be, were correlated. After his visit on Tuesday, he wouldn't be thinking about fun and running with his friends rather than work.

At the far end of the room Thomas 215 and Cynthia 216 were gathering forks into bouquets as if they were flowers found on the tables. They were working together, quietly talking, unaware that Jason had spotted them.

He found a partially eaten roll that fit his hand like a baseball. He set down the dinner plates, stepped back, away from the table, and wound up like a pitcher about to throw as hard and fast as he could. He glanced to the left, as if checking the runner, waved off the sign from the catcher, then threw the roll. It sailed from his fingers and began a steady if shallow climb, smacking the wall about two inches from Thomas 215's ear and slightly above his head.

Startled, Thomas 215 jumped, dropping the forks. He looked around angrily and saw Jason 215. He pointed a finger, and yelled, "That wasn't funny."

"It was very funny."

Thomas 215 saw a slice of bread. He snagged it, rolled it into a tight ball, and threw it as hard as he could at Jason 215. Rather than dodging, Jason 215 caught it, wheeled and threw it back. The bread slapped Cynthia 216 on the shoulder. She squealed, dropping the forks she held.

"Get him, Thomas," she said.

Jason 215 dodged to the right, around the end of the table, then crouched behind the molded plastic chair. With just his eyes above the surface of the table, he scanned for more ammunition. He found a tomato that had a brown spot on one side that suggested it was spoiled. He leaned forward, grabbed it and dropped back into hiding.

Now Thomas 215 and Cynthia 216 were joined by two

younger boys, Frank 219 and Russ 219. Each of them had a handful of discarded food. They dropped it on the floor near them and hid behind the table.

"No fair," said Jason 215. "I'm outnumbered."

But he was joined by Susan 213 and Debbie 212. They had no ammunition, just strong arms from playing baseball for a couple of extra years.

Jason 215 sat down with his back to one of the plastic chairs and searched for more ammunition. He pointed to a spot about halfway down one of the long tables, where a bowl of fruit had gone nearly untouched. There were two oranges, an apple, a pear, and three bananas.

To Susan 213, he said, "Grab that fruit."

Crouching low, as they had seen on some of the history disks, Susan 213, using the table for protection, eased her way to the fruit.

Work in the communal dining room slowed, then stopped, as everyone began to join one side or the other. It had little to do with who the two leaders were but more with which side of the room they happened to be on when the fight broke out. They fell in with those closest to them.

Jason 215, remembering a phrase from one of the history disks, ordered, "Try to outflank them." He didn't know what it meant, only that it sounded military.

Susan 213 returned with the fruit and set it on the floor near Jason 215. She kept her head down, out of the line of fire, but that was more instinct than any sort of training. She just didn't want to get hit with a pear.

Jason 215 began to direct his makeshift army, spreading them out on their side of the dining hall to cover the door, block a retreat to the kitchen, and to hold what would become the strategic trash barrel, where the uneaten rolls, bread, and bits of fruit were being collected for recycling. It was now an ammo dump, and he wanted to keep it on his side of the battle.

Just as he was to launch his attack, the kitchen door opened and an older man stood there, hands on his hips. He wore an apron to protect his clothes, rubber gloves to pro-

tect his hands, and a white hat that seemed to have no function other than as a symbol of his authority.

"Just what are you children doing?"

There was a hesitation, as if they had been unable to understand the question. Finally, Jason 215 stood and offered, helpfully, "Cleaning."

"It doesn't look as if much cleaning has been done.
Might I suggest that we hurry here. There are others waiting for us to complete our assignments so that they might
complete theirs. It is impolite to keep them waiting while
you play some sort of childish game."

Slowly, the others stood and began to move back to
their assignments. They kept their eyes down, not wanting
to look at the older man.

"Who is responsible for this nonsense?" he demanded.

No one pointed a finger, or said a word. They simply
picked up where they had been.

"Well, it doesn't matter. We'll figure that out."

Jason 215 didn't like the sound of that, though he
wasn't sure why. There was some sort of threat implied,
but he didn't understand it.

The man whirled and returned to the kitchen without
another word.

[9]

WALKING HOME IN THE SEMIDARKNESS THAT
suggested late evening, Jason 215, Thomas 215, and Cynthia 216 had to laugh. They stopped in the park, under the
cover of the orange trees, and looked up between the
branches at the twinkling of the lights above them more
than four miles away. It was the far side of *The Home* and
they understood that had they been on a planet's surface,
those twinkling lights would be stars trillions of miles
from them. Here, on *The Home,* they were the lights of another part of the spacecraft. They represented another part
of the city, the living quarters of other residents.

Jason 215 dropped to the soft, and now slightly moist

grass, leaned back against the relatively smooth bark of the tree, and said, "Adults sometimes suck the life out of living."

"They have accepted their responsibilities," said Cynthia 216. "Someday soon we're going to have to accept those same responsibilities and become complete residents."

"I don't see what having a little fun in the dining hall would have hurt," said Thomas 215. "Any mess we made, we would have had to clean up anyway. No one was hurt."

"What about all those waiting for us to complete the cleanup so that they could do their jobs. They probably wanted to return to their apartments, but they couldn't until we finished cleaning the dining hall, and we couldn't finish because we were playing."

"I don't think it would have made all that much difference," said Jason 215.

"It wasn't polite, and, besides, it could be said that we were wasting food. Waste not, want not," said Cynthia 216.

"The food was destined for the recyclers anyway," said Jason 215. "We weren't wasting it."

"Still . . ."

"Ever wonder what those people up there are like?" asked Thomas 215.

"Just like us," said Cynthia 216. "What do you think?"

"Ever meet any of them?"

"Once, in the mall, I saw a group of them," said Cynthia.

"If they're just like us, how could you tell?"

"My mother said that the Crew live up there, closer to the navigation computers and the flight decks. They were wearing Crew uniforms."

"Really?" asked Jason 215, interested. "What did they look like?"

"You've seen the flight uniforms on the disks," said Cynthia 216.

"Yes, but it's different when you see them yourself,"

said Jason 215. "Then you know the stuff is right. Not some picture invented to fool us."

"Why would you say a crazy thing like that?" asked Cynthia 216.

"Because," said Thomas 215, "he thinks more than he should. That's why."

"Well," said Cynthia 216, "they looked just like the pictures we see on the disks. Though I thought the men were taller than anyone else. And they looked smarter, too."

"What were they doing?" asked Thomas 215.

"Simply walking along, looking around. Sight-seeing in our side of *The Home*."

"Did you talk to them?"

"No. No one did. They stopped to stare, then moved aside so that the Crew could pass."

Jason 215 sat up erect. "Maybe we should go over to the other side of *The Home*. We could see some members of the Crew. Maybe we could talk to them."

"It's a long way over there. Too far."

"Well, not tonight," agreed Jason 215. "But on Saturday we only have half a day of school, then free time until dinner. Maybe Saturday afternoon."

"I don't know," said Cynthia 216.

"Sure. It would be fun."

"We're not supposed to travel if it's not necessary," said Cynthia 216. "Uses valuable resources. A good resident keeps to himself."

"But we'd be on a learning excursion," said Jason 215. "No one could object to that."

"Well . . ."

"It's settled," said Jason 215, taking charge. "Saturday we'll travel to the other side of *The Home* to look for the Crew."

"You ever been there?" asked Cynthia 216.

"No," said Jason 215. "I haven't ever been away from our side here."

"You think it'll be all right for us to travel over there?" asked Cynthia 216.

"Sure," said Jason 215. "We'll be on a learning trip, and no one can object to that."

"Okay," agreed Thomas 215. "We'll go look for the Crew. See what they're really like."

Both of them looked at Cynthia 216, and she hesitated only a moment. "Sure. I'll go."

"We'll meet here right after school on Saturday," said Jason 215 as he stood up. He dusted the seat of his coverall. "I'll see you then."

[10]

JASON 215 WAS SURPRISED TO SEE ALL THE lights on when he returned to his apartment. His mother, Janet 189, and his father, Randolph 185, were sitting on the molded plastic couch. Sitting in the chair opposite them, looking a little concerned, was Bruce 185, the family counselor. Jason 215 stopped in the doorway, holding it open, almost afraid.

"Come on in, Jason," said Bruce 185. "There is nothing to be afraid of."

Slowly, carefully, Jason 215 closed the door and took two steps forward, staying nearly as far from any of the adults as he could.

"Jason, come in and sit down," said Randolph 185, more than a little annoyed. "Bruce is here to help you."

"Do I need help?"

Bruce 185 grinned, showing nearly perfect teeth. "Well, that might be a little strong, but there have been some strange events these last few days."

"I don't know what you mean."

"Jason, come in and sit down," said his mother. She looked worried, almost afraid.

"Yes," said Bruce 185. "Let's all relax a little bit here. There is nothing to worry about."

Jason 215 walked into the living room and sat down on the couch, as far from his parents as he could get. He looked as if he was going to spring forward and flee at any moment.

"Now, Jason," said Bruce, "why don't you tell me about that little fight . . ."

Jason 215's mother gasped, and said in a high, tight voice, "Fight?"

"It's not what you think, Janet," said Bruce 185. "A little childish display in the dining hall."

"Jason," said his mother, exasperated.

"I didn't do anything."

Bruce 185 smiled, and said, "Well, now let's think about that a little bit. You and the others had the task of clearing the tables, sorting the silver, plates, glasses, and leftover foods so that the kitchen staff could complete their jobs and head home for the evening. Is this not true?"

Jason 215 felt a fluttering in his stomach and looked down at the floor. "Yes, sir."

"Did you not throw a roll at one of your friends?"

"Yes, sir."

"An act of aggression?" said Randolph 185, astonished. "You committed an act of aggression?"

Bruce 185 held up his hand and smiled. "Well, it's more in the category of a playful act. Teasing a friend more than an overt act of aggression."

"Well," said his father, looking at Jason 215.

"I think the real problem is that the children began to take sides into two groups, one centered around young Jason here and the other around his friend, Thomas 215."

"That Thomas has been nothing but trouble since he moved in here," said Janet 189.

"Let's not go blaming others," said Bruce 185. "Jason was right in the middle of this, and he committed the first act. The blame is clearly his."

"What are we going to do?" asked Randolph 185. "We've tried to raise a good boy."

"And you've done a fine job. Sometimes there is just a little more that needs to be done. Not the fault of anyone. We'll take Jason to the Med Center tomorrow rather than wait until Tuesday and see what we can learn. Maybe apply a treatment. Everything should be fine tomorrow evening. Nothing to worry about because all these transgressions are of a minor nature. We'll simply head them off now."

As Bruce 185 stood up, Randolph 185 said, "We'll have him at the Med Center tomorrow, first thing."

"Well, it's not quite that important. I think ten would be appropriate."

"He'll miss some school," said Janet 189.

"I think this will benefit him more."

[1 1]

THE MED CENTER WAS ACROSS THE PARK, BACK toward what would be considered the rear of the ship, if the residents thought about it that way. There were glass bulkheads that allowed residents to see inside the ultra-modern waiting room. As they entered, both Jason 215 and his father held up their wrists so that their implants could be scanned, logging them in.

Although neither Jason 215 nor his father had ever been in an Earth-based building, they had seen pictures of them. Had they not known exactly where they were, they would have believed that they were on a planet's surface, walking into a building there. The lobby was large, bright, spacious, and surprisingly quiet. One wall looked as if it had been made of glass and looked out over a green meadow filled with wildflowers and sloped gently to a slow-flowing river. There were deer near a clump of trees, and a breeze rippled the grass.

The loop for the holographic view was so smooth that there was no jump as it started again. The deer disappeared into the trees and walked about again, the river just kept flowing, and nothing slipped in to obstruct the view.

Centered in the lobby and leading to a second floor was an escalator. Jason 215 and his father walked to it, climbed on, and got off at the second floor. They crossed to the receptionist, a young woman with short dark hair, dark eyes, and soft, nearly white skin. But even with the variations, she still looked like a member of the family.

She said nothing to them, and Jason 215 slipped his wrist under the scanner. When information appeared on her screen, she said, "First door on the right. First door beyond that."

"Thanks."

They entered another part of the building, with wide halls, bright lights, and a slightly artificial odor, one of chemicals and cleanliness. There was another door close by, and they opened it. There were two chairs, a bench that was about waist high, a small sink, and a little cabinet that had artificial wooded doors.

"What do you think, Dad?"

"I don't think this is much of a deal," said Randolph 185. "When I was your age I went through much the same thing. Just some questions and a little additional medication."

"What if I don't want the medication?" asked Jason 215.

"Why wouldn't you want it?"

"Because I'm not sick."

Randolph 185 pointed at one of the chairs, and said, "Have a seat, and let's talk for a moment. I want you to understand that sometimes we feel fine but can still be sick. Though not our fault, our brains sometimes play tricks on us, but the medication makes everything better. Helps us understand our world here and makes us better residents."

Jason 215 felt his head spin, and said, louder than he meant to, "You mean my brain is sick?"

At that moment the door opened, and a man walked in. He wore the traditional white coat of the medical profession, but he looked like everyone else. The only difference between him and most of the people Jason 215 knew was that the doctor was older than most, and his hair was sprinkled with white.

"Well," said the doctor, in a reassuring voice, "I think that is something that we need to determine, but I doubt that your brain is very sick."

"But everything feels fine," said Jason 215. He looked up at the doctor. "My brain is fine."

The doctor laughed and crouched down so that he could look Jason 215 in the eyes without looking down at him. "Of course it is. You have nothing to worry about."

"But my dad said . . ."

"Yes," said the doctor, interrupting and looked at Randolph 185, "dads often say things because they worry about their children. They're concerned and want everything to be wonderful, but sometimes they make mistakes, too."

"Then there is nothing wrong with my brain?"

"Well, since you're here, why don't we check some things out before we draw any conclusions. Let me make sure that everything is in tip-top shape."

"Dad?"

"It will be just fine, Jason. The doctor knows what he's doing."

Jason 215 didn't say anything.

The doctor ran through a quick routine, looking deep into Jason 215's eyes and ears and listening to his chest. These tests had become nearly meaningless because there were better ways to access patients' state of health, but the personal contact and the seeming concern of the doctor relaxed the patients. It was now part of the bedside manner, though the monitors in the room had already provided the same information for the doctor.

The complete analysis of Jason 215 had been completed, the data collected as he had used the bathroom that morning, as he had eaten his breakfast, and as he had passed various scanners that took readings from his implant. The doctor already knew what the treatment would be and how it was to be administered.

"Well, Jason, everything looks fine."

"Then we can go?"

The doctor grinned, and said, "I've never seen a young man so eager to leave. You have a girl waiting for you?"

Jason 215 thought momentarily of Cynthia 216 but, of

course, she was just a friend and not a girlfriend. Jason 215 shook his head.

"Well, then, let me do this." The doctor patted the bench, and said, "Hop up here."

Jason 215 did as told.

"Now, we're going to give you a little bit of a relaxant so that you won't be nervous. Then we'll ask you some questions. When we're done, you can go home."

Jason 215 looked at his father, and asked, "Dad, do I have to do this?"

"It's all right, Jason. It's for your own good."

A nurse entered the room, without being summoned, and pulled at the sleeve of Jason 215's coverall. She touched his arm with a metallic tube, and he felt nothing. She left immediately.

The doctor said, "If you don't mind, I'd like to finish this alone."

Randolph 185 sat for a moment, as if he didn't understand, then nodded. "Of course."

"Dad . . . Wait."

Randolph 185 stood up and looked at his son's half-closed eyes. He said, "You'll be fine."

When Randolph 185 left the small examination room, the doctor pulled a chair close to the bench, turned so that he could see the flat-screen, and said, "This will just take a few minutes. Please answer each of the questions with the first thing that comes to mind. Do you understand?"

"Yes."

He ran through the list of questions quickly, listening carefully to Jason 215's responses. When they were finished, he waited for a few moments, then the diagnosis appeared on the screen. To Jason 215, he said, "I'm going to give you a shot, you'll go to sleep for only a few minutes, and when you wake up, you'll be able to go home. How's that sound?"

Jason 215 didn't say anything because he couldn't refuse. He would be given the shot no matter what he said because the adults were always doing these sorts of things for your own good. Didn't matter what he thought, because he was going to get the shot.

And then, suddenly, he was awake, sitting on the bench, feeling as if he could run home. He was happy, content, and without anxiety.

The door opened, and Randolph 185 said, "Let's go home."

[1 2]

ON SATURDAY AFTERNOON, WHEN HE WAS SUP-posed to meet Thomas 215 and Cynthia 216 for their expedition in search of the Crew, Jason 215 was sitting at his computer studying. He had forgotten about their plan and hadn't noticed that neither Thomas 215 nor Cynthia 216 had been in school on Friday afternoon.

At recess he had stayed in the room, playing games on the computer rather than joining the others outside in the park. Normally he would have been encouraged to get out and play, but this time the teacher, Jessica 192, had let him sit by himself. She had been told it would be better for the next few days.

So Jason 215, rather than going out to play on Saturday afternoon, rather than joining his friends to search for the Crew on the other side of *The Home,* just sat by himself, letting the computer entertain him and letting it be his friend. He didn't know that it would be his only friend for a while.

CHAPTER TWO

YEAR TWO TWO SEVEN

[1]

ALTHOUGH THE COMPUTERS CONTROLLED THE flight, and the engines were set into a gigantic pod that seemed to trail the ship, there was a flight deck that was reminiscent of the bridge of an old-style aircraft carrier. It was a large room, thirty or so feet long and another twenty wide. There were four chairs that faced the flat-screens, and another half dozen that were set facing various sensor arrays, engine instruments and navigational aids. Though the flight deck was designed for ten people, in fact, flight of *The Home* could be accomplished from anywhere on the ship by one man or woman who had a computer input and the right access commands.

William 157 sat in what had been designed as the Captain's chair though he was not the Captain. William 157 was a short man with graying hair, brown eyes and a thick nose. He didn't look as if he was a resident. He didn't look as if he belonged on *The Home* because of his stature and his facial features. In a society that wasn't supposed to recognize such things, he had been denied the top spot because he didn't have the right look. He had been relegated to the second echelon of the Crew, where he had a certain power over everyone else on *The Home,* but he would never make it to the first echelon.

William 157 sat with one leg up on the arm of the chair. He wore the standard Crew uniform of a one-piece black coverall, black boots, and the gold piping of the Crew. There were two and a half gold rings at the bottom of his sleeves, telling the residents that he was an officer of high rank, but not the highest. He was an important member of the Crew, but not the most important.

And that's what bothered him. Had he not been competent to be Captain, that would be one thing, but to be denied the top slot because his body was stockier, his face fleshier, and his eyes not quite the right color was something else. He could live with being the second-shift navigator if that was all that he could do. But he knew better; he had all the talent necessary, and he knew why he had been denied the top spot.

That was the problem with computer records. The computer geeks could erect all the fire walls they wanted, they could install all the security they could think of, and they could limit access to a few with the proper passwords and identification, but they couldn't keep the determined hacker out. William 157 had been able to breach security and read the notations on his file. He would never be considered for the role of Captain because he wasn't the right type. Education, intelligence, training, and ability had nothing to do with it. He didn't look right. He didn't look like a resident of *The Home.*

William 157 sat there in the Captain's chair, and looked at the large flat-screen display in front of him. It showed space around the ship. The points of light that marked the distant stars, the smudges of nebula and galaxies, and the

larger balls of light that represented the closer stars. One of
them, on the right and near the corner, also had four planets revolving around it. They were all gas giants, five or
ten times the size of Jupiter, and therefore uninhabitable.
That system, though closest to *The Home,* would be of no
use to them. Distant scans had revealed no smaller, Earth-
like planets.

The hatch irised open, and Sally 176 entered. She
looked more like a resident. She had the proper tall, lean
body, the dark brown hair, and the blue eyes. Of course her
hair was turning gray, but that happened to everyone and
hadn't marked her an as outsider.

"I didn't expect to see anyone here," she said.

"Just making a quick check. The nav program is working flawlessly."

"Would you expect anything else?" she asked as she
dropped into one of the other chairs.

"No." He pointed toward the flat-screen. "I just like to
look at the stars."

"That slightly red one," she said, "a little off center is
our destination."

"Yeah. I know."

Sally 176 shot a glance at him, then grinned. "Of
course. You're nav. You know all that."

"I also know that we'll never see it without the aid of
the enhancement programs."

"How far is it?" she asked.

"Several dozen light-years. Captain ran a routine distance program last week. We're now only 250 years out, if
we continue to accelerate and don't begin braking until the
last possible second, then brake as hard as we can. Cuts
some of the travel time."

Sally 176 reached up and slipped her fingers into the
Velcro holding her uniform top closed. She ran a finger
down with the sound of ripping cloth, and said, "Little
warm in here."

William 157 frowned because the temperature in *The
Home,* or on the flight deck, never varied more than a de-

gree or two. It was set to keep everyone as comfortable as possible.

Without thinking about it, she shrugged her shoulders so that the coverall slipped down her arms. She grinned broadly, and said, "Now that's better."

"Isn't the Captain scheduled to make a tour of the bridge in thirty minutes or so?"

"I think that's been canceled. I think he decided to make a walk around in the engine pods. Give the engineers a little bit of a thrill."

Now she turned her attention to the navigator, and said, "You know, William, my husband is assigned to agronomy this week. He's spending all his time over there, sleeping in the dorms. Doesn't like the commute. So I'm all alone."

William shot her a glance. She was naked from the waist up. He looked at her carefully, surprised at how firm her body was, for a woman of her age, though he wasn't sure what that meant. He found her very interesting.

"Hasn't been home for several days and won't be home for several more."

William 157 suddenly felt trapped. The rules were quite clear. There could be no aggression. But anything consenting adults wanted to do was not outlawed. The watchword was discretion. No one wanted to create a scene, no one wanted to create emotional distress, but there was not much in the way of enforced exclusivity.

The problem was that William 157 felt no desire. Sally 176 did nothing for him. She had no power, she could not help him climb the ladder, and her husband, though nearly as powerless as she, knew people. He could cause more trouble than it was worth if he decided he didn't want his wife to play around with another man.

Politics. That was the problem. *The Home* was supposed to be free of politics, but it wasn't. Those with power helped their friends and hindered their enemies. Oh, it was subtle, but it happened. The right word, hint, in the right place, and a person suddenly found himself or herself promoted a little faster than normal.

William 157 wished he had realized that a little earlier

in his life. He could have done a few favors here and there in the hope they would be remembered when positions opened up as people retired or died. Nothing elaborate. Nothing obvious. Just a favor or two so that the Captain, or the higher-ranking members of his staff might remember his name. Or those whose parents held power might think kindly of him.

But now Sally 176 was next to him on the nearly deserted flight deck, half-naked, and he was sitting like a lump. He made no move, and although she had no power, her father, Ralph 149 certainly did. He had the ear of the administrator, and if William 157 didn't do something, then Sally 175 might become annoyed and tell her father.

William 157 stood up and looked at the hatch, wishing that he could lock it. But, of course, there was no lock on the flight deck. In the event of an emergency, and if access was needed immediately, they couldn't have people searching for a key or someone with the authority to open it. There was nothing on the flight deck to be stolen, and a member of the Crew was usually there anyway.

He stepped in front of Sally 176, slipped a finger under the Velcro, and opened the front of his coverall from throat to crotch. It was obvious that he was ready.

[2]

GEORGE 148, WHO WAS KNOWN TO MOST OF the residents simply as the Captain, sat quietly in his living room. It was twice as large as most. He listened to the whirring of the microwave oven as it cooked his evening meal. He had put the package into the oven nearly five minutes earlier because he didn't want to be surrounded by residents at the community dining hall, he didn't want to answer the same questions over and over tonight, and because he sometimes enjoyed his privacy. He was not required to take his meals outside of his apartment when he didn't want to. It was one of the privileges of his rank.

The Captain, because of his age, looked a bit different

than most of the residents. He was taller, thicker, with darker skin, darker hair, and brown eyes. His heritage, which he proudly traced to Zululand in nineteenth-century Africa, had not been completely blended into the population of *The Home* as they strove for a racial harmony. But he was still within the acceptable range of different, or he would not be Captain. And he knew that.

The Captain hadn't been on the committee that had made the decision, and had he been, he would have voted against it. He believed, given the finite number of residents in *The Home,* that the mixing of people of various backgrounds would have eventually reached a single race in which the differences would be little more than cosmetic. The genetic manipulation to reach that goal in just a couple of generations rather than ten or twelve over a century or more bothered him.

But that made little difference to him. There was nothing he could do to stop it, it had been going on for more than seventy-five years, and the results were startling. The youngest generation all looked as if they had come from a single family with their height varying little more than a couple of inches, the hair and skin color all of the same basic shade, and a physique so similar that it was sometimes difficult to tell the girls from the boys.

George 148 heard the quiet bong from his microwave, but stayed seated. He was watching, to his great amusement, William 157 and Sally 176 engage in sexual intercourse. Not everyone on *The Home* could tune into all the various security cameras, but as Captain, he could. Although it could be argued that the Captain didn't really need to be able to see into the ag pod, or the maintenance pod, or into any of the living areas, he, as Captain, claimed that no one knew where a problem would arise that could affect the operation of *The Home*. He needed to be able to access any camera anywhere at any time without having to wait for permission from some bureaucrat.

He watched as Sally 176 stood up and slowly removed her coverall. She turned slowly, letting William 157, and the Captain, get a good look at her body. She then reached up and slowly rolled her panties down her thighs.

There was another bong, but this time it came from the front door. The Captain, like all those at the top, had the privilege of locks on the doors. And like those of privilege, he didn't have to get up to see who was there. He touched a button on the remote and the scene on his flat-screen shifted from William 157 and Sally 176 to the front door.

His executive officer, Christina 160, stood looking right up into the camera so that there would be no confusion as to who it was.

Still sitting on his couch, he touched another button, and the door unlocked and swung open automatically. He called out, "Come on in."

Christina 160, whose racial heritage was almost impossible to detect given the genetic manipulation that had taken place between the birth of the Captain, and those conceived in the generation after him, was in uniform. She stopped near the Captain, stood at attention, and waited.

"Is this a formal visit?"

"Yes, sir."

"That would explain the uniform. Why don't you sit down and tell me why you're here?"

"I would prefer to stand."

The Captain grinned to himself, but he couldn't fault her for the formality. He had often insisted on the respect and the courtesy that his position demanded. Given his position, he tried to stay somewhat separated from the rest of the Crew and certainly from the residents. To his exec and some of the other top officers, when they were alone, or off duty, he allowed some of the formality to slide.

"Then why are you here?"

"You're aware of what is happening on the flight deck?"

The Captain touched a button, and the view from outside his door returned to that of the flight deck. William 157 was now naked, as was Sally 176. All he could see, given the angle of the camera, was William 157's naked butt bouncing up and down. To the Captain it didn't look very dignified, and it certainly was less than erotic.

He gestured at the flat-screen.

Christina 160 turned and looked. "Oh."

"I certainly don't condone the actions, but he is where he is supposed to be."

"But he is not monitoring the sensor arrays as he is supposed to."

The Captain shrugged, and asked, "Is there something else going on here that I failed to notice?"

"Sally has a husband."

"Has he complained about this . . . liaison?"

"No, Captain, but I don't think it makes for a very happy Crew."

The Captain took a deep breath, then said, "Please sit down."

"Yes, sir." Christina 160 took the small chair to the right, where she could look at the flat-screen and out the small, polarized window that was another privilege of high station on *The Home*.

"Are you suggesting that this will breed disharmony among the Crew?"

"Her husband is working in the ag pod now."

"Yes," said the Captain, "which seems to be the point. He is out of the picture at the moment, and I have heard nothing to suggest that he is unhappy with his arrangement with Sally or with her."

"Still," said Christina 160, "William is not paying attention to his job."

"I have to say, Christina, that if I were worried about this, I would be on my way to the flight deck right now. But the monitors will alert him to anything unusual. I'll be notified automatically, as will the Mayor and his council. I don't see the problem here."

"Then how about the fact that William is Sally's immediate supervisor?"

"But she initiated the activity," said the Captain. "There will be no reward for her because of this. I see no rule broken here. Just a little activity to ease the boredom of a long afternoon watch."

"Yes, sir."

"You put on your uniform to come over just to tell me about this?"

Now she grinned. "Well, I thought I should make this a formal visit in case you weren't aware of what William was doing on the flight deck."

The Captain glanced at the flat-screen where it showed that William had slowed down and was now flat on his back, with Sally sitting astride his hips. She was moving very slowly. He said nothing about her or her technique.

"So there will be no consequence?" asked Christina 160.

The Captain leaned back and put an arm on the rear of the sofa but kept his eyes on the screen. "I can't see where anything has been hurt here. He's where he is supposed to be and can react in a moment. We know what is happening and can monitor the sensors as well."

"Yes, sir. Then I guess I'll be going," said Christina 160.

The Captain suddenly remembered his dinner, cooked and now probably cold. He said to Christina 160, "If you'll wait for me to change into uniform, we could go to the senior dining room for dinner."

"Yes, sir."

[3]

THE HOME'S GOVERNING COUNCIL WAS NOT elected by popular vote, but appointed by the computers that had been programmed to search the residents for those who had the right combination of leadership, intelligence, and ability. It did not search only the databases of those who wanted the jobs, but those of everyone, so that the best and the brightest could be appointed to the council for long terms. A high rate of turnover in governing bodies could lead to fragmented ideals, incomplete planning, and

unnecessary changes in policy because of the whims or de-
sires of the new leaders. Democracies on Earth and Mars
had all suffered from that sort of turnover, which wasn't always a negative.

Michael 177 had been the Mayor for more than a
decade, having taken the job when the old Mayor, Caleb
117, had died in an explosion in the water treatment pod.
A combination of sewer gases and chemical cleansing
agents had been trapped when a vent had failed. An electrical spark from what should have been a shielded con-
nection had ignited the gases, causing an explosion that
took out a third of that water treatment pod and killed fourteen people, including Caleb 117.

There had been talk at the time that someone had
clogged the vent, then exposed the wires to create the explosion, but the only one to really benefit was Michael
177, and he had no way of knowing that he would be selected as the new Mayor. There seemed to be no real mo-
tive unless someone simply liked to see things explode;
but the counselors at the Med Center, not to mention the
computers, had found nothing to suggest that.

Now Michael 177 sat in the center of a curved table
that described about a third of an arc, with the other council members seated on either side of him. These were men
and women appointed by the computers with a little input
from the Mayor. The original programmers had realized
that sometimes people didn't get along because of a per-
sonality conflict. Decades of psychological research had
never found a reason or a cure and could only say that
sometimes these things happened. So, the Mayor, with
good reason, could dismiss a council member. That, of
course, placed a great deal of power in the hands of the
Mayor.

Michael 177, who was young for the position, sat quietly as the other four council members entered the chamber. They were Roger 171, who coordinated the ag
products; Stephen 168, who was responsible for security;
Linda 168, who oversaw flight operations in a general
sense; and Jane 158, who was the advocate for the resi-

dents and their various elected and appointed boards. There was a single "at large" councilor, Gary 169, who was the genetics representative.

Michael looked at the flat-screen mounted in the desk in front of him and situated so that only he could see it. The agenda scrolled past him so that he would know what all had to be discussed, then returned to the top of the page and held there, waiting for him to give the computer a command.

"First item," said Michael 177, "is the outbreak of juvenile vandalism. Incidents have increased in the last month, and I find the trend disturbing."

"It's spring," said Jane 158. She was a dour woman, which meant that something had gone wrong in the birthing process so that she had a negative outlook on life. She looked like everyone else, though her face seemed a little flatter, her eyes drooped slightly, and her hair had been gray for decades, as if there had been no pigment for it.

"How does that explain anything?" asked Michael 177.

"It's the season," she said.

"Nonsense," said Michael 177. "That is meaningless on *The Home*. We have no regular seasons, there is no alteration in the light levels from one season to the next, the magnetic field is not changed, and our growing cycles have been established to reflect a need for continual harvest, not based on the growing seasons controlled by the weather."

"Our biology is not that far removed from that of our brothers and sisters on Earth," said Jane 158.

"We have, over the course of the flight of *The Home*, changed that biology so that when we arrive at The New Home, we will be better suited for that planet. I say again, nonsense."

Gary 169, who looked like he had been the model for the residents, was tall, slender, with the dark skin and dark hair that all had been told was the ideal. He had light-colored eyes that might have been blue, or hazel, but were sometimes the color of water and other times nearly green.

"There had been," he said, "a genetic component that made spring seem to be the best time for mating, though I confess I don't know why. With a nine-month gestation, it would seem that late Fall would make more sense . . ."

"Is there a point in there somewhere?" asked Michael 177, a little sharply.

"Simply that any genetic cause can be ruled out. The predisposition has been eliminated because it was found to be nonproductive."

"Hormones," said Jane 158. "Teenage bodies change, and those changes create strange urges that even your genetic manipulation can't eliminate."

Gary 169 looked at Jane 158 as if he couldn't believe what she had just said. He sighed, and said, "We compensate for that with additional doctor visits and various compounds added to the food of the youngsters at school. This is something that should not be happening."

"Simple solution," said Michael 177. "Test the food and make sure that the levels of the chemicals are appropriate. We might want to add something for the gym classes. A little boost until the problem resolves itself."

"We do not have an overabundance of the compounds," said Gary 169. "They're a drain on our resources."

"And children running loose, creating havoc are also a drain on our resources. I think that we need to begin a program of further education, which includes indoctrination about some of the more structured societies on Earth and less on the wide-open American ways."

"Do you think that necessary?" asked Jane 158.

Stephen 168 interrupted. He was a tall, slender man, who looked like all the others on *The Home*. He said, "There have been any number of studies in Earth-based societies that have shown that violent behavior displayed through various media teaches children behavior that is not learned in other forums. Simply, they see a program with violent actions when those actions are praised or used in conflict resolution, and they learn the lesson that violence is an appropriate solution. We need to look at the programming and select it with an eye to violence. Or rather, not select those with a violent theme."

"Shakespeare was very violent, and his work doesn't lead to violent behavior in youth," said Jane 158.

"Not directly," said Stephen 168, "but I'm looking at the lessons here. Defiance of parental authority, fighting in the streets, and killing opponents. All these lessons can be learned in *Romeo and Juliet,* but that is not the message we want transmitted to our young people."

Michael 177 touched his flat-screen, pulled up the scientific studies on juvenile behavior and the influence of violent programming on the young mind. He scrolled through it, seeing that there was a correlation between violent programming, violent sports—which was why they had banned football and soccer—and violent behavior of youngsters. The effects seemed to wear off, but the correlation was there.

Michael 177 didn't think that watching violence on the flat screen or being exposed to violent episodes in Earth history had made him into a violent person, but they had to be so careful on *The Home.* They were flying through a hostile environment in which one mistake could kill everyone, and they were out of range of help from anyone. Radio signals sent to Earth took years to get there, and it would be years before they could get any sort of response. They were on their own, in a self-contained, limited environment that could collapse if they weren't careful.

He said, "I see no reason to take a chance here. Stephen, with Jane, I want you to review both the shipwide programming and the lessons in the educational arena. I want our violent past to be cut from the programs for the time being. Let's move on to the increased sexual programming and see if we can focus attention on that area." He grinned at the thought, and of what the security cameras might reveal as the youngsters began to experiment with sex.

"If I might be so bold," said Linda 168. She was a small woman who looked like a three-quarter-size replicate of a resident. The doctors couldn't find a reason for her smaller size. The gene that controlled growth had either failed to switch on at the proper time, or switched off early. She wasn't a dwarf or midget, she was just smaller than everyone else.

"I believe," she continued, "that part of the problem might be the computer games . . . in fact, in all games that children play. All create a competition that in the end is unhealthy."

"You're not suggesting that we eliminate the games, are you?" asked Michael 177.

"No, Mister Mayor. Many of them promote hand-eye coordination and some of the strategy games teach critical thinking, as well as developing the mind for advanced thought. Instead, I'm thinking that we change some of those games. Rather than making a big production out of winning . . . some of these games proclaim at the end, 'You won,' in all capital letters with exclamation points. Instead, a note that suggests, oh, I don't know, maybe 'You have succeeded,' or something of that nature."

"Please," said Stephen 168, "aren't we going overboard here? I played all these games growing up, and I don't think it had an adverse affect on me."

"Not the point," said Jane 158. "We know that it can have adverse effects, so why not eliminate it? No one is harmed by this elimination. The games, for the most part, still exist in the computer, and the children can play them. But we change the nature of the competition."

Michael 177 nodded his approval. "I think all these ideas are good ones. I'll want to see some proposals in the next few hours, then we'll make a decision. I can't see any problems except for the production of the various medications, but that can be handled at the production level."

He glanced at the people assembled around the table, then said, "Let's call it a day here. Closed-circuit meeting after lunch."

[4]

THE CAPTAIN, GEORGE 148, ACCOMPANIED BY
his executive officer, Christina 160, the chief of navigation, Murray 162, and the chief of engineering, Carmen
155, entered the tube that would carry them out to one of
the gigantic engine pods. Had anyone looked down on
them, they might have thought it was some kind of a family outing. All were about the same height, had the same
coloring, and the same body type, sorted only into male
and female. The Captain would be thought of as the father,
and the others as his children. They looked that much
alike.

The engine pods were set away from *The Home* proper,
to protect the inhabitants from any radiation generated.
They were attached near the center of *The Home* so that
they could thrust in either a forward or backward direction
depending on the orientation of *The Home*. Smaller
thrusters, scattered around the perimeter of *The Home* allowed them to rotate the ship so that thrust could be produced in any direction needed. Directional changes were
actually large, looping turns that had to be handled very
carefully given the size and mass of *The Home*. The engine
pod wasn't the best system ever devised, but it worked.

The hatch that allowed access into the main tunnel
opened as they approached, the computer having recognized the Captain and members of the Crew. It recognized
that each of the residents had clearance to the engine pod,
so it made no effort to stop them. Residents who were not
members of the Flight Crew, if they had approached the
door, would have been warned off, and had that failed, Security would have been alerted. If, in any fashion, the residents had breached the hatch, they would have been
stunned by electrical charges. And had that failed, for
whatever reason, they would have been electrocuted. The
engines had to be protected at all costs.

The Captain and the others entered through the hatch,
which closed behind them. A conveyer belt on the floor
would move them rapidly toward the pod. They could

walk along the "resident mover" for more speed if they wanted.

The Captain stopped walking, leaned back against a waist-high barrier, and turned to look back at his Crew. He said, "This is simply a routine inspection."

"Which we could have done on the flight deck," said Murray 162.

"Yes, but this access tunnel is one of the few places that isn't monitored all the time."

"And why is that important?" asked Murray 162.

Christina 160 took a deep breath and sighed. "Why not allow the Captain to talk?"

"I've been thinking about the overall command of *The Home*," said the Captain. "We have a dual command structure here. Civilian and military. There are times when these two lines of command come into conflict with each other."

"What are you suggesting?"

The Captain held up a hand as they passed the halfway point of the tunnel. There was a camera array there, in case someone penetrated the security at the hatch. When they had moved beyond it, the Captain said, "I'm suggesting only that we think about this problem and how it might play out on The New Home."

Murray 162 said, "I don't understand your concern. The system has worked well for over two hundred years, and we're not due to arrive at The New Home until long after we are dead and recycled."

"Well," said the Captain, "we're living in a closed environment, where our population is strictly limited, and the dangers of life have been eliminated to a great extent. If we pay attention to the rules of evolution, however, we see that we're breeding ourselves into extinction."

"What in the hell are you talking about?"

The Captain shrugged, and said, "I only want each of you to think about this. Survival of a species is directed by the strongest, smartest, fittest of the individuals. In our environment, the traits that would make for successful competition in such an environment are being slowly eliminated in favor of a docile, gentle, easily manipulated resident. The fittest in this environment are certainly different than the fittest that developed on Earth many centuries ago."

"That's not all necessarily bad, Captain," said Christina 160.

"On *The Home,* no. But once we arrive at The New Home, once we can no longer control everything to the degree that we do, these new, docile traits are not going to help us survive. In fact, they're going to work against us."

They were reaching the engine pod, where there were more monitors and another security screen. The Captain held up his hand to end the discussion. He said, "Remember, I'm only pointing out a flaw in the thinking on the civilian side of the equation here. I think we all would be better off if we thought this all the way through and made recommendations based on those thoughts. I'm not suggesting anything, other than we might have a problem with the overall programming that could be corrected with an added dose of military thought."

"Yes, sir," said Christina 160.

When the resident mover stopped, they stepped off onto the hard, stationary surface. The hatch into the engine pod was heavier than that at the other end of the access tunnel. The Captain put his thumb against the identification plate, looked directly into the lens of a camera, and said, "Captain. George 148. With a party of officers."

There was no response, but the hatch irised open so that they could step through. Once inside, they stopped at the edge of the railing surrounding the conversion engine. It was shielded to prevent the leakage of radiation as it throbbed and threw out a screen that scooped up hydrogen for fuel. There was nothing to see, other than the size of the engine. The monitoring could be done from the flight deck, and repairs were accomplished by computer and drone. Rarely did any humans enter the engine pod other than on a guided tour.

The Captain stood there, hands clasped behind his back, and stared up at the marvel of technology. Although the engines had been built more than two hundred years earlier, they had functioned with few repairs, little maintenance, and looked as if they had been brought on-line only days earlier. He would have thought that two-hundred-year-old technology would look, well, two hundred years old.

He didn't know what had been accomplished on Earth, what the state of interstellar flight was, though they were, more or less, in communication with Earth. He knew that civilization had survived and that the alien creatures that had flown by the Solar System, now more than two hundred years earlier, had not returned. They knew as little about them today as they had then. Apparently, whatever the aliens had been searching for was not available in the Solar System.

He looked out of the corner of his eyes at the men and women with him—the products of genetic engineering that had been an outgrowth of what someone else thought would be the best human for the long flights of the generation ships. Smaller than the average on Earth. Thinner, but smarter. Weaker but more harmonious. Trade-offs necessary for the enforced closeness of a ship traveling at below-light-speeds for other solar systems. All engineered so that the human race could move its eggs from their single basket. Engineered so that the destruction of one world did not mean the end of humanity.

The Captain took a deep breath and stared up at the nearly blinding overhead lighting reflected from the engine itself as it hummed along. There were no moving parts that he could see, merely a deep humming, more of a pulsation that he felt through the soles of his feet, and a high-pitched whine that was almost beyond the threshold of human hearing.

Christina 160 slipped closer to the Captain, and asked quietly, "Do you know what you're doing?"

George 148 turned and smiled, almost as if he were the father and she the bright daughter. "Of course. I've thought long and hard about this. It is something that needs to be done."

"I'm with you, but Murray . . ."

Murray had moved away from the group, along the catwalk to where he could look down into the bowels of the engine and see a blue flickering that might have been static electricity jumping from one metal part to another but was something more like an aura. It presented no threat to the functioning of the engine or to *The Home*.

"Murray will be fine," said the Captain. "He'll be slow to understand the problem; but he will, and he will then join us in our mission."

Raising his voice, the Captain said, "Everything looks to be working properly. I suggest that we retreat and see if we can find lunch."

[5]

FOUR DAYS LATER THEY ALL MET IN THE CAPtain's private quarters for a party. Although most of the bridge and navigation Crew were present, many of the engineers were not. George 148 didn't like it when members of the Crew were not present for his parties, and while he understood that some of the engineers were required to maintain the engines, and some of the navigation Crew were performing required duties on the bridge, he had hoped that everyone else would be there.

With the approval of the Mayor, the party was catered by the kitchen staff of Dining Hall Thirty-seven. They brought covered trays, warming dishes, silverware, plates, glasses, and they would be around for cleanup later. The Captain, who hosted the party, did nothing more than show up and partake in a little of everything provided.

The Captain circulated slowly, pulling from the Crew present the top officers and those most sympathetic to his point of view. He ushered them into his private study, a large room that looked like a library on Earth except that the shelves of books were all an illusion.

Through the library computer, the Captain had access to all the books of Earth without restriction, another privilege of rank. Home computers could only access certain books and information. Some computers didn't even contain a full index of everything available, but the Captain could look at anything he wanted.

The room itself was about twice the size of a lower-end family apartment, but it was furnished with the very best. There was a desk that looked like mahogany, but was, of course, plastic and steel, a conversation area that had a long couch that looked like leather but was synthetic, with chairs near it, and a table that was partially actual wood, taken and processed from two fruit trees that had died.

The Captain, a drink in his hand, circulated in the room, thanking all for coming. He then walked to his desk, sat on a corner of it, and said, quietly, just loud enough to be heard over the noise of the party in the other rooms, "I welcome all of you here, to the inner sanctum."

Christina 160, who was not dressed in a uniform but was wearing a short dress that seemed to be made of mesh, said, "This is the command structure?"

The Captain didn't like that question and shot her a glance. He said, "We have all agreed that some policy shift might be in order."

Christina 160 walked to the couch and sat down, slowly crossing her legs. She said nothing.

Murray 162, wearing his dress uniform, complete with medals and badges, said, "I think we might want to hold off any action until we're sure it's needed. I've seen nothing to suggest planetfall in the next fifty or sixty years. I don't understand what we're talking about here."

The Captain nodded, but said, "The educational programs are being changed even as we speak. The Mayor, in consultation with members of his staff, has decided that our society here on the ship is too violent. I'm afraid that in years to come all of the traits we'll need on that far-distant planet will be bred from us. We won't have the skills we need to tame that world. In time, there will be no one who remembers any of the old lessons learned on Earth. I think that we need to ensure the continuity of the information to ensure the continuity of our mission here and our race on The New Home."

Philip 188, a young navigator who had joined the group

because Sarah 190 had been included, said, "I have done a survey of the closest star systems, and I haven't seen anything that is promising. The two nearest stars have, between them thirty-two planets, and not one of them has a diameter smaller than that of Jupiter. There is nothing in any of them that would be of use to us, which means the mission will continue."

"That include the moons?" asked Sarah 190.

Philip 182 blushed, and said, "I focused on the planets, not the moons."

The Captain held up his hand, the ice cubes in his glass tinkling. He said, "I think that ending this discussion might be a bit premature."

"I was just saying, Captain, that we have plenty of time because there isn't any planet close by that we could use for The New Home."

"Thank you, Lieutenant, but I'm aware of what is around us. Sarah, there are three moons, two in one system and one in the other, that are about the size of Earth. They are orbiting with their planets inside the star's biosphere, but we have little or no indications of liquid water on any of them. That, of course, makes them unsatisfactory to us."

"Yes, Captain."

"The point," he said, raising his voice, "is that we are far enough out that we can be subtle. We don't have to act tomorrow. But we have to be aware that action will be necessary if the trends here don't change. We must keep a hard edge to the human race, or we will not be able to survive on the surface once we reach The New Home."

He waited for someone else to say something, but no one did. He held up his glass, and said, "I wanted each of you to see the others who are as interested in this as I. I wanted each of you to understand that we are not alone on this and that your fellow officers in the Flight Crew are with you. That we understand one another and that by each of us seeing the others, we would know where our strengths are."

Sarah 190, who was wearing her uniform though she had modified it slightly so that it seemed molded to her body, held up a hand. Residents who altered their coveralls in such an individual fashion would have been counseled about their lack of respect for their clothing. Members of the Crew were rewarded for their initiative.

The Captain said, "You are free to speak."

"Yes, sir. Should we be recruiting?"

The Captain was about to tell her no, but stopped. He closed his eyes for a moment, then opened them. "I would think that we might all approach fellow Crew and sound them out carefully. At this point, I don't think we should bring any residents into this. I simply don't know which way they might jump because they don't have the training that we do."

"Yes, sir."

"Now," said the Captain, "I want to propose a toast, which is why I have been waving this glass around like some kind of a banner. To our success, to finding The New Home, and to every member of the Crew."

Those in the room joined him. They took swallows from their glasses and began to move toward the door.

Christina 160 stood up and walked over to the Captain. He glanced down, saw her nipples through the mesh of her dress, and decided that he approved. He did enjoy looking at the female form, and if a woman put herself on display, she shouldn't be surprised that people looked.

As the last of the Crew slipped out the door, she asked, "Do you think that was a good idea?"

"What?"

"Exposing the whole conspiracy to so many. Everyone who is involved was in this room tonight. That might not have been a wise decision."

"I wanted everyone to know that he or she is not alone in this. That many members of the Crew had thought about the matter and joined us. I wanted them to know that we are standing together."

"And any one of them could tell Security tomorrow that we are unhappy with the civilian leadership."

The Captain finished his drink and set the glass on his desk. "So what?"

"Any one of them can identify all of us. Secret organizations always make sure that no one person has information on everyone else. Prevents one individual from giving away the whole group. Now everyone knows everyone else."

"Christina, this isn't Earth, and this isn't a conspiracy. All we're doing is talking about ways to improve *The Home.* No one is going to concern themselves with that."

"Captain, are you really that naive?"

"Meaning what?"

"You are suggesting that we take control away from the civilian government. They're not going to like that."

"I'm only suggesting that we have a say in the policy of running *The Home.* We're residents, too. And I think we have some ideas that will not only improve life here, but make survival on The New Home easier for those who finally find themselves on that planet."

Christina set her drink down and stepped closer to the Captain. "I think you're splitting hairs here, and I don't think it will make any difference."

"We'll we have to do something, and there is no one qualified to take our places. We are bargaining from a position of power."

"If you call it bargaining," said Christina 160 quietly.

"What would you call it?"

"Mutiny."

[6]

STEPHEN 168 STOOD IN FRONT OF A WALL made of flat-screens. By using his mouse, he could access information from anywhere in *The Home,* punch up conversations so that he could hear what was being said, spy on people in their bedrooms or in the common baths, and in a hundred other places that they believed had complete and total privacy. Although everyone knew there were cameras that monitored behavior, they did not know how extensive the system was. Very few knew that cameras could see practically everything, and only Stephen 168 and his top two assistants knew it could see *everything*. Not practically everything, but *everything*.

There was a single room where there were no cameras and monitoring systems, and he was standing in it. There was no one to guard the guards. That was the flaw in the system, and no one had figured out how to defeat it. Even if another, outside security had access to everything, there was still someone who stood at the apex of the system. The only solution was to put the final review into the hands of the computer, and no one wanted that sort of power given to a machine. So, there were security officers at the apex of the system.

Stephen 168 turned to the right, where Julie 201 sat at the console that controlled the screens. She was looking down at the flat-screen there, and said, "Do you want all rooms?"

"Just the library from the other night."

The scenes in front of him vanished and were replaced by the party that had been held in the Captain's quarters. Stephen 168 studied Christina 160 as she moved around the room, talking to other members of the Crew. It wasn't that he was interested in her activities; he was fascinated by her dress. It left little to the imagination.

Stephen 168 watched as some of the Crew entered the library, then as the Captain spoke. He listened to the speech, thinking that there was little of a subversive nature in any of the actual words, though the meaning was quite clear. He watched as they agreed with the Captain, then filtered from the room. And he watched as Christina 160 suggested that they had been talking about a mutiny.

"Clear it," he said. "Bring up the Captain now."

Seated in a room across *The Home,* the Captain was eating his lunch. Near him were three members of the Crew who had been at his apartment and in his library during the talk. They were alone in the dining room that was for the exclusive use of the Crew. No residents were there.

"We can get three of them," said Julie 201.

"Wasted effort. We need to take them in a public environment, so that the lesson won't be lost on the residents."

"Still, cut off the head . . ."

"Show me the other conspirators."

The screen seemed to fragment, and suddenly there were two dozen smaller pictures, each centered on one of those who had been in the Captain's library. Each was in uniform. A few were in their apartments. More were on the flight deck or attending to other duties. Two were in the pedestrian mall, walking among the residents and acknowledging their admiration.

"We have security close to all of them?"

"Yes, sir. At least two per Crew member."

Stephen 168 rubbed at his chin, thinking. It was time to end the mutiny. There were enough of the Crew in public locations that the lesson would not be lost. Within an hour the residents would be talking about what they had seen, or what they had heard. Within an hour the Mayor, Michael 177, could be on every flat-screen suggesting that the danger was over. In an hour, everything could go back to the way it was.

"The teams are ready," said Julie 201.

"Here's what I want to do. Keep everyone in position. I'm going to supervise the arrest of the Captain."

"Even without an audience?"

"We have enough of the Crew out among the residents so that the message will be clear. Might be better to take him in private. Won't frighten the residents that way."

"Yes, sir."

Stephen 168 walked back to the control console where Julie 201 sat. He touched a button, then leaned down, toward the wire-thin microphone. He said, "Security teams, stay with your targets. We go on my command. Kim 188 to the control room."

Julie 201 looked up but said nothing.

Stephen 168 said, "I want a senior member of the team on hand here in case there is a breakdown in communications."

"Yes, sir."

Without another word, Stephen 168 left the control room and walked swiftly to the locker room. He opened the locker assigned to him and removed his taser. He hooked it to his belt, took out his pepper spray, then his leather-covered sap. He thought about the tangle foot, which was little more than an electrically charged net that wrapped itself around the feet and ankles and gave off periodic pulses to interrupt the neurological impulses; but that seemed too extreme. The other nonlethal weapons wouldn't be necessary. He, with two others, should be able to subdue the Captain and those with him. He wouldn't need any of the old slug throwers or lasers locked in the arms vault.

He left the locker room and walked out of the Security Building. It was down the street from the court. But unlike that structure, with its artificial stone edifice, the Security Building was small and looked like any other part of *The Home*. It was made of metal bulkheads, with steel hatches and no windows.

He hurried along a steel-and-aluminum corridor, turned down another, and walked out into the central park area. He followed the designated path to another corridor and slowed as he walked along it.

Residents who saw him moved to one side or hurried into a compartment, apartment, or office to get out of his way. They weren't afraid of Stephen 168, and had he been in a regular coverall, they probably wouldn't have noticed him. But, because of the arrests to be made, he was dressed in his uniform of black with the red piping of Security.

In fifteen minutes he reached the Crew's private dining hall. He spotted his two security officers, a man and a woman, standing where they could watch the hatch but couldn't be easily seen. Both were wearing resident coveralls, but when they saw Stephen 168, they pulled their security hats out of their equipment packs and put them on.

Stephen 168 approached them, and said, "What have you got to report."

The man, James 194, said, "There are four of them in

there now. The Captain and three of the lesser officers. They're still eating their lunch."

The woman, Elizabeth 186, said, "They haven't seen us. They are relaxed, eating slowly, and talking about living to see The New Home."

"All right. Standard arrest. I'll speak for us and tell the Captain that his antiharmony activities have been observed and he is to come with us. If they cooperate, then we take them to Security for interrogation. If not, use pepper spray first and tasers second. I want to do this with as little force as possible."

"Yes, sir."

Stephen 168 stepped to the hatch and touched the lock with his thumb. It cycled for a moment, recognized his print, and irised open. As he stepped through, into the dining hall, he whispered into his radio, "All teams are to go."

"You are not authorized in this facility," said the Captain, coming to his feet when he saw the intruders.

"That I have opened the hatch suggests that I am. Captain, George 148, I must inform you that you are under arrest for plotting to undermine the civilian authority of *The Home*. Your colleagues here, as well as all other members of the Crew who have plotted against the harmony of *The Home* are being arrested as we speak."

"I will not allow this," said the Captain.

As he stood up, so did the other members of the crew. Jackie 199 was the youngest. Hal 189 moved to the right as if to outflank Security. Lawrence 191 moved to the left.

"Captain," said Stephen 168, "this is unnecessary, and it will be your people who get hurt."

"You had better get out of here. I'm going to take this up with the Mayor."

Jackie 199 moved then, toward the female security officer. Elizabeth 186 responded with her pepper spray. She aimed the tiny can at Jackie 199 and pushed. The jet of spray caught Jackie 199 on the throat and chin. She leaped then, grabbing at the hand that held the can, but, with her eyes closed, she missed.

Elizabeth 186 sidestepped easily, grabbed the hand of

Jackie 199, lifting. As she did, she punched once, feeling her knuckles against the soft flesh of Jackie 199's abdomen. Jackie 199 cried out in surprise and fell to the floor, doubled up in pain, trying to catch her breath.

Before the Captain could move, Stephen 168 drew his taser and, without a second thought, fired. The two darts hit the Captain in the upper chest and pulsed once. Without a sound, the Captain fell to the deck.

At that moment the other two Crewmen froze, one raising his hands.

Stephen 168 asked, "Everyone all right?"

"We're good."

Jackie 199 was sitting up, breathing deeply. She slowly climbed to her feet.

"You will all accompany us to Security."

"We've done nothing wrong," said Lawrence 191.

"That is for the judicial panel to decide. In the meantime, you'll come with us."

Stephen 168 touched the button on his radio, and said, "Status report."

He listened as the others checked in, each reporting success with the arrests. He nodded once.

The Captain was by then sitting up. His face was gray, and he was sweating heavily. He managed to ask, "What's going to happen to us now?"

"You should have been thinking about that earlier."

"How did you know?"

Stephen 168 grinned broadly, and said, "Christina told us. We've known since the very beginning. She'll be promoted to Captain now."

CHAPTER THREE

YEAR TWO THREE FIVE

[1]

ONLY RARELY DID JASON 215 MISS LIVING WITH his parents. Only rarely did he think about their tiny apartment, his unlimited access to the computer, and the benefits of having someone else take care of him. Now he was on his own, living in a cubicle that was one in a long line of cubicles across a narrow corridor from an identical row of cubicles.

His cubicle was, of course, like all the others. It was small, little more than eight-by-ten, holding a cot with a thin mattress, a small desk to support the flat-screen and keyboard, and a shelf with a pole running under it to hang his clothes. There were almost no personal items in the cubicle, except for a picture of a sunset on Earth that had been there when he moved in. Pictures of his parents, friends, graduations, and winning teams were stored in the computer, to be reviewed when the mood moved him.

He had grown since the day his friends had moved, disappearing from his life almost as permanently as if they had died or returned to Earth. His father told him that their fathers or mothers had been transferred into the industrial park some eight miles away and seemed to think that those who lived and worked there were somehow below his station. Although he had not forbidden a trip to the industrial park, Randolph 185 had made it clear that if his son traveled there, he would be disappointed in him.

So Jason 215 had tried to communicate with his friends through the computer net, but somehow the messages were lost, or misdirected, or never acknowledged. In a few months, as the school year progressed and new students arrived from the engineering center or the ag center, Jason 215 forgot about Thomas 215 and Cynthia 216.

Now he rarely saw his parents, who lived in the same apartment as they always had, but he was at the far side of *The Home,* living in the university area. He was studying astronavigation, with an eye to joining the Flight Crew upon graduation. There were fewer students in that field and those related to the operation of *The Home* after the scandal of 227.

Jason 215 sat on his cot, but he could see the flat-screen on his tiny desk. He could see the opening of his paper, due at the end of the week, but he didn't feel like working on it. The topic had been chosen for him, and it wasn't something that he really wanted to know. A survey of the gas giants in the nearest four solar systems did nothing for him. Better to look for smaller, Earth-like planets where they might be able to establish The New Home rather than study gas giants that were, at best, in the way.

Helen 214 appeared at the opening of his cubicle, one hand up on the top of it as she leaned against the wall. She was a hair taller than most of the residents and seemed to be a little thinner, though she weighed a little more. She was wearing shorts and nothing else. Her long, dark hair had been piled on the top of her head.

"You going to eat soon?" she asked.

Jason 215 looked at her but tried not to stare. He was still young enough that the differences between the boys and the girls interested him. He could, by walking down to the shower, see a number of girls, completely undressed, and, of course, there were the intercourse chat rooms where he could not only look at the girls, but talk to them, through the network, while watching them. It wasn't a big deal, but it was something that was more fun than studying, say, the photographs of the gas giants of the four nearest systems, which weren't at all interesting.

But the problem with the girls in the chat rooms was that they were on the computer screen and couldn't be touched. Too often, they were in another segment of *The Home,* and travel into those areas was severely restricted. Without the proper permissions and passes, he couldn't just drop in to see them even if they invited him over. On the other hand, Helen 214 was standing right in front of him, offering him an opportunity to forget all about the gas giants in the four closest systems.

"Sure," he said. "Why not?"

"Let me grab a shirt, and I'll meet you at the door."

Jason 215 swung his feet down and stood up. He glanced at the flat-screen. His report sat there waiting, the cursor blinking slowly, almost as if to remind him of the work he needed to finish. He touched a button, and the screen darkened into the standby mode.

He saw Helen 214 standing near the door wearing a coverall and sandals. She was talking to two other residents, one male and one female. As Jason 215 approached, she said, "Donna and Zeke thought they would join us."

Jason 215 thought about telling them to get lost, but that wasn't done. No matter how private a conversation, all residents were invited to join. No matter what Jason 215 might have thought about the invitation by Helen 214, they couldn't exclude others on a whim. All residents were equal. Instead of suggesting that he had planned to dine with Helen 214 alone, he smiled, and said, "Two more just makes it a better time."

They walked out of the dormitory, crossed a pathway, and turned left on another. They walked past a series of low buildings that housed administration and computation services, and a library that held a number of computer terminals, though Jason 215 never understood the reason for such a structure. All the information in the various starship libraries could be accessed from any of the computers, including the one on his desk. Jason 215 didn't understand that the reason the library annex existed was for the interaction of the residents rather than because of the information available.

As they entered the dining hall, they swiped their wrists at the scanner, which registered their presence. They moved to a line similar to those in any cafeteria on Earth, selected what they wanted for dinner, and swiped their wrists at the scanner at the far end of the line. The food they selected was also noted. Had they been eating too much that was of little overall nutritional value, had they been eating meals that weren't properly balanced, at some point the computers would have noticed and it would be suggested that a better diet be planned. All residents had their eating habits monitored and often dictated when they began to slide into poor nutrition.

They sat at one of the long tables, taking seats two abreast on opposite sides. They used the plastic utensils to eat off plastic trays made of recycled materials.

Once settled, Jason 215 asked, "Anyone want something to drink?"

Helen 214 said, "Sure. I'll go with you.

That left the other two sitting at the table as Jason 215 and Helen 214 walked to the front of the cafeteria where the drink dispenser sat. He took a cup, scanned his wrist implant, and let the liquid fill.

"It's nice to be able to relax a little," said Helen 214.

"Well, it's not as if we're working for a living," said Jason 215.

"What do you mean?"

"We're in school, learning."

"Which is our job now. We're to learn as much as we

can as fast as we can so that we can be of service to *The Home*."

When his cup was filled, Jason 215 moved it out of the way. He took a sip and for the twentieth time was certain it wasn't as sweet as it had once been. He kept thinking that he would check out the formula and see if he could find out if it had been modified in the last few weeks, but by the time he got back to his computer, he had forgotten about the problem.

To Helen 214, he said, "I can't think of it as a job. We produce nothing, perform no service, and *The Home* sees no real benefit in what we do."

"Sure, now. But when we graduate, then we'll be productive residents. *The Home* is investing in us so that it will benefit in the future." She was beginning to sound like one of the counselors at the Med Center.

When she had her cup filled, they walked back to the table and sat down with their friends. Jason 215 asked them, "Do you think of what we do, as students, as a job?"

Wendy 212 said, "Of course. It is our duty to learn as much as we can as quickly so that we might relieve the burden of our elders and give them some time to enjoy life before the end."

"And you?" Jason 215 asked Zeke 211.

"Certainly. Don't you?"

Jason 215 sipped his drink, then set the cup on the table in front of him. "Not as a job. Sure, it's important for us to study, learn our lessons, but it's not a job. Residents aren't relying on us."

"Sure they are. They are relying on us to learn our jobs and become full residents of *The Home*."

Jason shrugged, and said, "If you all insist."

[2]

WHEN HE WOKE UP IN THE MORNING, TO THE slightly insistent chirping of his computer, Jason 215 felt a little tired, a little sad, and more than a little annoyed. He didn't like the way things had been structured for him. Four years of "infancy" when his only "duty" had been to develop into a thinking human so that any training he received would be retained. Then it became his "job" to learn, first at elementary school and eventually, after years of schooling, at the university. Learn all that he could so that he could become a productive resident.

No one had asked his opinion of this. It had been decreed before he was born and would be the way long after he died. Residents were not asked what they wanted to do. They were told. From the moment they were born, even if they couldn't understand the instructions, until they died, they were told exactly what to do.

Jason 215 had wanted to be a member of the Crew, maybe a pilot, or even the Captain, but he was satisfied with being in navigation. He would eventually join the Crew, be issued the black coverall with the gold piping, and have the responsibility of plotting the course for *The Home*. He would be a productive resident who had an important job. He was lucky that his ambition coincided with the needs of *The Home*. Had they not, he might have found himself as a maintenance worker in the bowels of *The Home*, covered with grease doing a job he hated.

As he sat up, blinking, and the overhead lights came on signaling that it was time for everyone to rise, he felt anger. His class schedule had been prepared for him when he arrived at the university, along with his assigned dorm cube, and even the social circle in which he moved. Nothing had been left to chance, and sometimes he wished it had been. He wanted a little random excitement in his life.

Thinking about it before he got up, he remembered that long-ago discussion he'd had with his teacher and his parents, when he had wanted to know how he knew that the material being taught was accurate. How did he know that it hadn't been manipulated to make him think it was true when it might not be?

Yes, he could see that two plus two was four because mathematical truths were mathematical truths, but what about the material he couldn't test. He couldn't know for certain that the reason for the launch of *The Home* was alien contact. He couldn't know for certain that there were any aliens out there because he hadn't seen them. All he had seen was the computer records, and he knew how easily those could be altered. All it took was someone with a keyboard or voice input, a little time, and some programming knowledge. A clever resident could alter the computer record, and there would be no way to discover that.

Jason 215 stood up, stripped off his underwear, then walked naked down the corridor to the communal shower. He slid in, between two classmates, one male and one female, and turned on the shower. It sprayed for just twenty seconds, allowing him enough time to get wet. He then soaped, scrubbed, and took another twenty seconds to wash the soap from his body. He then stepped in front of a blower that dried him. There was very little waste because they had so little to waste.

He returned to his cube, dressed, and before he could join the line for breakfast, a quiet bong on the flat screen told him he had an incoming message. He turned, touched a button, and saw, "Jason 215, you are required at the Med Center at 1000 hours for your routine, yearly examination. Thank you."

Jason 215 sat down on his cot and stared at the message because it didn't make any sense to him. His routine physical wasn't for another six weeks, and he'd seen no indication that anyone else had been required to come in early.

"Me and my big mouth," he said out loud to no one.

If he pretended that he was like everyone else and accepted everything that was said, he wouldn't have to make those unscheduled and sometimes frightening extra trips to the Med Center.

Helen 214 appeared at the cubicle opening, and said, "I was hoping to catch you."

He looked at her, annoyed, because he felt she had betrayed him. He believed that she had told someone about his questions at dinner and the report had somehow gotten to the doctors at the Med Center. He said, somewhat coolly, "Well, you found me."

"You going to breakfast?"

"I'm not very hungry this morning. I have to go to the Med Center."

"Oh, really?" She sounded excited. "How come?"

"Annual physical, though it's early this year."

"Well, it's your duty to eat. You must maintain your health for the good of *The Home*."

He was about to say something snappy and maybe a little sarcastic when he realized that it wasn't the wise course of action. He didn't know who might be listening and who might turn him in to the authorities.

"Yes, you're right. I need to keep my strength up."

"Let's hurry," said Helen 214. "We don't want to be at the end of the line.

"We sure don't."

[3]

WHEN JASON 215 ENTERED THE MED CENTER fifteen minutes early, he was escorted to the second floor and taken to one of the small, treatment rooms. There he stripped his coverall and hung it up. Then he sat down and quietly waited for the doctor.

Two men entered the room, both older than Jason 215. Neither wore a name tag but both were dressed in white coats over their white coveralls.

One of them turned to the flat-screen, touched the keyboard, and read what appeared. He said, "Well, this isn't much of a problem I see."

Jason 215 said, "I was told to come in early for my annual physical."

"And so you have," said the doctor at the screen. He stood up and took a loaded injector from the drawer, looked at the label on the bottle inserted into the top, and moved toward Jason 215.

"Just a little booster here for you."

"You're sure I need that?" asked Jason 215.

"Not afraid of a little medication, are you?"

"No."

The doctor grabbed Jason 215 by the upper arm, held him tightly, and placed the nose of the injector against the flesh of his shoulder. He squeezed the trigger, there was a quiet thump, and a sensation of coolness.

Jason 215 looked at the doctor and grinned weakly. He felt suddenly dizzy, as if the room had begun to spin while he stood still in the center of it. He thought he was going to be sick, then thought he was going to fall down. He put out a hand to steady himself, and the next thing he remembered was lying on one of the examination tables.

The doctors were long gone, but there was a nurse standing there. Julie 193 reached out, touched his wrist, as if to take his pulse, but that was being done automatically. Hers was a gesture designed for human contact and comfort, not one born of medical necessity.

"You're awake," she said.

"What happened?"

"Reaction to the medication. Happens sometimes. It's nothing to worry about."

"I feel fine now."

Julie 193 helped him into a sitting position. "When you feel strong enough, you can go."

Jason 215 had a sudden headache. There was a pounding behind his eyes and a rushing in his eyes. Black began to descend again; and then, as quickly as it had begun, it ended. The headache was gone, and the room was bright.

"I guess I'm up to it," he said.

"All right. I'll leave you here."

As Julie 193 walked out of the room, Jason 215 began to put on his clothes. He realized that he felt calm, almost relaxed, except for the paper hanging over his head. A survey of those four systems was needed and while he thought others were doing the same work, it didn't hurt to have another corroborate the findings. That made for good science.

[4]

THE DORMITORY WAS IN CHAOS WHEN JASON
215 returned. All the lights were turned on, computers
were screaming for attention, and residents were literally
running around. Helen 214 hurried up to Jason 215, and almost yelled, "Have you heard?"

"No."

"Blight in an ag pod."

"What?"

"Some kind of blight in an ag pod. Spreading rapidly,
destroying crops."

"Crap," said Jason 215. "What are they going to do?"

"Everyone has to report to the ag pod now. Everyone in
this dormitory."

Jason 215 looked at the flat-screen and could see the
face of Michael 177, the Mayor. He was talking quietly
while a series of pictures appeared behind him, showing
one of the ag pods. Jason 215 didn't stop to listen to the
Mayor. He already knew what was being said.

"You need to wear your boots, coverall, and take one
spare set of everything. We're not going to be able to get
back here anytime soon."

Jason 215 looked around him. He saw his friends beginning to move toward the door. All were dressed the
same, all prepared for labor in the ag pod. He sat down on
his cot, listening to the chaos. He kicked off his sandals
and put on his boots. He took his oldest coverall and put it
on. Into the pockets he shoved everything else that he
would need. His personal items such as his toothbrush,
clean underwear, and clean socks fit nicely into the pockets.

Helen 214 stood watching him, and said, "Hurry up.
We've got to be ready to go."

Days earlier, Jason 215 might have asked what the rush
was because the blight wasn't going to spread that fast. He
might have suggested that the Mayor was overreacting to
a minor situation, but now, today, he was caught up in the
excitement. He felt his heart race and his head seem to

spin. His fingers seemed to be the size of sausages as he tried to lace his boots. Finally, he stood, ready to join the fight, to stamp out the blight that threatened the ag pod.

He almost pushed Helen 214 out of the way as he tried to join the line forming at the door. They stood side by side as the main doors opened, and they marched out to the waiting farm techs who would lead them up toward the ag pod. He didn't ask why they had to walk in such a tight formation, nor why the blight had been allowed to spread. All he knew, all he cared about, was that they had to do something quickly or great amounts of *The Home*'s food supply would be lost with no way to recover it. They couldn't buy it on the open market from those other countries that found themselves with a surplus. They had to solve the problem, or they wouldn't have enough food.

When everyone from the dormitory was standing outside, one of the techs, dressed in the light green of the ag workers, yelled at them, "If you will please follow me. We have no more time to waste."

The man turned and began to jog away, toward the central park, where the access tunnels to the ag pods were located. The students, Jason 215 included, followed, running along with him. They formed four lines, running in step with each other, almost as if they were in a military formation and heading toward battle. They carried nothing, other than the few personal items that didn't fit easily into their pockets.

Jason 215 felt good about this. Not that a blight had struck, but that they were moving rapidly to do something about it. He was surrounded by people he knew. Smart people, just entering into their adult lives, ready to battle the latest threat that confronted *The Home.* He was glad for the opportunity to contribute something to the rest of the society. Something that was more tangible than a report on the gas giants of four nearby planetary systems.

Around him the others seemed to feel the same way. Many were smiling as they ran, following the man in the light green coverall. There was a rhythmic pounding of their feet, as if someone had told them to run at a certain pace with each fourth step a little heavier. They were out to fight the problem and to contribute to the health of the starship.

Jason 215 didn't have time to run out of energy, or to get winded, before they reached the access tunnel. The leader held up a hand like an infantry officer ordering a halt. Then he walked to the hatch over the access tunnel and waved his implant under the scanner. The hatch irised open, but this was larger than most of the other access tunnels. It was wide enough for two wagons to pass one another. It was designed so that equipment could be taken to the ag pod as it was needed and the produce brought out as it was harvested.

Without a word, the man waved at the students, and the first, of them began to walk forward. They entered the access tunnel, and Jason 215 followed. He had never been in either this access tunnel or this particular ag pod. The flooring under his feet moved when he stepped into the tunnel, but he didn't stop walking. Instead he moved forward more quickly, surrounded by the other students, all maintaining their formation without command or direction.

They reached the far end of the access tunnel and stepped out onto the catwalk that provided admittance to the whole pod. There they stopped for a moment as their leader tried to find out where they were needed first.

Jason 215 hadn't expected what he saw. As a youngster, he and two friends, including Thomas 215, had sneaked through a tunnel and found themselves in one of the other ag pods. It looked to Jason 215 like the inside of a large building, with the floor and part of the walls covered in dirt and streaked with green. Overhead had been banks of strangely colored lights that simulated the sun. It was sort of a curved farm with an extended growing season, rain that came from overhead sprinklers and only when needed, and a sun that was regulated by computer and rheostat. The growing day had been extended to the point where the plants grew at an alarming rate, almost so fast that anyone watching could see the changes in the vegetation.

This pod was not like that other. It held large, shallow vats covered with green, growing plants and surrounded by metallic walkways. The overhead lights were not as bright, but there was an oppressive feel in the pod. There was a heaviness of the air that made it a little hard to breathe and a little uncomfortable to move around.

The man in the green coverall said, "I want everyone to remain here until I learn what we need to do."

Without another word, he punched a button on the metallic wall, and a door slid open. He disappeared inside.

The students all began to drift toward the railing so that they could look down onto the floor of the pod. There were already residents there, working at a fast clip. Some of them were walking in the vats of knee-deep water that were covered with vines. Some were pulling gourds out of the water and tossing them to others. Some were pulling at the vines, ripping them free and piling them on the metal walks between the vats. A few were moving around the vats, inspecting the crops, looking for signs of the blight.

Jason 215 couldn't wait for the opportunity to get down into that area and begin to work. He wanted to leap over the railing, but knew that would do no good. They needed to wait until the farmers and the computers decided in which area they should work. It wouldn't be long before he could join the fight.

[5]

JASON 215 DIDN'T KNOW HOW LONG HE HAD been wading in the tepid, knee-deep water, but he did know that he was tired. His back ached from the constant bending at the waist, his feet hurt because there was no way to sit down to take the weight off them, and his hands were bleached nearly white from the chemicals in the growing vats.

He worked at finding the gourds, pulling them out of the water, then cutting them free of the vine. Then he pulled the vines free, rolled them up as much as he could, and handed them to one of the residents on the metallic walks. He worked with five or six other residents in the vat. When they reached the far side, they turned, moved to the right five or six paces, and began another sweep.

The lights above them dimmed, almost as if the sun was beginning to set. The timer had not been touched after the blight had been discovered. When it was almost too dark to see, the lights blazed back, making it suddenly too bright.

Jason 215 tripped and almost fell before he straightened up. He grabbed at the shoulder of the man standing next to him.

"Take it easy," the man said.

"We have a lot of work to do before we can get to bed tonight," said Jason 215. "I want to finish."

"We'll finish."

They worked their way across the vat again, but this time there wasn't much to find. They pulled all the vines, picked all the gourds, and were stirring up the thin layer of mud at the bottom to make sure that nothing had been missed. They needed to make sure they had everything.

Jason 215 climbed out and started to walk toward another vat, but someone yelled, "Hold up."

He turned. A woman in a green coverall, one of the farmers, was waving at him. "Come on back."

When he joined the rest of the group, she said, "That's going to be it for tonight. We'll start again in six hours. Each of you is to take a shower and try to get some sleep. In the morning, dress in the same clothes. We'll destroy them when the work is done here."

Jason 215 said, "I'm feeling fine. I . . ." He waved a hand to indicate all those with him. "We could work another hour or two."

"That's not necessary. We're now in isolation. There is no chance of the blight contaminating any of the other ag pods. This crop is lost."

"Then why the hurry?" asked someone.

"Because we needed to isolate the pod, and we needed

someone to work in it. We need to get this pod back into production as quickly as possible."

They were led away from the vats, along a metallic trail that seemed to echo with their footsteps. They came to a set of double doors reminiscent of a barn on Earth. The farmer pulled on a handle, and the doors swung open, revealing a small dormitory complete with a shower facility at the far end. All water used would be recycled in the pod but not into the ship's supply.

"Some of you will have to sleep on the floor, and you'll have to take turns in the shower. Get cleaned up, and we'll get you something to eat."

Jason 215 entered the "barn" and walked to the shower area. There were only four nozzles, which meant it would take more than an hour to get everyone through, and they probably wouldn't get clean. Without thinking about it, he stripped his boots and coverall, setting everything on a bench. He walked into the shower, turned it on, and closed his eyes. He turned slowly, letting the water play over him for the allotted twenty seconds. He used a bar of soap to scrub his body, concentrating his efforts on his feet, which felt dirty.

Finished, he turned on the water, letting it wash down his back. He felt someone grab him, playfully, and opened his eyes. Helen 214 smiled, and said, "Waiting for me?"

"Well, no," said Jason 215. "I thought I'd get a shower before the line formed."

"Yeah. Some of us thought we would grab a bed first. You're welcome to share mine."

"I'm not sure that's going to make a difference tonight," said Jason 215. "I've had a full day."

"Hey," yelled a male voice. "Let's hurry it up. There are others out here."

Jason 215 laughed. "You done?"

"I need more than a spray of water," said Helen 214, "but given the circumstances, I'm done."

They left the shower room but could find no towels or blowers to dry them. Instead, they stood together talking quietly, letting the air dry them slowly.

Helen 214 stepped to the bench and picked up her soiled coverall. She looked at the stains, the mud splattered at the knee and close to the waist, and held the garment away from her body as if it smelled.

"I really don't what to put these back on."

"Then don't," yelled a male voice. "No one is going to complain about the view."

"Juvenile."

"That I am."

Jason 215 laughed. He slipped into his coverall but didn't close the Velcro. He picked up his boots. Finally, he said, "You know. I'm not all that hungry tonight."

"We all missed lunch. How can you not be hungry?" asked Helen 214.

"Maybe it's you," said Jason 215, knowing that the real reason was that he was tired. Too tired to eat. He could eat in the morning.

Almost as if reading his mind, Helen 214 said, "Well, we can eat in the morning, which, according to what they said, isn't all that far in the future."

"So we could try out that bed you claim to have captured," said Jason 215.

Helen 214 took his hand and led him through the crowd waiting for the shower. She reached the bed, pushed someone's coverall off it, and sat down.

"Not too wide, but it'll do."

Jason 215 walked around and sat down with his back to Helen 214. He leaned back onto his elbows and looked up into her face. Her hair was wet, hanging down, and there were droplets spread across her shoulders. She looked like most of the other people, with the same hair color, eye color, and skin color. Her features were a little rougher than some, but not anything that was unattractive.

Jason 215 thought it would be nice to snuggle up against her back as tightly as he could. It would give him a chance to hold on to her and to slip forward, but as he had the thought, he was suddenly, overwhelming tired. All he wanted was to go to sleep.

Helen 214 turned around, lifting her legs so that she

could stretch out. She rolled to her side and Jason 215 joined her, holding her. And, in an instant, he was asleep.

[6]

THE LIGHTS CAME ON, AND SOMEONE WAS standing near the doors shouting. Jason 215 couldn't move because Helen 214 was lying on his arm, pinning it to the cot.

She opened her eyes and grinned at him. "Fell asleep, did you?"

He smiled back. "Yep."

She sat up and swung her legs out of bed. She sat with her back to him while he ran a finger up and down her spine. Finally, he reached around, cupped her breast, and let his fingers slide lower, across her stomach.

"Now you get horny. Thanks a lot."

At the front, the farmer stood, his hands on his hips, and shouted, "It's time to get to work. Let's get going."

Helen 214 said, "Give some people a little power, and it goes straight to their heads."

"He's doing an important job."

Helen 214 turned to look at him, as if she couldn't believe what he was saying, as if she had never heard him talk like that. Instead, she said, "Then we'd better get up."

As she stood up, Jason 215 got out of bed. Now he was hungry, and he didn't like the idea of putting on the dirty coverall from the day before, but those had been his instructions. It made sense, though. Why get another set as dirty when these would provide all the protection he would need? Why stain a clean pair when there was no reason to do so?

With little talk, everyone in the barn began to move, putting on their clothes and straightening the dormitory. They formed two lines at the door as the farmer pointed first to the right, then to the left.

"We have a lot of work to do today," he said. "I've been

informed that breakfast will be delayed by two hours, so we might as well get right to it."

Jason 215 found that he was disappointed in the announcement, but he didn't complain. No one complained. It meant that when breakfast came, it would be that much better.

They filtered out of the dormitory, spreading around the large vats holding the remainder of the diseased crop. This time Jason 215 avoided getting in the vat. He stood outside and helped stack the gourds and later some of the vegetables that were being recovered. The vines and the stocks were ripped from the vats and piled on the metallic walks in piles that were nearly six feet high. Had they been on Earth, had they been outside on the planet, they might have burned everything as they tried to destroy the disease. Here they could only attempt to isolate it and use chemicals to defeat it.

A young man, apparently part of another party, looked up at Jason 215, and asked, "What do they do with this?"

"Don't know," said Jason 215. "Never been through anything like this before."

"I'm Rod 212," he said.

"Jason 215."

Those in the vats reached the edge again, and one handed Jason 215 an armload of vines. They were dripping and had mud clinging to their shallow root systems. Jason 215 took them and lowered part of them back into the muddy water in the vat to wash the soil from the roots. That done, he dropped everything into one of the piles.

"Think they'll process into food?" asked Rod 222.

"Don't know. They'll do whatever is best for *The Home*," said Jason 215.

They moved slowly from one vat to the next until they reached the end of the row. Standing there, against the rear wall, were another dozen students who had finished their work a little earlier. They were watching as the remaining teams worked to complete their sweeps through the vats.

As they stood there, Jason 215 realized that they hadn't been given their breakfast. They had been told it would be a couple of hours, but now it was nearly noon, and they hadn't eaten yet. He didn't like that because he was feeling hunger pangs.

He sat down and looked up, toward the rows of lights ninety feet or so above him. They looked like miniature suns, putting out rays that could be converted by the plants. The whole ag pod had to be nearly a mile long and half again as wide. On Earth it would have been about half a section, which was a good-sized farm. Of course with the techniques used on *The Home,* not to mention the always perfect growing weather, the crops flourished. There was always a bountiful harvest, and there was no need to wait through long winter months until they could plant again. The whole thing was based on the life cycle of the crops rather than on what the weather would allow.

But, something had gone wrong in this pod.

Helen 214, looking hot and tired, with sweat-matted hair and large mud stains on her coverall, walked over and sat down next to him. She said, without really thinking about it, "I hope this is the only ag pod infected."

"Damn," said Jason 215. "I hadn't thought about that."

CHAPTER FOUR

YEAR TWO THREE FIVE

[1]

MICHAEL 177 SAT IN FRONT OF HIS FLAT-
screen which was now split into quarters so that he could
see the faces of the four people he needed to consult. Each
quadrant was labeled because the four people all looked
remarkably alike. Other than gender, he wouldn't have
known which quadrant held which person.

At the top left was Susan 199, who was an expert on
crop diseases and had found herself in trouble. She should
have caught the blight before it had spread as far as it had.
Some were talking about a demotion for her, if not some
sort of stronger punishment. There was even talk of a special section at the Med Center that would help her forget
these problems and make her into a productive resident of
the society.

At the top right was David 181, who was in charge of all the ag pods. He, too, was in trouble. Maybe more than Susan 199 because the whole farming system was his responsibility and the loss of the farms, even in a single pod, was a disaster that couldn't be easily fixed. At the moment it hadn't been labeled a disaster, but people were worried about the blight.

Below, in the right-bottom square, was Evan 200, who was manager of the pod in which the blight had developed. He had spent the last few hours explaining why everyone else was to blame, and although he had annoyed Michael 177, it was beginning to look as if Evan 200 was right. He was not to blame. Or rather, the blame did not belong to him alone.

In the last square was Doris 188, who had little to do with ag but might have some ideas on how to stop the blight. She was a botanist who had been working to develop various strains of plants so that they would have a selection of crops resistant to a variety of diseases when they reached The New Home.

Michael 177 said, without preamble, "Is it contained?"

"Well," said David 181, sweating heavily, "we have had no reports of further outbreaks."

"Which doesn't answer my question."

"Inspections are ongoing," said David 181. "No one has reported anything else to me. Under the circumstances, I believe that it has been contained."

Michael 177 rocked back in his chair, surveyed those on the screen, and said, "I don't have to tell you the importance of the ag pods. The little produce that grows in the main cabin of *The Home* cannot possibly sustain the level of occupancy that we currently enjoy. Those are the nice-to-have luxuries and not the life-sustaining necessities."

David said, "I have been running the figures, and if nothing else happens, if no other crops are affected, then the impact will be negligible. Only a few calories eliminated from the daily meals, a critical eye on the recycling of the food, and we'll be in good shape."

"What about cross-contamination? Contamination into the other ag pods?"

Doris 188 said, "I've found no evidence of it, but we do have to be very careful. The people who are in that contaminated pod now need to undergo a decontamination process and be kept out of all agricultural areas until we're sure that the blight has been eliminated."

"The food products from there?"

"I can't see any way of saving it without endangering everything," said David 181. "I believe we have it isolated in a single pod, but if we try to use the materials, we could cross-contaminate."

"How in the hell did this happen?"

For a moment all of them were quiet, each hoping that one of the others would venture a guess. Finally, Doris 188 said, "Spores could have lain dormant for decades. Something triggered them. The sterilization processes used on the dirt brought in could only do so much. We couldn't, and didn't, want to kill everything in the soil. Had we done that, it would have been as useless to us as the sand from inside an hourglass. We had to be careful on the selection of soils. Something might have defeated the screening process."

"You mean it lay dormant for more than two centuries?"

Doris 188 shrugged. "The alternative is that this blight, and by the way, that's not quite the right term, but this disease is something that developed here out of one of the benign and useful bacteria in the soil. At least that seems to be the most likely source of it."

"How could you tell?"

"DNA analysis might provide us with a clue. We'd have to do the testing on a genetic level. Once we have it isolated, then we could probably develop a way to eradicate it without harming the other bacteria."

"How long would that take?"

Doris 188 shook her head. "I don't know. Weeks certainly. Months probably, depending on how much research time is devoted to the problem and how much computer time I have access to. This is a rather complex problem."

Michael 177 rubbed his chin. "We can take that pod out of production until planetfall if that's necessary. But then we're going to have to reevaluate some of the decisions that have been made."

"What are you going to do with the vegetation from the pod?" asked Michael 177.

"What we should do is collect it and shove it all out into space, then clean and sterilize everything in that pod. When we're sure we have eliminated the disease, we then begin to reintroduce bacteria and other soil supplements and finally begin agriculture again. I hate losing that vegetable matter, but I think anything else is too dangerous."

"Time frame?"

"Six months. Maybe a little longer."

"Crap," said Michael 177.

"That is the worst-case scenario," said David 181. "We probably could have the first crops going in three months, but we don't want to cut any corners."

A red light began flickering in the corner of Michael 177's flat-screen. He ignored it for the moment, believing that the most pressing matter was the discussion under way. To Susan 199, he said, "Is there anything that you need to add here?"

"David has it under control. I would, however, be careful about bringing those residents back into the main part of *The Home*. We need to be sure that we have rid them of any sort of contamination. If it spreads into other areas, we could be in big trouble."

Michael 177 now wished that he had paid more attention during the last navigation briefing. He had thought that one of the nearby systems had been identified as suitable, meaning there was an Earth-like planet with a biosphere, though it was larger than Earth, and they had yet to get a good reading on the atmosphere.

The size of the flashing red light continued to grow, signaling its importance. Michael 177 glanced at it, and announced, "I have to take a call. Excuse me."

He touched a button and the images of the others faded. They were replaced by that of a single woman, whose face was unnaturally white, as if she was very scared. The instant she saw the Mayor, she said, "We have the blight in a second pod."

[2]

STANDING ON THE METALLIC CATWALK ABOUT fifty feet above the deck, looking out over the farming pod, Betty 205 could see patches of brown where there should have been only bright green. The crop, a genetically engineered variety of wheat that produced nearly three times the grain of regular wheat, was beginning to wilt. If it had been later in the growing cycle, or if they had been on Earth, where weather could create havoc, she might not have been so worried. But on *The Home,* at that point in the growing cycle, there should be nothing but unbroken green.

A moment later she was joined by David 181 and Susan 199. She didn't say anything to either of them. They stepped to the rail and looked down at the brown splotches that were twice as big as they had been the day before.

David 181 said, "What is it?"

"Some kind of rust," said Susan 199.

"Why now?"

"I don't know. If we were on Earth, I would give you a dozen different answers, but here we shouldn't have this problem unless someone has done it on purpose."

"Why in the hell would anyone do something like that? It would be cutting his own throat along with that of everyone else on *The Home?*"

"I'm saying that it is an odd coincidence that we have an outbreak of another crop disease in another of the ag pods at this particular time."

David 181 turned to Betty 205, and asked, "Have you been down there?"

"Not since yesterday."

"Maybe that is the first thing we should do. See if we can get any clues about this."

David 181 turned and moved toward the elevator. He touched a button, and the door opened. Along with the others, he stepped in and waited as the doors closed. There wasn't much in the way of sensation, then the doors opened on the lower level. Ten yards in front of them, over a low metallic rail, was the wheat.

"If we walk out there, are we going to spread the disease?" asked David 181.

"I wouldn't think so," said Susan 199. "I'll have to gather some samples anyway."

David 181 looked at Betty 205. "You've been out in the fields?"

"Of course."

"If I might suggest," said Susan 199, "that after we complete the inspection, we change into clean coveralls. We'll need new boots, too. We can cut down the possibilities of cross-contamination that way."

"If we lose this pod . . ." began Betty 205. She didn't bother to finish the thought.

"We are not going to lose this pod," said David 181, though he didn't believe his own words.

Betty 205 lifted a short section of the railing, flipping it over and out of the way. David 181 stepped around her and out into the field. He felt the soil give under his weight and saw that it was dark and wet, as it should have been.

He walked along slowly, looking right and left. As he neared one of the larger areas of brown, he began to see small patches of a deep red spotting some of the plants. At first it was widely scattered, but farther into the pod there was more of it. He knew that the rust was spreading throughout the field and didn't know how they were going to stop it.

He halted and looked at Susan 199. She was crouched, holding a leaf in her hand, fingering at it gently, examining it carefully, closely.

"Can we stop this by cutting out the bad sections?" asked Betty 205. "Or maybe eliminating the infected parts of the field."

"I think it might have spread too far for that. I think we might be too late."

"Can we hold it in this pod?"

"I would have thought so an hour ago, but we've lost another ag pod already. Not to the same disease, but to some disease. I don't know what might happen," said Susan 199.

David 181 crouched, a knee in the moist dirt. He reached out for a leaf and looked at it carefully. There were but two tiny splotches of red on it, but that signaled the beginning of the rust. The plant was already infected.

"We can save part of the crop," said Betty 205. "If we harvest now, we can save part of it."

In a world where the resources were finite, a partial crop was better than no crop at all. An immature crop would not produce the bounty of a crop that had time to grow and mature, but it was still better than nothing.

"We'd better get started," said David 181. "We don't know how fast this will spread."

"Do we have any time?" asked Betty 205.

"Almost none."

[3]

MICHAEL 177 SAT AT THE END OF THE TABLE. He looked into the eyes of the Crew who had been summoned. They included the Captain, Christina 160, the chief navigator, Ryan 171, and Douglas 176, who was the planetfall expert. All except the Mayor were dressed in their black uniform coveralls. Christina 160's had extra gold braid, at the shoulders and around the cuff showing that she was the Captain. The others had lesser amounts of braid, which indicated they were important officers but were not the Captain. The lowest members of the Crew had very little gold.

Michael 177 wore a gray coverall that could have used a needle and thread. There was a tiny rip at one elbow, and the cuffs had seen better days. He was trying to set an example for the rest of the residents, showing them that coveralls didn't need to be discarded simply because there were a couple of holes in them or because they had begun to fray.

Michael 177 waited until everyone looked up at him, then said, "I want to know how fast we can make planetfall."

"Why?" asked Christina 160.

"We have the beginning of a crisis that might only be resolved with planetfall."

Christina 160 shook her head, as if to say that civilians and residents panicked much too easily. She could think of no reason they would need to abandon *The Home.* All problems could be resolved if given enough thought by those in charge. Still, it was an interesting question.

"There are five planetary systems we can reach in about a year to eighteen months. Four of them are made up of huge planets, none of which are suitable for our purposes. The fifth system is the farthest away, and we have recently begun the mapping project there. I believe we have detected a number of smaller, inner planets. The composition of that system resembles, to a large extent, the Solar System."

"There was some discussion of the moons of those larger planets in the closer systems."

Christina 160 looked at Ryan 171 but didn't wait for him to say anything. She said, "In an emergency, I suppose, but the problem is that we'd be on a moon of a larger planet, and I wouldn't want to guess about the stability of the orbit or the possibility of a collision with another moon. All the large planets in the Solar System show remnants of moons destroyed either by the gravitational fields of the planets or by collision with other, large objects. The rings of Saturn are the best example, but the ring systems of the other gas giants suggest dangerous gravitational forces."

"In a pinch?" asked Michael 177.

Christina 160 decided that she didn't like the direction of the conversation. She wanted more information. She needed more information before she could make any sort of an informed recommendation. She asked, "What is going on?"

Michael 177 waved a hand as if to brush aside the question without bothering to answer it.

"We," said Christina 160, indicating the other members of the Crew at the table, "cannot make intelligent comment if we are working blind. There might be circumstances that demand we pick the closest available planet or moon and others that suggest we might wait for a better, more appropriate choice, not to mention The New Home."

"How long to The New Home?" asked Michael 177, even though he knew the answer as did everyone else in *The Home*.

"At our current speed, with no navigational problems or errors, and keeping everything comfortable for the residents, seventy-five years."

"At maximum?"

"If we begin to accelerate, then brake at the maximum, we could be there in fifty-two years. Shuttles could put some of the residents or, at the very least, some of the Crew on The New Home in a little under fifty years."

"Well, that's out," said Michael 177.

"Again. What is the problem?"

Michael 177 took a deep breath, and said, "Right now I'm only looking at our options. We're having some trouble in the ag pods, but I'm not sure that it is going to impact heavily on us. If we can get control of the problem, then our food supply will remain constant, and there will be no problem. If not, we could be in for some lean years."

"My God," said Christina 160. "Are the residents aware?"

"Only those who have been involved in the fight against the disease, and they're isolated in the ag pods where the problems exist."

"You said, 'Pods'?"

"Two of them have been infected. We've lost the crop in one, but I think we can save some of the crop in the second. We'll get new crops growing as soon as possible."

"What sort of backup food supply is there? How much has been stored?" asked Christina 160.

"We've been tapping the reserve for quite a while," said Michael 177.

"Meaning?" asked Christina 160.

"Meaning, simply, that the reserve is down, and we don't have a great deal of leeway here. If we can't reverse this problem in the near future, there could be consequences. If we can't end it quickly, the only real solution is to make planetfall as quickly as possible."

"We can launch some exploration ships to look at the conditions on some of those moons," said Christina 160. "We might even find something there that will help us fight off this new problem."

"What are the odds that we'd find anything that is compatible?"

Christina 160 shrugged. "We haven't been looking at moons because they are, frankly, moons. Besides, our surveys have not been to find a place for The New Home. That has been designated for decades. We wanted to know what was in the galactic neighborhood that might be of some use to us."

"So you have nothing to help us," said Michael 177.

"No. I haven't said that. I have said that most of the planets close to us, relatively close, are gas giants. There are a number of moons, twelve, I think, that are of a size close to Earth. Each might have an environment that could be exploited by us. We haven't looked closely."

"Then you have no answer."

"At the moment, no. I can have a survey of those moons completed in a week or two depending on the location of the high-speed probes. But why don't we refurbish the dirt in the ag pods?" she asked.

Michael 177 shrugged. "I'll have to get with the ag people to find out if that might be a problem."

"Worst case," said Christina 160, "is that we'd have to sterilize the dirt, at least to my way of thinking."

"Too many questions for me to answer," said Michael

177. "I'll need to call a full meeting of the ag committee to figure this out."

He looked at Ryan 171, the chief navigator. "How soon can you find out something from the probes?"

"In a matter of hours, if all goes well. If we want to put a crew on one of the scouts at full acceleration, that'll take a couple of weeks for the closer systems, couple of months for those farther away."

"Is there anything promising?"

Ryan 171 looked at Christina 160 because she had already answered that question. To him, it suggested a note of hysteria. Things might be worse than the Mayor was letting on.

He said, "Couple of things. Our best bet at the moment would be the fifth system, but even a probe would take a long time to reach it, and we don't have to worry about acceleration or deceleration pressures with no human crew aboard."

Michael 177 found himself getting bored. The tone of the meeting had shifted from the crisis at hand to the launching of scouts and probes. Christina 160, as the Captain, could make those decisions without his help. That was her territory, and if she felt a probe or a scout was necessary, she didn't have to consult with him to authorize it.

Instead, he was concerned with what was happening in the ag pods. That was his immediate responsibility, and if they had a complete failure of all the crops, they would be in trouble in six months to a year. If they could get everything replanted and could boost the growth rate, then in six months the problem would be resolved.

He looked at the Captain and her chief navigator, and said, "I want to have a plan for the probes and the scouts on my desk in the next three hours." He started to stand to signal the end of the meeting.

Christina 160 banged her hand down sharply. The sound startled both the Mayor and the chief navigator. She then smiled sweetly, and said, "I will proceed with the plan simply because it is in the interest of *The Home* to do so. You will not usurp my authority because you have made an error, and we are facing a crisis. You will not give me orders."

Michael 177 dropped back into his seat and looked at her with both contempt and anger. And then he realized that now was not the time for any sort of fight over power in *The Home*. He said, "I'm sorry. I was thinking of what has to be done. I didn't mean to imply I was giving orders."

"All right then. Three hours."

[4]

JASON 215 WAS AGAIN KNEE DEEP IN MUD, but this time the majority of the water had been drained from the vat. He reached down, dug his fingers into the mud, and tried to scoop up any vegetable matter than might remain in it. Finding nothing, he repeated the process, working his way across the vat with a group of others doing the same thing. When they reached the opposite end, they turned around, slipped to the right, and started across again.

They kept at it through the afternoon and into the evening without stopping except to move from one vat to another or to use the bathroom facilities. They kept moving, bending, pulling their feet free of the mud only to sink into it again. The whole process was tiring, the mud seeming to suck the energy from them. The high humidity that had characterized the pod because of the water-filled vats and the need for moisture given the nature of the crops and the growth medium contributed to the misery. They sweated in the high heat of the artificial atmosphere.

Finished with the vat, Jason 215 climbed over the edge and stood on the metallic walkway. He sat back on the edge of the vat and mopped his forehead and face with the upper sleeve of his coverall. He felt drained, as if he didn't have the energy it would take to fall over.

His coverall was nearly stiffened with the grime of the last three days. Rings of salt sweated from his body marked the area under his arms, around his waist, and down his back. He was hot, tired, and more than a little annoyed, but had no energy to even complain.

Helen 214 climbed from another vat close to him, seemed to stumble, then sat down in front of him. He could see into an opening in her coverall and stared at her chest. There was something exciting about seeing it when it was supposed to be covered. At least to his tired mind there was something exciting about it.

She wiped at her face, looked at her hands, and said, "This is not what I wanted to be doing."

"I would like something to eat," said Jason 215. "They're not getting the food to us regularly."

"I think we're under quarantine," said someone. Jason 215 didn't see who it was.

"I heard that, too," said Helen 214. " About the quarantine. They're trying to keep this whatever it was from spreading into the other ag pods."

Jason took a deep breath and exhaled audibly. "That's no reason not to feed us on time."

"Logistics," said Helen 214. "I think they might be having trouble getting enough food in here."

Jason 215 reached up and ran his fingers under the Velcro of his coverall, opening it to the waist. He'd thought he might be cooler, but he felt no breeze. He felt nothing, other than the heat and humidity.

The overhead lights began to dim, telling them the day had ended. They were released to the dormitory. Jason 215 stood up and held out a hand for Helen 214. He pulled on her arm, helping her stand.

"I didn't realize how tired I was," she said. "I think I would prefer to sit here for the next ten or twelve hours. I don't want to move."

"I think we must be about done in here," said Jason 215. "We've cleaned the vats. We've cleaned them more than once. We've cleaned everything except the dirt."

They walked slowly toward the double barnlike doors. They stepped inside and removed their dirty boots. In bare feet, they walked toward the rear, where the showers were located, but now there was a line.

Jason 215 shrugged out of the top of his coverall and knotted the sleeves around his waist. He watched as those in front of him stripped, showered as much mud from their bodies as they could, then relinquished their position under the shower to those standing behind them.

Finally, Jason 215 and Helen 214 had reached the front of the line. They kicked off their coveralls and stepped under the fine spray. Jason 215 turned slowly and, once the spray stopped, used his hands to rub the dirt and sweat from his body. When it started again, he rinsed, then stepped out of the shower. He didn't feel very clean.

He looked down at his dirty coverall, and said, "I can't put that on again." He picked them up, holding them away from his body so that they couldn't contaminate him.

Naked, he walked from the shower area and stopped at the cot he had shared with Helen 214. Clean, fresh coveralls lay there, folded neatly. He dropped the dirty garment to the floor and looked at the new coveralls.

"I think we're done here," said Helen 214.

He turned and looked at her. She was standing next to him, equally naked.

Jason 215 picked up a clean coverall, opened it, and stepped in. Then he sat down on the cot and watched as Helen 214 dressed.

"I haven't felt this good in days," he said.

Before Helen 214 could reply, someone near the double doors said in a raised voice, "May I have your attention, please? If everything works out, tomorrow you will be returning to the university. We have completed the cleaning, and it will be several days before we are ready to replant."

That brought a quiet cheer.

The man speaking held up a hand, and said, "Well, I don't blame you. Anyway, tonight, in a few minutes, we'll have our final meal together. We've tried to arrange something a little special in way of thanks."

That, too, brought a cheer. Had they known what was happening, they wouldn't have been nearly so happy.

[5]

MICHAEL 177 SAT IN FRONT OF HIS OVERSIZE flat-screen and looked at the sequence of boxes spread across its surface. The full governing council and the command structure of the Crew were present. Michael 177 could, at his whim, silence any of them, with the exception of the Captain. She had a similar power. It was usually unnecessary to use it unless the meeting degenerated into a shouting match, but that rarely happened.

Michael 177 took a deep breath, and said, "I guess we had better get this going. First, I think we need to get the latest from ag. David, what have you got?"

"At the moment, we have the disease confined to two of the pods. One has been sterilized, and we're working in the other. That part of the operation is completed or will be completed soon, but that's not the disturbing news." He stopped talking and looked at the camera.

Michael 177 saw, on his flat-screen, the questioning look that David 181 gave him. He said, "This is a closed meeting. You may feel free to speak here."

David 181 looked down at something out of camera range, then looked up again. "The only way to explain the outbreak of these two divergent diseases in two areas at basically the same time is sabotage."

There was momentary quiet, then an explosion of sound as everyone tried to talk at once. One by one, Michael 177 cut off the microphones so that there was only silence. Those talking took the hint and fell silent. Order restored, he looked right at David 181, and said, "Are you sure?"

"Not completely, but there really is no other explanation for this. There seems to be nothing in any of the samples we took or in the review of security that would suggest this is a natural by-product of our form of agriculture."

Michael 177 sat for a moment staring into space, trying to figure out a way to identify the saboteur. Nothing like this had ever happened. The closest was when George 148 had tried to engineer a destruction of the civilian side's au-

thority in a rather poorly executed mutiny a number of
years earlier. He had wanted to control both the military
and the residents. That had been dealt with quickly by Security.

Michael 177 opened the mike for Stephen 168, who still
commanded the Security Section. He said, "Is there anything that you can do?"

"We can review all the access disks to see who might
have tried to sneak in; but if it was sabotage and the person was supposed to be in the pods, then we'll have a hard
time finding him or her. Especially if he or she was merely
doing a job."

"Can't you see who was in the infected areas?"

David 181 was waving, trying to get Michael 177's attention. Michael 177 opened all the mikes at that point, and
said, "David?"

"I wanted to say that if it was someone authorized in the
pods, there wouldn't be much evidence. All he or she had
to do was brush the disease spores on a coverall and walk
through the pod. Thinking about it, he or she could have
brushed it on someone else's coverall and let that resident
walk through the pod."

Michael 177 nodded and turned his attention back to
Stephen 168. "Is there anything you can do?"

"I can review the record of everyone who has been in
both these pods, assuming that it is only one person . . ."

Michael 177 seemed to be astonished by the comment.
He interrupted, saying, "Why would it be more than one?"

David 181 said, "Because we're dealing with two pods
and two different types of disease. I can think of no one
who would be able to create the diseases for two different
types of crops in two different types of environment and be
able to get in to infect both crops."

"Then maybe we are dealing with a coincidence," said
Michael 177.

Stephen 168 said, "I don't think so. I think this is a case
of sabotage. We have the disks that will show us all that we
need to know. A complete review should provide us with,
at the very least, a list of suspects. We can go from there."

Jane 158, the advocate for the residents, spoke for the first time. "Can we isolate those two pods . . . in fact, can we isolate all the ag pods so that we won't have additional trouble."

"We can restrict the access in any way that we want or can think of," said Stephen 168. "That's the least of the problems we face."

Michael 177 realized that they had become diverted. The real problem, the immediate problem, was not who had done this, if someone had, but what they could do to remedy the situation. Again he turned to David 181.

"What has this done to our production?"

"Our production remains high, except in the infected areas. All other ag pods have been checked, and I have seen no indications of any disease."

"But we've lost crops."

"We've lost everything in the hydroponics pod, but we might be able to replant there. In the second pod, we've only lost part of a crop, and we're trying to isolate the disease."

"Will that work?"

David 181 shrugged helplessly. "I don't know. I suspect not, but I can only hope."

Michael 177 rocked back in his chair and surveyed the flat-screen, looking from face to face. There was one question that he had. One question that needed to be answered. He said, "Can you stop this disease?"

"I think so."

Michael 177 turned his attention to the chief of Security, Stephen 168. "Can you catch the saboteur?"

"If there is one, yes, we can catch him. But we might need to add some security to do it."

Michael 177 nodded, then said, "Here's where we are. If no other pods are affected, then we'll face a little bit of a lean time, but no one will die. We are now checking various systems, looking for a world that we can inhabit if the contamination continues to spread. And, we are cleaning up the mess. We have many options."

"And if there is sabotage and more ag pods are infected?" asked David 181.

Michael 177 didn't want to say anything about that, but he was afraid that the situation would then worsen. Residents would die, and the mission would be in jeopardy.

[6]

DAVID 181 KNEW THAT HE NEEDED MORE INformation. He knew that the crops in one ag pod had been ruined, that the crops in a second were infected, but didn't know how far the problem had spread. If it was contained, then no new action by anyone was required. They could finish the cleaning, they could eradicate the diseases, and begin again. If, however, any of the other ag pods had been infected, then the options were limited. He needed to know if any other ag pods had been infected.

His first task was to use the computers to survey the crops, looking for any anomaly. For comparison purposes, he looked first into the hydroponics, which were little more than dried vats and piles of decaying vegetation, into the wheat pod, which showed more of the rust infecting the plants, and finally at the corn pod, which seemed to be healthy, at the soybean pod, which also seemed healthy, and into the first of what he thought of as the truck farm pods. These held vegetables such as peas, brussel sprouts, tomatoes, and other crops.

The computers had detected nothing, so David 181 began a visual search, using the various cameras mounted throughout the pod. He noticed, at first, some wilting on the brussel sprouts, but he had also expected that. It was getting close to harvest, and the plants were ending their cycle of life.

As he switched over, looking at the tomatoes, he began to spot brown leaves and an overall wilting of the plants. He sat up and focused in on one plant, increasing the magnification. He could see that the leaves were not only wilted, but had deep brown spots on them. The tomatoes,

which should have been a light green or maybe a pale yellow, were, in a couple of cases, tan. They were rotting on
the vine.

That could mean, simply, that one plant was diseased.
Or it could mean that something was beginning to infect
the tomatoes; but the disease could easily be something
natural. They might be able to eradicate it with a simple
spray, by changing the watering cycle, or by altering the
light-and-dark cycles. It could mean nothing important.

But David 181 didn't think so. Not with what had happened in the last few days. Shutting down his computer, he
stood up, walked to the door, exited, and began a stroll
through the park, toward the access hatch to the ag pod. He
took his time, looking at the fruit trees, but saw nothing to
suggest they had been infected with any sort of disease.
The fruit looked to be growing well.

He reached the access tunnel, let the computer scan his
wrist implant, then stepped through. He let the resident
mover carry him upward until he reached the top, where he
was scanned again and allowed to enter the ag pod.

As in the other pods, he was standing on a catwalk some
twenty or thirty feet above the deck. He looked down, at
the rows and rows of vegetables. From that perch, he
couldn't see anything wrong with the crops.

He took the elevator down to the deck and walked out.
The lights overhead were still on brightly so that David
181 had no trouble seeing the plants. There was nothing
wrong with the brussel sprouts that he could see. The
plants looked healthy. He crouched near some of them and
examined them closely. They were healthy, producing
dozens of sprouts.

He walked over to the tomatoes. Most of the plants
looked to be healthy. A few had bright red tomatoes ready
to be harvested. They held dozens of other, smaller tomatoes that ranged from the size of a pea to some about the
size of a tennis ball. They ranged in color from a dark,
deep green, to a paler shade, to yellows, and finally to red.
Most of the plants looked to be healthy.

But then, at the far end of the pod, near the farmers' dormitory, he found the beginnings of disease. Centered around half a dozen plants was a blight that seemed to be wilting the leaves and causing brown spots on the tomatoes themselves. Even with a quick examination, it was clear that one plant had been infected and the disease was spreading to the plants around it.

David 181 entered the dormitory and spotted Mickey 203 sitting on a bed, resting. He looked up as David 181 entered, and called, "Hello. What can I do for you?"

"Spotted something on the tomatoes. You seen it?"

Mickey 203 stood up and walked toward the door. "I haven't seen anything that I would worry about."

David 181 stepped back and gestured out into the pod. "Let's go take a look."

When he pointed out the plant, Mickey 203 said, "I've seen something like that over near the bulkhead. I checked the pH in the soil, water level, and for fungus. I've got a couple of the tomatoes in the lab for analysis."

"You didn't report anything."

"Didn't see the point now," said Mickey 203. "If I isolate the cause and correct it, then no harm done. If not, I report up the chain and let you figure it out."

"When did you notice the problem?"

"Couple of hours ago."

David 181 crouched near the tomato plants, one knee in the soft, wet soil. "You didn't notice this?"

Mickey 203 knelt next to David 181 and fingered one of the leaves. He turned it over and pulled it from the plant. He sniffed it, then crumbled it between thumb and forefinger.

"This looks like what I found, but I didn't see it here. It's another part of the pod."

David 181 stood up, looking like a farmer who had acres of land in an Earth-based society. He wiped a hand across his forehead and smeared the sweat on the front of his coverall. He understood exactly what was happening in the pod even if Mickey 203 did not. To Mickey, he said, "I'm going have to report this."

"But it's not really that big a deal, and I haven't seen any of the other plants infected."

"We have to stay on top of this," said David 181, but he already knew the magnitude of the problem. The pod was contaminated, and it was only a matter of time before all the crops began to die.

To Mickey 203, he said, "I've noticed that the brussel sprouts are ready for harvest. Let's get that taken care of right now. And any tomatoes that are red or turning red should be picked as quickly as you can."

Mickey 203 didn't understand why he was being given these orders but nodded, and said, "Of course."

David 181 looked back toward the elevator but didn't move right away. He didn't want Mickey 203 to suspect that anything was wrong, but he knew what the small outbreaks of blight on the tomatoes meant. More of *The Home*'s food was about to be ruined.

[7]

MICHAEL 177 HAD LISTENED TO DAVID 181'S report with growing apprehension. A third pod had been found to be infected, and that surely meant that if disease hadn't developed in the other pods, it would shortly. *The Home* was being killed. Slowly.

He sat in his private apartment, in what he called his library, though it held only a computer so that he could access all the information available on *The Home*. There were a desk, a couple of chairs, and an old couch that should have been recycled a decade earlier.

Christina 160, holding a glass filled with bourbon, sat on that couch. She was wearing her uniform and thought of the visit as official, even though she was drinking. She hadn't liked being summoned, but the note of desperation in Michael 177's voice had inspired her to forget protocol and political maneuvering.

"I have news," he said.

"Good or bad."

"Bad," said Michael 177. "The worst. We have found evidence of disease in another of the ag pods. I believe that we will eventually find disease in all of them."

"Then we're doomed unless we take radical action," said Christina 160.

"You mentioned that we might begin to probe the systems closest to us. That we might find a world that we could make into our New Home."

Christina 160 drained her bourbon and set the glass on the deck near her feet. She straightened up, and said, "You are aware, I'm sure, that with luck there will be a single planet in a star system."

"Yes."

"And if that planet happens to be a gas giant, it would be wholly inappropriate for us. The mixture of gases in its atmosphere would probably not support human life, not to mention the effects of the much higher gravitational pull."

"Yes."

"So, our search might have to encompass a dozen, two dozen systems before we find anything that might remotely be suitable for us. It fact, we might be lucky to find one planet in a hundred star systems."

"I understand the odds, but at the moment, all I can see is that we're going to run out of food," said Michael 177. "We are all going to be in trouble at that point."

"I don't know what you want me to do," said Christina 160. "We have probes out. We have scouts searching. About the only thing more we could do is launch some of the smaller shuttles. Put some of the residents in space."

"How does that help us?" asked Michael 177.

"Well, if we find something promising and have a shuttle in the area, we can do the preliminary recon right then. We don't have to launch from here, which could take extra time. Speeds the process a little bit."

Michael 177 stood up and walked around his desk. He leaned back against the front of it and looked down at the Captain. "Given the circumstances, don't you think it in our best interests to begin preparations for that?"

"Well, Mister Mayor, I don't want to waste our resources. We might be using resources that we can't replace and will need later."

"I think, given the deteriorating nature of the situation, we had better begin."

Christina 160 grinned broadly, and asked, "How are you going to select the residents who go on the mission?"

"I believe that the computer will do that for us. All I have to do is provide the guidelines."

[8]

JASON 215 WAS GLAD TO BE OUT OF THE steaming environment of the ag pod. He hadn't liked the humidity, the heat, or the backbreaking work. Now, back at the university, where his bed was more comfortable, the showers a convenience rather than a necessity, and the meals scheduled and eaten at regular intervals, Jason 215 realized how lucky he was. Clearly he was not going to be assigned to ag duties. He was being educated in flight operations, which meant he would eventually be assigned to the Crew.

There was a quiet bong from his flat-screen and Jason 215 rolled over on his cot and tried to see what the message was. Failing, he got up, leaned on his desk, and used the mouse. All he could see was that he was to report to the flight deck for a special assignment.

Given what he had recently endured, Jason 215 was convinced that he would be used in some kind of maintenance crew to help out. He grinned broadly, having just thought he was finished with manual labor only to be ordered into more of the same. It was the price he would have to pay for his luck.

As he straightened up, he saw Helen 214 approaching. She looked a little frightened. She stopped in the hall in front of his cubicle, and said, "I've got another assignment."

"So do I," said Jason 215. He pointed to his flat-screen. "I'm to report to the flight deck."

Jason 215 raised his eyebrows in surprise, and said, "So am I. Now."

"Then let's go." She started to walk to the door, then stopped, looking back at Jason 215. "Why do you think they want both of us?"

"Don't know," said Jason 215. "Let's be glad that they do."

"I'm not sure this is a good idea," she said.

"Whenever you're summoned it's not good—but sometimes it all works out."

"Yeah."

[9]

THERE HAD BEEN A WARNING, BUT IT HADN'T been believed by the Mayor, the Captain, or any of the other authorities. The instant message, appearing on computer flat-screens all over *The Home* had been simple and direct. There would be an explosion in one of the official buildings by 1800 hours. They should be prepared for the worst.

Michael 177 had alerted Stephen 168, who in turn had alerted his security forces. Though they attempted to learn who had issued the warning by backtracking through the messaging system, whoever had sent it knew enough to hide his or her identity because it looked as if the Mayor had sent the warning. There were dozens of computer programmers on *The Home* who could have done it and no real way of finding the culprit.

So Michael 177 sat in the Security Center his eyes flitting from screen to screen as he searched for some sign that the threat had been carried out. He couldn't help but think that it was just that, a threat, and nothing would happen. Not here, on *The Home*.

But Stephen 168 became more nervous as 1800 hours approached. He found that he couldn't sit still. He got up and walked around in a small circle, orbiting the chairs where the others sat. He would stop, stare at two or three of the screens, watch the scenes shift, then start another orbit.

Finally, Michael 177, who wasn't as calm as he tried to appear, snapped, "Will you sit down?"

Stephen 168 looked surprised at the tone and dropped into the closest chair. He said, "Sorry."

Michael 177 said, "Forget it. Do you really think that anything will happen?"

Stephen 168 began to relax. He was being asked his expert opinion. It was something that he could handle. He said, "Well, the problem here is that we know there are some residents out there who wish to harm *The Home*. First the food supply and now this threat. Either way, he or she has managed to disrupt our lives."

"Will anything happen?"

Stephen 168 nodded, and said, "Yes. This time I think something will happen. Next time, maybe not."

"Next time?"

Stephen 168 turned from the flat-screens and looked at the Mayor. "Of course. You didn't think this was going to be a one-time event, did you?"

"I thought . . ."

"This represents resentment against our society here, on *The Home*. Those behind it, and I believe there has to be a conspiracy, feel that they have been abused by us. This is a way of getting even."

"Conspiracy," said the Mayor nearly shouting.

"A conspiracy is any two residents acting together to accomplish a goal. Clearly there is more than one involved here. The attacks on the ag pods demonstrate more knowledge and ability than a single person could possess. Add to that the ability to post that message without leaving a trail to follow and to use explosives and we have more than a single individual. That means conspiracy."

"Then do something," demanded the Mayor.

"What would you have me do that I am not already doing? What actions should I take?"

"Patrols," snapped the Mayor.

Stephen 168 pointed at the flat-screens, and said, "I

have every available security officer on duty around every building structure or area that might be attacked. I have additional officers, not to mention some of out top computer residents, trying to backtrack the message. I don't know what more I could be doing here."

"There must be something more that you can do."

"I don't know what it would be."

The clock snapped over from 1759 to 1800. Michael 177 stared up at it, then turned his attention back to the flat-screens. There seemed to be nothing there. He began to relax as the seconds ticked off.

And then the alarm sounded. Just a low buzzing that wavered up and down, calling attention to itself without the insistence of a siren.

The main screen slipped from a view of residents in one of the parks to the main court building. Smoke was pouring from the shattered front windows, being sucked up toward the filters. Debris was scattered on the ground, and three or four residents were lying in front of the building. Security officers and firefighters were running toward it.

"Jesus," said the Mayor.

Stephen 168 leaned closer to a microphone. "I want all the security disks reviewed. I want the location of the explosion identified, and I want anyone who has been near there in the last forty-eight hours questioned."

The Mayor, his face drained of color, sat staring at the destruction. He watched as the security officers pulled residents from the building, lining them up for treatment, or moving them to a smaller group for the dead. Two security officers walked along the lines of the injured and the dead, trying to identify them.

Stephen 168 directed the Security operation, ordering his officers from other locations, moving them around the burning courthouse. The fire was extinguished in minutes, but smoke still rose toward the filters. Medical residents arrived and were treating the injured.

"We'll fan out from there," said Stephen 168. He looked at the Mayor for a response.

"Fine."

"We'll find out who did this."

"Sure," said the Mayor, but his voice seemed to be detached. He was distracted. Finally, he said, "This means we have to hurry now."

Stephen 168 didn't understand.

"It means," said the Mayor, "that we have to get the exploration going faster. We're running out of time on *The Home*."

CHAPTER FIVE

YEAR TWO THREE FIVE

[1]

JASON 215 STOOD IN THE HANGAR POD AND looked up at the shuttle. He had seen pictures of it his whole life, and he had read descriptions about it taking the residents of *The Home* down to the surface of The New Home, but he had never seen it personally. He had never stood close to it and looked up at the gleaming white sides, the short stubby wings that were aeronautically designed but provided little in the way of lift, at the rear, where the huge engines that could force the craft off a planet and push it into orbit were mounted. He had dreamed of seeing it in person and believed, as he studied at the university, his career path would bring him to that point, but he had not expected it so soon.

He walked around the craft, studying it as if it were

some sort of an alien artifact. There was a cockpit set high so that the pilots could visually see the landing area, but that was unnecessary. Cameras mounted around the craft gave the pilot a complete and probably more accurate picture of the landing area and what was happening near the craft than his eyes could. If, for some reason a critical camera failed on landing, the pilot could then acquire a visual sighting.

The shuttle sat on a tricycle landing gear of gigantic tires designed for a variety of surfaces, and if necessary, they could be retracted in favor of skis and pontoons. Any open area long enough for the landing roll could be used by the shuttle.

Jason 215 had believed from the first time he saw a picture of the shuttle that he would never have the opportunity to ride in it. His was a generation, like that of his parents, and their parents, who would be born on *The Home* and would die on *The Home* because The New Home was so far from Earth. But now, here he was, looking at the shuttle, not in a holo or on a flat-screen, but in person.

He walked out onto the hangar deck, which looked like a hard black surface but was soft and yielding. Most of the overhead lights were out, giving the impression of twilight on a planet's surface. At the far end, opposite the huge hangar doors, was a control room. It was brightly lighted, and the technicians circulated inside were preparing for the launch. They were too busy to notice Jason 215.

"You're early," said Helen 214.

Startled, Jason 215 turned around. He smiled, and said, "Yes. I wanted to get a better look at the shuttle."

"Big," said Helen 214.

"Bigger than I thought it would be," he replied.

"Well, when you think about it, the shuttle has to carry a hundred or more people down to a planet's surface. That takes a lot of space."

Jason 215 nodded and realized that those who eventually reached The New Home would have to take everything they needed to the planet's surface with them. That meant huge numbers of trips, or large shuttles. Large shut-

tles didn't require as much fuel to accomplish the mission
because there were significantly fewer trips.

They walked forward, toward the front tires of the landing gear. When they reached them, Jason 215 stood for a
moment, staring, then touched the hard rubber.

Helen 214 said, "This is going to be interesting."

"Well, yes."

The lights came up suddenly, and it was as if the sun
were focused on the hangar deck. Jason 215 blinked in the
sudden brightness.

Quietly, as if afraid that he would be overheard, he said,
"I'm not sure I'm ready for this."

"Nothing to be ready for. The Crew will pilot the craft.
We'll simply make observations when we reach the target.
You sat right there in the same briefing I did and heard the
same instructions I did."

Jason 215 smiled. "I know that. But we're about to
leave *The Home*. I'm not ready for that. I never expected
anything like that in the first place."

"If you had, the computer probably wouldn't have selected you to participate."

Jason 215 shrugged.

A hatch on one end of the control room opened, and two
people exited, both dressed in flying coveralls. These were
of a light blue with darker piping on the sleeves, down the
legs, and at the shoulder. Silver wings gleamed on the left
breast of both, signaling that they were pilots.

The older of them, Ken 197, turned toward Jason 215
and Helen 214. Ken 197 was slightly taller than everyone
else and had skin that was a little lighter. His nose looked
odd, but that was because it had been broken when he was
a child, the result of a playground accident that hadn't been
properly repaired. Ken 197 didn't look as if he belonged
on *The Home* because of this. He looked almost alien to
them.

Sarah 202 looked like everyone else, though she cut her
hair shorter than normal. She said it was because of the
equipment the pilots were required to use, but Jason 215
thought it was an affectation designed to make her stand

out in the crowd. Residents would ask her what she did, and she could tell them, with more than a little pride, that she was one of the shuttle pilots. In the past, that made no difference, but with this mission, she became one of the local heroes. She was going out into space in a relatively small craft to save all of humanity on *The Home*.

Ken 197 asked, "Anything wrong up here?"

Jason 215 shook his head. "Nope. I was looking at the tires."

"It's going to be another four hours before you can board. We've got to do our preflight and check out the systems before we can launch."

"You think anything is wrong?" asked Jason 215.

They were joined by Sarah 202, who had heard the question. She grinned, and said, "Everything should be fine. Flight Crew has inspected the ship, but you know, they're not going to be flying in it. We are. So we make another check, looking for anything that might have been missed."

"You ever find anything?"

Sarah 202 shook her head. "No. They've always found all the problems and repaired them before we arrive on the scene. But then this is the first time we'll be traveling away from *The Home* to such a distance. No one around to help us if we get into trouble so a few extra precautions can't hurt."

Jason 215 looked from one pilot to the other, but both seemed to be calm.

Sarah 202 said, "Why don't you wait in the control room, or even in the ready room while we finish up out here. You'll be bored otherwise."

Jason 215 thought about going back into the main body of *The Home,* but, of course, the access had been restricted. In fact, access was restricted throughout *The Home* until those who had damaged the crops, tried to destroy the mainframe, and attempted to blow up the main court building could be caught. Everyone was restricted to his or her own part of *The Home* with no travel between the various facilities or communities without special permission or a pressing need. The Mayor and his advisors believed that the restrictions would prohibit the saboteurs from committing any other acts of violence.

With Helen 214, Jason 215 walked back across the hangar deck and exited through the hatch. Standing on the other side, with a nonlethal sidearm, was a member of the security force. Jason 215 didn't recognize him but thought he looked to be young to be on the security team.

They walked along the access tunnel, avoiding the resident mover, preferring the little exercise they would get by walking around. Helen 214 reached out and took Jason 214's hand. It was something that wasn't done by the residents. Affection for one another was encouraged, but not outside the apartments where others could see it.

Jason 215 didn't pull his hand free. He knew that it made no difference because, in a matter of hours, they would be launched into space. They would be away from *The Home*, searching for a suitable place to land so that all the residents could be relocated.

Helen 214 stopped walking and turned to face him. He noticed that she was pale, as if she was about to be sick. Her eyes were wide and bright.

She said, suddenly, "I'm scared."

[2]

THEY STARTED AT THE NOSE, USING SHORT ladders to climb up so that they could poke into access ports, check small servos, and even inspect the landing strut of the shuttle to make sure that there were no foreign substances, oil, grease, or anything else, that might cause trouble or hint at future trouble. Ken 197 and Sarah 202, working as a team, inspected, checked, and examined everything they could get at, poked into the service crawl spaces, and reached in to feel where they couldn't see, trying to find anything that didn't belong.

Finished with the interior of the shuttle, they opened the hatch and crawled up into the cockpit. Ken 197 flipped a switch, and the instrument panel powered up. The dials lighted, the needles on various meters flickered to life, and the master caution panel brightened. He scanned everything quickly and saw nothing out of the ordinary. Everything was in the green, at one hundred percent and working perfectly.

"Take out the checklist," he said.

Sarah 202 reached around between the seats to a small pouch and pulled out a small handheld computer. She flipped it open, then scrolled through the pages until she found the prestart checklist.

"Got it," she replied.

Together they worked through the checklist, first making sure that everything was turned off, then turning on those items they needed to start the engines. They kept at it until they were satisfied that all systems were functioning as expected and nothing hinted at failure.

Ken 197 touched a button, and said, "Control, we've completed the preflight."

"Roger that. We'll get the rest of your crew gathered, and we can start loading."

"Roger."

Ken 197 leaned back into the soft cushion of the seat. He felt it seem to embrace him, providing support that was unneeded on the hangar deck but would be necessary if they penetrated the atmosphere of a planet.

Sarah 202 said, "Here they come."

The far hatch irised open and several residents came through. Two of them were carrying personal duffels in addition to other equipment. They walked across the hangar floor, ignoring the residents inside the control room, and stopped at the side of the shuttle.

Sarah 202 had left the flight deck and stepped down into the cargo area, which had been reconfigured for the mission. She spun the wheel on the hatch, then pulled in and lifted up, pushing the door out of the way.

The first thing through was a duffel that one of the men tossed in. He followed it, picked it up, and walked toward the rear. Billy 209 was assigned as the astronomer. He would be looking at the solar system, studying the planets, and attempting, with little in the way of observation time, to figure out the orbital mechanics in the system in case they might interfere with their exploration.

Right behind him, carrying the other duffel, was Leslie 207. She had tossed it up, into the shuttle, and then picked it up after boarding. She carried it to the rear, dropping it on the deck next to the one other duffel. She was going to study the various planets and moons, trying to establish if they were suitable for human habitation. She'd been trying to determine the range of temperatures, the composition of the atmosphere, and anything else that she thought important from the observatory on *The Home,* but such long-range observations, even with modern technology, were often in error.

Behind her was Jason 215, who was assigned as the navigator, though the position was almost superfluous. The pilots and Billy 209 would be watching where they were going. Jason 215 would be trying to keep track of *The Home* so that they would be able to return to it when the mission ended.

Helen 214 followed him. She walked to the first seat she could see and dropped into it. She was assigned as the botanist and planetfall expert, which meant that she was responsible for checking the local flora, if there was any, to make sure it wouldn't compete with their plants, and if it would, she was to find methods to eradicate it.

Finally, was the zoologist. Martha 212 would be responsible for a survey of the fauna. She would have to determine if there was anything dangerous, and if there was, decide if it posed a major threat to the residents. There was little reason to send her along; though, from a cost basis, it didn't matter. If there were animals, she might be of real use.

Jason 215 watched the others store their duffels as he buckled in. He relaxed slightly, because they were finally going to get under way. The chances of some sort of catastrophic accident were remote, but he was still apprehensive. He'd watched, as a child, some of the old videos of the first steps into space and seen the spectacular failures. He'd seen rockets explode on the launchpad as balls of bright orange fire engulfed them. He had seen pictures of rockets that lifted off only to explode in the air as parts of them cartwheeled away.

And he'd seen the pictures of the first American astronauts killed in space. Although the event was now hundreds of years in the past, being able to watch it, repeatedly and in color, changed it from something that had no effect on his life into something that was as real to him as if it had happened to the residents who lived at the time. He thought of it as something that had happened to residents he knew.

Helen 214 reached over from her seat and took his hand again. This time he was grateful for the human contact.

They couldn't see, from the rear of the shuttle, what was going on up front, where Ken 197 and Sarah 202 were checking all the systems one last time. They made sure that the shuttle was airtight, that the heating system was functioning properly, and that they had a sufficient supply of air, and the equipment to recycle it, to last for the mission. Satisfied, they called the control room and told them that the shuttle was were ready for launch.

"You are cleared for preliminary roll," came the clipped response.

The lights on the hangar deck suddenly turned red, and a Klaxon began to sound. In front of them the hangar doors began to open, though, at first, they couldn't see much. Then a black line appeared as the doors separated. The line widened, and the lights began to dim even more. There were only a few stars visible through the opening.

Ken 197 pushed forward on the yoke, and the shuttle, after a hesitation, began to move slowly. The doors continued to open until they had folded out of the way. Ken 197 accelerated then, and the nose of the shuttle pushed on through. A moment later they rolled into the blackness of space. The Milky Way was spread out to the right, galactic center glowing brightly. To the left were fewer stars, some of them extremely bright and the others tiny points of light nearly invisible in the distance. There was a single, bright nebula, but Jason 215 wasn't sure exactly which one it was.

Ken 197 reached forward, pushed a button, and a thruster fired. It moved them away from the slight gravitational pull of *The Home.* They were now in free space. They were as alone in space as *The Home* was, but they were much smaller and much more vulnerable.

[3]

THE INTERIOR OF THE SHUTTLE HAD BEEN CON-figured to provide some privacy on a rotating and limited basis. There were several cabins in the rear with doors that closed, beds so that any of the crew could stretch out for a nap, and a single, small shower that trickled water.

The thing was, the shower was actually a marvel of engineering given the nearly weightless environment in which it worked. The water tended to "fall" toward the rear of the shuttle so that the head rested on a bulkhead that was on the nose side. The water tended to drift to the rear, but had little in the way of weight and sometimes, rather than falling, collected in large drops that floated around the human body. Still, it was better than nothing, and sometimes trying to break the cohesion of the water so that the body could get wet made an entertaining game. And sometimes it was interesting to slide a hand along the body, letting the water coalesce into larger and larger drops that would orbit a body much like a planet around a star.

The rest of what was called the cargo compartment had been arranged around high-backed acceleration chairs, the equipment and sensors for monitoring the planets, and closed bays that held the portable devices that would be used if they landed and ventured out into the planet's atmosphere. There was lots of equipment for the few residents assigned to the mission.

Beyond that, at the front, was the cockpit that could hold four crew. There was also an access panel that would allow the technicians to climb below, into the inner work-ings of the shuttle in case some sort of in-flight repair was needed.

As the shuttle floated in space, near *The Home,* Jason 215 got his first look at *The Home* from outside. Most of the sky was taken up with *The Home,* telling how massive it was. Jason 215 thought it was almost impossible for an object as large as *The Home,* which had been constructed by human beings, to maneuver through space, and yet here it was, light-years from Earth and the Solar System.

Helen 214 leaned close to him, and said, "I never knew *The Home* was so big."

"Certainly get a different impression from outside," said Jason 215.

There was a sudden pulsing from the rear of the shuttle, and *The Home* began to fall away. They were accelerating away from it, moving off toward a solar system in the dis-tance. As the angles changed, they could see the bright star at the center of the system as displayed on the main flat-screen. They could also see two of the large planets with only a minimum of magnification on the screens. Their destination didn't seem all that distant.

They sat quietly, feeling the increase of force as the ac-celeration continued. And then, as quickly as it had begun, it seemed to end. The forces seemed to equalize, and though they knew which way the rear of the shuttle was, based on the continued force, it wasn't as strong as it had been.

Jason 215 unbuckled the seat belt and pushed himself out of his seat. He walked over to one of the consoles and sat down in front of a screen. He touched the mouse, zoomed in, and magnified the scene so that he could get a better look at the star system. One of the gas giants had an arrangement of rings that rivaled those of Saturn. The other seemed to be surrounded by bright points of light that marked some of its moons. He counted thirty-one before he lost track.

Helen 214 joined him, standing behind him, but holding

on to the back of his chair. She leaned forward and tapped the screen. "I think that is our target."

Jason 214 looked at the bright, white light that was standing off from the large, orange planet. The rings dominated the view. He isolated on the moon, increased the magnification, then glanced down at the sensor readout.

The moon was a shade under the size of Earth, something like seven thousand miles in diameter. There was a blue glow about it, suggesting water in abundance, or at least that was what he believed. There seemed to be points of white and gray, which could indicate cloud cover, and there was what looked like a single mass, which could be a continent. He didn't know if all the land was contained in the single continent, or if there might be others, hidden behind on the dark side or obscured by the clouds.

Helen 214 said, "It looks good."

"How far away is it?"

"Shuttle will take a long time to reach that system, then a week or so to slow into orbit around that moon. We have lots of time."

"Looks like it might have indigenous life on it," said Jason 215. But all he really meant was that the planet looked a little like Earth, and that meant there could be some form of life, animal and vegetable, on it already.

"Nothing to indicate an industrial society," said Helen 214, misunderstanding him. "Nothing at all to indicate intelligent life."

Jason 215 rocked back into the soft padding of the chair. He stared at the screen and the glowing little moon dominated by the planet it orbited. He said, "Well, we know that intelligent life exists out there somewhere. Maybe there are no detectable indications of intelligence, but that doesn't mean that there isn't any intelligence there."

"Why not?" asked Helen 214.

"Well, we might be looking for the wrong thing."

Helen 214 snorted, which might have been a laugh. "If there was an intelligence on that planet, we'd know it."

[4]

JASON 215 FOUND THAT BOTH THE SIZE OF the shuttle and its maneuvering through space were slightly disorienting. He was used to an environment in which some of the bulkheads, walls, and structures were lost in the distance, or in the curvature of *The Home*. On the shuttle everything was within sight, and the lack of down or up as established by a gravitational field, as they had on *The Home* confounded him, until he realized that down or up was whatever he decided it was. Once he made that discovery, he felt better about being in space.

Now he drifted toward the rear of the shuttle, barely touching the deck, which he had decided was down, looking for Helen 214. She had abandoned her post an hour earlier, saying that she was tired and nothing was going to happen for a while anyway. She had looked directly into Jason 215's eyes, as if there was some deep meaning to her words, but Jason 215 didn't understand. He sat there in front of his flat-screen, working out the navigational problem that would take them to the new system. Of course, the shuttle crew already had the information. Jason 215 thought that he could use the practice.

He reached the closed door of one of the bedrooms and tapped on it before he reached down to open it. He pushed it open slowly, carefully, and peeked around slowly, in case Helen 214 had gone to sleep.

She wasn't asleep. She was stretched out on the bed with a net over it to keep her from drifting up off the bed and floating away. She had stripped off her coverall, and it had been thrown onto the deck, though it was now about two feet off it, rotating slowly.

Helen 214 was about a foot above the bed. She had looked back, over her bare shoulder at Jason 215, and grinned at him. She said, "Sometimes you're not too fast on the uptake."

Jason 215 tried to lean casually against the bulkhead, standing where he could get a good look at her body. She looked as if she were standing with her ankles crossed, but she was floating horizontally, with her right hand seeming to support her head.

"You look good," said Jason 215.

"Why don't you come in here and close the door. I've been trying to wait patiently because I didn't think you'd miss the hint. I didn't think you would, but I was beginning to wonder."

Jason stepped into the tiny cabin and closed the door. "Well, sometimes I don't pay close enough attention."

Helen 214 tried to roll so that she was floating on her back. She uncrossed her ankles and lifted her arms as if to embrace him. "No, sometimes you don't."

[5]

ALTHOUGH HE THOUGHT OF THE EXPLOSION as the most important of the recent events, Stephen 168 thought his best shot would be trying to find whoever had contaminated the ag pods. He had isolated the relevant portions of the disks and noted the activity, which, in and of itself, looked innocuous. When cross-indexed with other disks and scanned for furtive motion, a picture began to develop. One man walking among the plants in the ag pod meant nothing, but when he was found to have met with a woman who worked with biological substances, and who had made contact with a geneticist who was attempting to improve the yields of some of the crops, a picture began to emerge. Especially when certain crops began to wither.

Even with all the computer time he had needed, it took quite a while to establish the chain that led from one to the next. He found that Jack 218 had met with Cheryl 209. Jack 218 had access to the ag pod, and Cheryl 209, who worked in a lab, was friends with Hillary 211. Hillary 211 worked in genetics and was often in the lab after her colleagues had gone home, supposedly working to catch up. But close scrutiny showed that her late-night work was un- related to her day job. And though she tried to be careful, aware that there were cameras around her, Stephen 168 saw her pocket test tubes.

Stephen 168 thought he had at last found some of the conspirators. They had both the knowledge and access to the ag pod. All he had to do was make sure he was going in the right direction. He made notes of what he had seen, where to access the information, then made copies of the relevant parts. That way he could show it all to the Mayor without having to swap disks or access different parts of the mainframe.

He locked everything and stood up. Without a word to anyone, he left the Security office and walked out into the central plaza area. Fruit trees were in full bloom, there was a new bed of flowers off to the right, and children were running through the park.

He walked along a pathway of crushed gravel and reached the main research lab. He would move slowly and see if he could learn anything more. The investigation was continuing, but he wasn't ready to arrest anyone. Since they didn't know that he knew, or what he knew, time was on his side.

[6]

KEN 197 HAD STAYED ON THE FLIGHT DECK for nearly twenty-four hours. He had stayed there simply because the shuttle had entered the planetary system several days earlier and was now approaching a gigantic planet with many moons. He wanted to be sure that the computer was not suddenly overwhelmed by all the incoming data. There was no real reason for him to stay on the flight deck, because the computers could guide the shuttle toward the planet and its many moons. He simply felt better being there. Besides, there wasn't all that much else to do.

Jason 215 and Helen 214 were sitting side by side at there workstations watching the approach to the planet in real time, with little in the way of magnification. The approach gave him the impression they were moving rapidly in space. Had he not been watching, he would have felt no real motion. It would have been as if they were hovering.

Jason 215 had little to do now that they had reached their destination. He could watch the show as if it was a program back on *The Home*. He could inspect the planet, its moons, and not have to worry about a test later.

The planet gave off a bright orange glow. The atmosphere was thick, with clouds in stratification, making the planet look banded. There were two minor spots and one larger one that might have been swirling storms of incredible strength. The cloud layer flashed periodically in what might have been lightning. Though Jason 215 and those on the shuttle had never seen lightning in its natural form, they were familiar with static electricity and the blue sparks it generated.

Helen 214 had been watching her own flat-screen, but they were still too far out for her to find anything of interest to her. She'd have the chance to explore the plant life once they made planetfall.

"I think that moon is our best bet," she said quite unnecessarily, gesturing at the screen.

"Earth normal," agreed Jason 215.

She leaned back in the deep chair, and asked, again, "What do you think it will be like? On the surface?"

Jason 215 replied as he always did. "Just like on *The Home,* only we won't be able to see the other side. The stars at night will be stars and not the lights from the other side."

"Think it will be cold?"

Jason 215 hadn't thought about that. *The Home* was kept at a constant temperature for the comfort of all the residents. But there wouldn't be a computer regulating the temperature. Or the wind. Or the brightness. They would be exposed to the whims of nature.

"Or hot, or windy."

"You sound as if you are looking forward to it."

"Well," said Jason 215, "it'll be a new experience. If

we haven't liked something, we could alter our environment so that it pleased us. Now all we can do is relax and hope for the best."

"I don't want it to be cold," said Helen 214.

"Then you can stay inside the shuttle. Besides, we might not land at all. Might be some reason that this moon is unsuitable."

"We haven't found anything wrong with it yet."

"Maybe there are already residents on it."

She grinned because this was the direction Jason 215 always took. He imagined alien life that had spread out over all the land, filling it with cities and factories and hundreds of thousands of residents.

"But we haven't seen anything like that. If some alien species came upon *The Home*, they would see that there are intelligent residents on it."

"Yes, because a large manufactured object in space suggests a certain level of intelligence. But we've seen no evidence of intelligent life on that moon. Even the ancient Egyptians would have left something for us to detect."

Helen 214 was growing tired of the same old discussion, but she held to her part a moment longer. She said, "But if we look back a little farther, our ancestors wouldn't have been easily visible from space."

"But would have been from orbit. We can find them if they exist."

Helen 214 fell silent and watched the approach to the moon. She leaned forward as if to get a better view. She was watching sensor input scroll across the bottom of the screen.

Jason used his mouse and changed the angle and the picture several times. He scanned the land, looking for signs of industry or a city—any indication that there was intelligent life on the moon—but found none.

Helen 214 examined the continuing readouts, and said, "I've got signs of plant life here. Maybe some concentrations of animals as well."

From the flight deck, Ken 197 called out, "We've entered into our orbit. We're about two hundred miles above the planet."

For a moment Jason 215 was confused, then realized that Ken 197 meant they were above the moon. He adjusted his flat-screen and watched the moon slip beneath the shuttle. He got a good look at the major continent on the bright side of the moon, saw oceans that were a deep blue, and clouds in the atmosphere, including thunderstorms filled with bright flashes of lightning.

As they moved around to the dark side of the moon, he saw two more continents, one much smaller than the other. There were ice caps at the poles, and had he not seen thousands of pictures of the Earth taken from centuries of orbiting spacecraft, he might have thought they had found their way back to their home planet.

The one thing that was absent was any sign of civilization. Jason 215 believed that any concentration of intelligent beings, no matter their level of civilization, would be visible, whether it would be just preindustrial-age towns or the agriculture of an agrarian society.

He thought, for a moment, he had found that proof in a blotch of bright light on the dark side, but as he increased the magnification, he realized that it was a raging forest fire. There didn't seem to be anyone around to fight it.

His conclusion, and that of the others on the shuttle, was that no intelligent life existed on the moon. They found abundant plant life, sporadic indications of animal life, but no sign of any intelligence.

Atmospheric pressure, combination of gases in the atmosphere, gravitational pull, and temperature all seemed to be in the range to support human life. Jason 215 thought they might have found the salvation of *The Home*. He thought they might have found their New Home.

Ken 197 took his own readings, made his own observations, then announced, "I think we should land."

There were no objections.

CHAPTER SIX

YEAR TWO THREE FIVE

[1]

WITH AN EARSPLITTING ROAR, THE SHUTTLE touched down on a long, smooth plain that seemed to stretch to the snow-covered mountains in the distance. At least Jason 215 assumed that the mountains had snow on them though he had never seen real snow. He had seen pictures on *The Home*.

They bounced along, slowing, and finally rolled to a stop. The engines were shut down, and suddenly they were wrapped in silence, with only the quiet popping coming from the rear as the exhaust ports cooled.

Ken 197 opened the door that separated the flight deck from the rest of the shuttle, stood there for a moment as if searching for some monumental words, but settled for,

"Well, we're down in one piece. I think we'll be able to take off again when we need to get out of here."

Jason 215, conditioned by a life on *The Home,* sat in front of a flat-screen as the shuttle's cameras provided the view of a plain filled with brightly colored flowers and a long, thin grass of a green that bordered on blue. It was more of a teal than a real green like that on *The Home.* He could have been up, at the ports, looking out onto the real scene, but somehow, seeing it on a screen made it seem more real to him.

In the distance, barely inside the one-to-one resolution of the cameras, were trees. These weren't the fruit-bearing trees of *The Home,* but tall things that nearly scraped the sky and had umbrella-shaped branches near the top. They looked more orange than green.

"Outside atmosphere is nearly ideal," said Helen 214. "Traces of inert gases, maybe a little high in oxygen content but breathable."

Ken 197 moved toward the sensor arrays and dropped into the seat in front of them. He glanced at them without really seeing them, and asked, "We have anything about bacteria?"

Martha 212, the zoologist, said, "Well, I haven't detected anything that would be harmful to us. I doubt that we'll have to worry about disease. Any pathogen that evolved here would probably be incapable of infecting us. Different biologies. We should be safe."

"You sure?"

"Yeah." She was going to make the argument about species-specific disease on Earth but didn't bother with it. Ken 197 would either believe her analysis of the situation or he wouldn't, and no amount of argument would make any difference to him. She fell silent.

"Anything larger out there that we need to worry about?" he asked.

Martha 212 said, "I have found nothing on the scanners. A little movement, but most of that is small stuff getting out of our way, I think. Something like rodents and probably large forms of insects, or insectlike creatures."

Having completed the mundane shutdown procedures, Sarah 202 finally left the flight deck and joined the others. She sat in one of the passenger seats and turned so that she could participate in the conversation. She asked, "How soon until we are able to leave the shuttle?"

Jason 215 looked at her, surprised. That was something that he hadn't thought about much. Get out of the shuttle. Walk on the surface of a moon without more of the ship above him, or around him or under him. Walk out in the open, with a sun shining down, breathing air that hadn't been endlessly recycled, where no one was controlling the temperature, or the animals, or anything else. Walk out and pick a flower because no one cared about a single flower. Drink the water without a thought about where it came from originally and how many bodies it had gone through. Look at an endless supply of air and resources and not have to worry about using too much or wasting too much or how to replace that which might be lost. Just to walk free in the fields and the flowers and simply not worry.

Ken 197 rubbed a hand through his short hair, and said, carefully, "Well, I think we want to make sure that there is nothing harmful in the environment out there. Nothing that will injure us and no damage that we might do."

One by one they shut down the equipment or left it in the "standby" mode. They lined up at the hatch, with Ken 197 standing in front of it. He glanced back, at each of them, looking them in the eyes.

Finally, he reached out and put a hand on the wheel to open the hatch. "I can't think of anything to say," he said, "except, here goes."

He spun the wheel, saw the locking bolts retract. He pulled in and lifted up, pushing the hatch out of the way. Then he took a step back, as if to give those behind him a better view of the new world.

Jason 215 felt, for the first time in his life, the fresh air of a planet, moon actually. It felt cool, not unlike what came from the blowers on *The Home*. It tasted different, sweeter, and held none of the contaminants he remembered from the recycled air. At first the air seemed to sting his lungs, and he coughed. He took a deep breath, felt the air flow into his lungs, then felt his head spin.

Behind him, Leslie 207 said, "I feel faint."

"Sit down," commanded Ken 197, and, as he spoke, he slipped to the deck, his head low.

"Close the hatch," ordered Sarah 202.

"No," snapped Ken 197. "We'll be fine. We just need to get used to the air."

Jason 215 stepped back, away from the hatch, but he could still look out on the bright plain. The lights in *The Home* had never been as bright as the sun high overhead. He blinked rapidly and felt his eyes begin to tear. It was another new experience for him.

Ken 197 stood up, breathed in the new air, then jumped down, to the ground. He stood upright for a moment and dropped to his knees.

"Ken," yelled Sarah 202. Without thinking, she reached up to grab the hatch.

He turned slowly and smiled. "It's so soft. The ground is so soft."

"Damn it, Ken, I thought you were hurt. Don't screw around like that."

"I'm fine." He stood up shakily and took a step forward. Over his shoulder, he said, "I can't believe this. I simply can't believe this."

Sarah 202 exited next, and Jason 215 followed her. He stood with his back to the shuttle and looked out, over the plain. It seemed to go forever with no upward slope. The sky overhead was a deep blue, with a cloud here and there, but nothing above him but open sky. He began to feel anxious, almost afraid, as if there was too much space around him. He began to crave the interior of the shuttle, where he could see and feel the limits. He wanted to be enclosed.

Helen 214 joined him. She stretched as if she had just gotten out of bed, and said, "Isn't it magnificent? Isn't it the greatest thing you've ever seen?"

"It's overwhelming," said Jason 215, meaning it, but it also scared him.

Ken 197 said, "We need to get our camp established.

We'll want to have guards up around the clock. We'll need to gather samples of the plants, any animals we can catch, and I would like to get some water samples for later analysis."

"But we'll spend the night in the shuttle, won't we?" asked Jason 215. "We'll be inside during the night?"

"Why would you want to do that?" asked Ken 197. "We're free to roam out here."

"But we can?"

"Well, yes," said Ken 197. "But there is nothing to frighten you out here."

In the distance was a new, strange sound, which reminded Jason 215 of a bearing that was going bad. He didn't like the sound, but no one seemed to notice.

[2]

THE NIGHT HAD BEEN PEACEFUL, WITH A SKY ablaze with stars and a smear near the horizon that looked like spilled luminescent paint but was the heart of the Milky Way. A tiny moon appeared, raced across the sky, and vanished in a matter of hours. It glowed a dull red. Later, a larger moon rose and hung in the sky looking like pictures of the Earth's only satellite. And, of course, there was the hint of the huge planet around which their moon circled. Jason 215 had to keep reminding himself they were on a moon circling a planet that circled a star.

And though nothing came near them, they kept their lights burning all night as one of them stood guard over the others. They heard strange sounds in the distance, but it was not unlike the ever-present whining of servos and small motors on *The Home*. The tones were different and certainly didn't have the regularity of machinery, but they were only distant noise that posed no threat to them.

The sun rose in a flash of red and gold that slowly changed into the yellow rather than the nearly normal white light of *The Home*. Jason 215 stood in the hatch, having slept on the shuttle, and watched the sun as it first faintly painted the sky and finally washed out everything else.

Around them were the calls and cries of unseen animals. Overhead the first birds appeared, soaring on the breeze that accompanied the sun. It was all new to Jason 215, and he was staggered by the beauty and the enormity of everything.

Ken 197, sitting on a chair pulled from the shuttle and eating one of the processed meals, said, "Today we explore the area around us. We gather the samples that we couldn't get from orbit. We get everything we need, then we'll talk about taking off tomorrow morning."

Martha 212 said, "I think we need some samples of the local fauna. I'll certainly work on that." She looked at Ken 197, and added, "I'd like to have the help of Billy."

"No problem."

Jason 215 took a deep breath, and said, "I suppose that I could look for a source of water. I guess I could get a sample of that, the plants near it, and even some of the aquatic creatures, if there are any."

"Good," said Ken 197. "You have a preference for a partner on that?"

"Helen."

Laughing, Ken 197 said, "Why is it that I'm not surprised about that?"

"Because you are a clever, observant individual," said Sarah 202.

Ignoring that, Ken 197 said, "Sarah, you'll remain here and check out the shuttle so that we'll be ready. You might want to check the plain for hidden dangers that could damage us. I'll work with Leslie 207 on gathering samples as well. We'll head off in three directions, each of us being careful to keep our bearings and return in five or six hours."

Sarah 202 clapped her hands, and said, "I think this would make a wonderful New Home."

"If everything is as it seems," said Ken 197.

[3]

THE COMPASS THAT JASON 215 HELD SEEMED to be little more than useless. The needle didn't move. It was as if there were no magnetic lines of force around the planet. Nothing for the needle to point to. Nothing that drew it around. He slipped it back into his pocket and looked back.

Their path through the tall grass was obvious. They had crushed the blades, turning and breaking them so that they were a duller color than the grass around them. They could follow their trail back to the shuttle, even if they lost sight of the tail assembly, which stood high above the plain.

Helen 214 found a rock and sat down for a moment. There was a light coating of sweat on her face. She was breathing deeply, as if she had run a long distance, but she was also smiling. She said, "Isn't this great?"

Jason 215 said, "I'm not so sure."

"Look at that," she said, pointing. "Those mountains are miles from here, and the place isn't jammed with people. We have the place to ourselves."

To Jason 215 that wasn't necessarily an argument in favor of the moon for The New Home. He was still bothered by the wide-open feel, though, now, in the daylight, it wasn't as bad as it had been.

"If you're ready?" he said.

"What's the hurry? I just want to enjoy this place. It's not like we have to be somewhere by a certain time." But she stood up anyway and began to walk forward, more slowly.

In the distance was a stand of trees, and Jason 215 believed that there would be water near them. At least, from his reading, he believed it. Once they had the water sample, and some plants and animals, they could get back to the shuttle, their mission accomplished.

But Helen 214 was walking slowly, as if it was all uphill. She stopped frequently to examine a flower or plant or something she had seen in the grass, collecting samples as she went along.

She picked up a pointed stone, and asked, "What's this?"

Jason 215 took the rock from her and felt the edge. It was sharp and looked as if it had been worked by an intelligent hand. He remembered seeing pictures of arrowheads fashioned by any number of primitive peoples.

"That was manufactured," said Helen 214.

"Well, I think 'manufactured' is being overly kind."

"You know what I mean."

"We saw no signs of any civilization," said Jason 215.

"This doesn't mean a civilization."

"No, but it does indicate technology and something more than scavengers."

He turned it over in his hand. The bottom was discolored, as if it had lain on the ground for a long time, but he didn't know what a long time meant. A year? A decade? A century? It could be the remnant of a civilization that had disappeared along with the people, the creatures, who built it.

"You know what this means, don't you?" asked Helen 214. She answered her own question. "This can't be The New Home. Not with an intelligent race living here."

"Then we might as well head back to the shuttle," said Jason 215.

"No," she said. "I want to see more. I want to be outside for a little longer with nothing really to worry about. I want to see a lake or a stream or a river; I want to see the trees and stand under them."

Jason 215 shrugged. He wanted to head back to the shuttle so that he could sit inside, where he could see the bulkheads and the overhead and feel a little safer. But he followed Helen 214 as she walked toward the stand of trees.

As they approached them, the grass seemed to thin, and the flowers got smaller, as if dwarfed by something. The trees were a hundred feet tall, with green, mossy trunks and only a few branches, all of them seventy or eighty feet in the air. The orange-tinted leaves were three or four feet wide. They formed a canopy over the area, creating shade, so that in the center of the stand it was much darker.

What they had found was a miniature forest, with a thick undergrowth and bushes with long, thin spines. There was a rattling on the interior, from under the bushes, which sounded as if there were things, small, unseen things, running around.

There was a trickling, splashing sound that might have been running water, though they could see nothing like that. Helen 214 pushed past the first barrier of low bushes and stumbled. She put a hand out, screamed in surprise and pain, and pulled it back quickly, cradling it.

Jason 215 reached her, and said, "Here. Let me see it."

Helen 214 held out her hand gingerly. Jason 215 looked at the palm. It was red and blistered, as if burned by acid. There were two thorns embedded in her flesh.

"It hurts, Jason."

Jason 215 didn't know what to do. They didn't encounter plants that burned the hand on *The Home*. But then, this was some sort of burn, and he knew something about treating burns. He took the water bottle that he had stuffed into his pocket, opened it, and poured the water on her hand.

"That feels better," she said.

Without thinking about it, he pulled one of the thorns out. There was a drop of blood, and she grunted with the pain. When she didn't say anything, he pulled the second free with one quick jerk. He then poured the rest of his water on her hand.

"I suppose we should wrap it in something," he said.

"What?"

"Cloth."

"I don't have any cloth."

Jason 215 thought for a moment, then tugged at the sleeve of his coverall but the seams were too well sewn and the cloth too tough to tear. He thought about one of his socks but was afraid that it would be too dirty.

"Maybe the air would be best," she said.

"I suppose."

"We should head back."

Jason 215 thought, *Yeah, now you want to head back*, but said nothing to her. Holding her uninjured hand, he turned and retreated from the tiny, dangerous forest.

[4]

KEN 197 HAD ACTUALLY THOUGHT THEY MIGHT be able to walk to the foot of the mountains even though, intellectually, he knew they were too far away. Conditioned by a life on *The Home,* he didn't have a concept of something being so far away that he couldn't walk there and back in a matter of hours. He started off walking quickly, arms swinging in a rhythm with his steps, with Leslie 207 right behind him. But after an hour, he was covered with sweat and feeling the first signs of exhaustion. The mountains looked as far away as they had when he started.

Leslie 207 finally said, "Can't we rest for a moment? You're walking too fast."

Ken 197 stopped and turned. She was bathed in sweat and breathing hard. She was pale and looked as if she was about to collapse.

"I'm sorry," said Ken 197. "You should have said something sooner."

"I thought you would stop to rest at any minute."

Ken 197 looked around, but there was nothing to sit on other than the grass. He dropped down and leaned back on his hands so that he was looking up at her.

"Finally," she said as she sat down.

The ground was slightly damp, as it was on *The Home* after an evening watering. And there were insects, or what Ken 197 thought of as insects. They were tiny creatures scurrying among the plants. He noticed that none of them had wings.

He looked up into the sky but saw no birds. There had been some circling at dawn, but now they were all gone. He wondered what had chased them from the sky. He held a hand up to shade his eyes and looked toward the sun. He looked right at the disk, stared at it, and finally looked away. Now, centered in his vision was a large, black disk. He could see to the right or left of it, but at the moment he couldn't see anything right in front of him. He wasn't worried, figuring the spot would disappear, the same way those back on *The Home* did when someone looked into one of the lights or someone used a flash to take a picture.

Leslie 207 said, "I should be taking notes for a map of the area."

"Why?" asked Ken 197, distracted by the black hole in the center of his vision.

"It's what I do."

"Shuttle can map the area in a matter of minutes."

"But it's nice to have a firsthand glimpse of the terrain. Add some detail to the maps that aerial photography or radar cartography can't add."

Ken 197 felt a sting on his wrist and jumped. He held his hand in front of his face, but couldn't see anything because of the black void. He held his hand off to the side and saw one of the insectlike creatures attached to his skin. He reached up with his other hand and pinched it between his thumb and finger. There was a satisfying pop as the creature burst. He pulled the stinger free and dropped it on the ground.

Leslie 207 said, "Shouldn't we be gathering the little beasties rather than squashing them."

"I suppose."

"So where do we head now?"

"I thought we might be able to get off the plain here and look at some of the other terrain."

"So let's see what we can find," said Leslie 207.

Ken 197 stood up and turned his head right and left, trying to get a look at the mountains and the path back to the shuttle. The blob of black seemed to be growing rather than disappearing. He blinked rapidly, rubbed his eyes, but still couldn't see much of anything.

"Maybe we should head back to the shuttle," he said finally.

Leslie 207 shrugged. "Makes no difference to me. Just let's slow it down."

Ken 197 was getting worried. The area around him seemed dimmer, as if the sun was setting. He turned his head slightly and could tell that the sun was still high overhead. Now he felt warm, hot actually, and frightened. He wanted to get back to the shuttle in the hope that he could find something to help his eyes.

"You lead," he said, his voice a little high and tight. "Good practice."

Leslie 207 stood up but didn't move. She said, "Is there something wrong?"

"I'm having a little trouble with my eyes. It's very bright out here."

"It sure is," she said. "I'm not sure that I like this at all."

She turned and began to walk back along the path they had created. Ken 197 followed her, turning his head right, then left, so that he could see her out of the corners of his eyes. He couldn't see the path and was aware of only a little of the vegetation around them. He couldn't see the mountains; nor could he see the tail of the shuttle.

Leslie 207 stopped, and Ken 197 walked into her. He bounced off, staggered a step, then sat down abruptly.

"Hey," she said.

"Sorry."

"Ken, what in the hell is going on here? Something's wrong."

He didn't speak for a moment and didn't move. He then rubbed at his eyes and looked up, to where he thought she was standing. Of course he didn't see anything except for bright circles around the periphery of his vision. He didn't want to put anything into words because that would seem to make it all real. If he didn't talk about it, if he didn't mention it, then it might go away. But he knew it wouldn't. He knew that he had done permanent damage when he had looked up into the sun.

Quietly, he said, "I think I'm blind."

[5]

By THE TIME THAT JASON 215 AND HELEN 214 reached the shuttle, Helen 214's hand had swollen so that it was nearly twice normal size. The skin had turned bright red and looked like a rubber glove. Helen 214 was dizzy, and pain was radiating up her arm, into her chest. She felt sick, and Jason 215 had to carry her the last hundred yards to the camp.

As they approached, he shouted, "Hey. We need some help here. A little help."

Sarah 202 dropped from the shuttle hatch and ran toward them. She tried to help but only succeeded in getting in the way. She asked, repeatedly, "What happened?"

"Don't know," said Jason 215. "She just touched the trunk of a tree. Something on the tree did this. I think it's some kind of poison. Or some kind of acid."

They reached the shuttle, and Jason 215 set Helen 214 down on the ground in the shade near the huge tires. She leaned back against a tire and sighed.

"I washed it as best I could with the water we had with us. I pulled out two thorns. I don't know if they injected the poison or if there was something on the tree that burned her. She barely touched it."

Sarah 202 nodded and looked at Jason 215. "You get anything on you?"

"Why?"

"Your face is quite red, too."

Jason 215 reached up and touched his skin. It felt dry to his touch and was a little sore. He said, "I don't think I got anything on me."

Sarah 202 said, "Well, sit down. I'll check the first-aid kits on the shuttle."

As she left, Helen 214 tried to smile but failed. She said, "I don't feel very good, Jason."

"Well, you just relax a little bit. Sarah will find something for you. We'll be all right now. We're back to the shuttle."

Sarah 202 dropped from the shuttle, walked over, and

crouched near Helen 214. She set down the large first-aid kit, opened it, and pawed through it.

"I don't see anything in here that might help," she said.

"Something to bandage the wounds from the thorns?" suggested Jason 215.

Gently, Sarah 202 lifted Helen 214's hand and turned it over. She could see the two puncture wounds, which had stopped bleeding. They looked clean, but she didn't know for sure. She didn't know what she should do.

"I can wash her hand in antiseptic, but that's about all I can do here."

"Maybe we should see what the computer can tell us," said Jason 215.

Sarah 202 ignored him. Instead, she took the antiseptic spray out of the kit, pulled the cap, and said to Helen 214, "I think this might sting a little."

Helen 214 nodded and clenched her teeth. When Sarah 202 sprayed, she cried out, and her eyes rolled back. Her head dropped as she passed out.

"Sarah!"

"Relax."

"She's fainted."

"I'm not sure that's such a bad thing to happen. Gives her a chance to rest."

She put the antiseptic back into the first-aid kit and took out one of the cloth bandages. This she soaked in water and used it on Helen 214's forehead. Finally, she tied it in place and poured more water on it.

Finished, she said, "Let's go see what the computer can tell us. Might have some suggestions."

"You think she'll be all right here?"

"Let her rest. When she wakes up, we'll move her into the shuttle."

Sarah 202 stood up and turned her head. In the distance she thought she had seen movement. She searched the plain, then saw Leslie 207 walking along with Ken 197, holding hands. She felt her blood boil though she had no claim on Ken 197. He was the mission commander, and they had done nothing except share the flight deck and work together. There was no reason for her to be angry with Ken 197 for holding hands with Leslie 207. No reason whatsoever, but she was angry. Such a display was not the professional attitude of the mission commander.

Leslie 207 raised her free hand, and shouted, "Somebody come here."

"Now what?" asked Sarah 202 angrily.

Leslie 207 and Ken 197 started to hurry, but Ken 197 stumbled and nearly fell. Sarah 202 stood flatfooted and watched as they crossed the last few hundred feet of the plain. It became clear that Leslie 207 was leading Ken 197. When she saw that, Sarah 202 ran forward.

"What happened to Ken?"

"I don't know," said Leslie 207.

"I can't see," said Ken 197. "Big black spot at first, and now it's all black."

"Anything attack him?" She realized she was acting as if he wasn't even there. As if somehow his lack of sight had rendered him incapable of answering any questions. She looked into his white, washed-out eyes, and asked, "Anything bite you? Anything attack you?"

"No. Not that I know. Bug bit me. Stung me, but I didn't have any reaction to it."

"Your face is very red. Do you know why?"

"No."

"Where'd the bug bite you?"

Ken 197 held up his hand and Sarah 202 examined it. She found a small wound that looked more like a pinprick than anything else. There was no discoloration around it, no sign of swelling, and no sign of tissue damage. The wound didn't look as if it had anything to do with Ken 197's sudden inability to see. It might not be related at all.

Finally, Sarah 202 began to lead Ken 197 toward the shuttle. It was the only thing she could think of to do.

Leslie 207 caught up, and said, "I didn't see anything. I don't know what happened." Then she spotted Helen 214, and asked, "What's wrong with her?"

"Tree sap or something," said Jason 215. "Some kind of poison or acid in it."

They reached the hatch of the shuttle and all stopped. Sarah 202 said, "Okay. We've reached the hatch. The ladder is not in place. I can set it if you need it."

Ken 197 said, "No. Just guide my hands, and I'll lift myself up into it."

Sarah 202 centered him in the hatch and placed his hands on either side of it so that he was holding the edges. She said, "You're all set."

Ken 197 felt around for a moment, touching the sides, then the bottom. Satisfied, he lifted himself up and turned so that he was sitting with his feet dangling. With his hands, he felt the deck, then the sides of the shuttle. He stood up and took a step back.

Once Ken 197 was inside the shuttle, Jason 215 escorted Helen 214 to the hatch. She'd regained consciousness, but was still very unsteady.

"Can you climb up?"

She looked at the entrance, four or five feet above the ground, and knew that she would have to use both hands to enter. She said, "I'll need some help."

Sarah 202 helped Jason 215 lift Helen 214 into the shuttle. She moved past Ken 197 and dropped into a seat. Bathed in sweat, Helen 214 was breathing heavily. Her face was bright red, as were both her hands and her arms.

Standing outside, near the hatch, Jason 215 said, "This isn't going well. We've got two serious injuries."

"And we don't know where Martha and Billy are."

[6]

BILLY 209 DIDN'T LIKE BEING ON THE PLANET, though he was delighted with the opportunity to study it at close range. To him, close range would have been from orbit. Better would have been from fifty or sixty thousand miles. Close enough to get a good look but far enough that he could see the whole planet at once if he wanted. It was the way astronomy had worked for thousands of years. Study the astronomical objects from afar.

The flora and fauna of the planet didn't interest him. The geology wasn't of much interest. He wanted to know about the atmosphere, and he wanted to know more about its relation to the gas giant that dominated the sky. And, he reminded himself, he really wasn't on the surface of a planet but on a moon.

Martha 212 wasn't staring up into the sky, but was studying the ground, searching for tiny animals to catch. She had already grabbed a small, hard-shelled creature with six legs and a segmented body that looked something like an overgrown ant. But it also had some kind of coarse fur and no evidence of eyes or antennae.

She had found something else that had four stubby legs and a long, thin body. She thought of it as a "protosnake" but it didn't have any teeth, and she didn't know what it could possibly eat. Not that she cared at the moment.

During their short walk, no more than two miles from the shuttle, she had picked up a half dozen creatures she found interesting. Some were colorful and others dull, as if designed to hide in the grass. Some had fur or hair, and others had a beaded, reptilian skin. Of course, she had never seen anything like them.

They came to an area where the grass was smashed flat in a circular pattern. In the center was a wooden post, or at least something that looked like a wooden post. There were carvings on it though neither Martha 212 nor Billy 209 could guess what they represented.

"You know what this means," said Billy 209 as he studied the carvings.

"Yeah. This place has an intelligent race. We can't use it for The New Home."

"It also means that we can now return to the shuttle. Any research we do is going to be wasted. You might as well turn those little creatures loose."

"They're of interest to me, even if we can't use this planet. Tells me something about evolution and might provide us with an insight to the rest of the universe."

Billy 209 looked at her, then said, "You don't seem to be overly excited by your find."

"What do you mean?"

"Well, here we are on this planet, this moon, and you've found a dozen new creatures. Something that has never been seen before, and you're acting as if it is an everyday occurrence."

"I have been preparing for this since we boarded the shuttle," said Martha 212. "I have speculated and planned, and I am now carrying out that plan. What would you have me do?"

"I would have thought that you might express a little excitement as you caught these little things."

Martha 212 shrugged, and said, "But I expected to find living things. Maybe as I study them, I'll feel the excitement you require, but right now I don't know anything. I haven't done anything that you or any of the others couldn't have done."

Billy 209 shrugged and dropped the discussion. Instead, he walked into the center of the circle to examine the post. The carving was crude, done with a tool that wasn't very sharp. He thought he could recognize something that looked like an animal, but, of course, he couldn't identify it. Only that it was an animal.

Martha 212 stood at the edge of the circle. The grass at the edge had been flattened carefully. The edge was crisp and sharp and not ragged. Clearly something intelligent had been working there. The carved post proved it.

"This should excite you," said Billy 209. "Evidence of another, intelligent race."

But she suddenly didn't feel excitement. She felt fear. Living, intelligent creatures were quite different than tiny insectlike living things. Intelligent creatures could kill for no reason. They could cause trouble simply because they could think. She said, "Maybe we should get out of here."

"Come look at this," insisted Billy 209.

Martha walked to the post and bent closer. She could see carvings of animals running among the strange trees, and, if she hadn't known better, a lion attacking a zebra.

"Interesting," she said without really meaning it.

"Just interesting. Without having to go far, we see a representation that suggests a type of survival of the fittest that was seen on Earth. A predator and prey. Gives us a clue about the dynamics of evolution here."

"That's what you see," said Martha 212, "and you might be right, but until we can find these animals and watch them in action, we don't know that. Your interpretation of these symbols might be in error."

Billy 209 shrugged, and said, "Might be. I just thought it was a little more than interesting."

He looked up then and saw that they were no longer alone. Standing at the edge of the circle were a number of creatures. He didn't know if they were intelligent or not. They were humanoid, but that was about all that could be said for them. Their legs were very short and their trunks long. The heads were bullet-shaped cones that sat on the shoulders, and Billy 209 thought about those pictures he'd see in the computer of the alien race that had passed close to the Earth so long ago. These beings didn't look like them, except for the shape of the head. But then no one had ever gotten a close look at the aliens.

He reached over and pushed Martha 212. She waved a hand at him, but kept her attention focused on the figures carved on the post. When he pushed again, she looked up, annoyed, and then said simply, "Oh."

"They don't look threatening," said Billy 209.

"No," agreed Martha 212. "But they don't look like they're friendly either."

"Let's slowly back up and get out of here," said Billy 209. "Real slow."

As they backed away from the pole, the creatures began to move as well. One step and then another. Billy 209 thought that maybe they should run, but he didn't want to frighten the creatures into doing anything.

"What do they want?" asked Martha 212.

"I don't know," said Billy 209, "but let's be real careful here."

Before he could react, the creatures rushed forward.

[7]

THE SUN WAS BEGINNING TO SET, BUT THE huge planet seemed motionless in the sky. The orange and yellow of the bands of clouds were reflected to the moon, and although it was darker than it had been with the sun high overhead, it was still bright outside.

Helen 214 was now only semiconscious. She was moaning in pain, and the swelling had moved up her arm to her shoulder. Her face was a bright red, as were both her hands and her forearms, to the point where they had been covered by her clothing.

Everyone who had spent time outside had red faces, including Sarah 202, though she was paler than the others. All were miserable, trying to keep from touching the red areas. They found some salve in the first-aid kit that reduced the stinging in the reddened areas and seemed to cool the fire on their skin.

Ken 197 sat in the rear of the shuttle. He kept his head moving, looking right and left, trying to see anything. Now he couldn't even make out shades of gray. Everything was a nearly uniform black.

Sarah 202 had used some eye drops that had been in the first-aid kit but they did nothing to help Ken 197 see anything. He was convinced the condition was temporary, but he was becoming frightened by it. He wished that they were back on *The Home* where a doctor could check him. A doctor who understood this sort of thing and could come up with some kind of treatment for him.

Sarah 202 checked the time, and said, "Billy and Martha should be back by now."

"Maybe someone should go look for them," suggested Jason 215.

Ken 197 said, "Let's keep everyone together. How overdue are they?"

"You said not to be gone more than six hours. They've been gone eight."

"What's it look like outside?"

"Getting darker," said Leslie 207.

"Then here's what we do," said Ken 197. "They know that we want to leave in the morning. They might have gotten lost, traveled a little too far from the shuttle and are having trouble getting back. Turn on the outside lights and fire a flare every hour or so. That way we create a beacon for them to follow back to us."

"And anyone else who might be around here watching," said Jason 215.

"Now, what's that supposed to mean?"

Jason 215 pulled the arrowhead from the pocket of his coverall. "In the confusion, with Helen getting hurt, and you getting hurt, I forgot. We found this." He held it up, then realized that Ken 197 wouldn't be able to see it. "An arrowhead. Crude, but something that shows us that someone, or something here, is or was making tools. Stone tools that suggest only the most primitive kind of civilization, but tools just the same."

"Crap," said Ken 197. "That rules this place out. If everyone was here, we could get out. Take off tonight and spend a few extra hours in orbit."

Sarah 202 asked for the arrowhead and examined it carefully. Finally, she said, "I think this is more of a spearpoint than an arrowhead."

"Doesn't really matter," said Jason 215. "It is clearly a manufactured object."

"How long until morning?" asked Ken 197.

"Ten or eleven hours," said Sarah 202.

"How dark is it out there?"

Jason 215 bent down and looked out one of the portholes. "It's not all that dark. Twilight. Looks like *The Home* as they begin to power down in the evening."

Ken 197 took a deep breath and blew it out slowly. He said, "Maybe we should go look for them, if you can follow their trail through the grass."

"Who would go?" asked Sarah 202.

"Have to be Leslie and Jason. Sarah, you have to remain healthy because you're the other pilot. I certainly can't go, and Helen 214 is injured."

"We already have two people missing," said Sarah 202 quietly, as if she didn't want to be heard.

"Well, I think we need to look for them. See if we can speed things up so we can get out of here," said Ken 197. What he didn't say was that he wanted to get off the moon's surface. He didn't like it. He only wanted to get back to *The Home*.

From the rear, in one of the two bedrooms, Helen 214 moaned in pain. She shouted once, but there were no words. Only a single cry of pain.

"And we need to get her to *The Home* for medical treatment," said Ken 197.

No one mentioned that *The Home* was a long distance away and that by the time they reached it the crisis would be over. She'd either have recovered or she'd be dead.

[8]

THE LIGHT OUTSIDE THE SHUTTLE HAD A strange orange glow to it. Everything was colored differently, oddly, and even those few things that were familiar to them didn't look right. It was the color of the light reflected from the giant planet that still dominated the sky.

The trail followed by Martha 202 and Billy 209 was fairly obvious. They had walked side by side, crushing the grass in two parallel paths. It wasn't a straight line, but nor did it meander all over the plain.

When they were out of earshot of the shuttle, Jason 215 said, "I don't like this."

Leslie 207 asked, "Why not?"

"Someone has been injured on two of the teams that have returned, and the third team is missing. There is a great deal not to like about this."

"You said that Helen touched one of the trees."

"Yeah."

"We'll simply avoid them."

"I've been thinking about that. If it was a poison, wouldn't it be based on the biology of the species found here, meaning that an Earth-based poison wouldn't work against the animal life here, and their poisons shouldn't work against us."

"Helen's injuries looked more like a burn to me," said Leslie 207. "Acid here should burn as badly as an acid created on Earth."

"That isn't very comforting," said Jason 215.

"Well, even if it was a poison, it still worked against Helen, so what's the difference?"

Jason 215 shrugged. He didn't have an answer.

They walked on in silence, both looking at everything around them, looking for trouble, looking for danger. Occasionally, Jason 215 looked up at the planet, but it was sliding toward the horizon and becoming more difficult to see. He didn't know how long they would have light and wondered how easy it would be to find their way back to the shuttle when it was dark.

There was a quiet pop behind them, and Jason 215 turned to look. A flare hung in the air a little above the shuttle. That, at least, answered his question. They could follow the light back if they got too far away.

"Maybe we should spread out," said Leslie 207. "Get a better picture of the terrain."

"All we're supposed to do is find Martha and Billy."

"Crap," said Leslie. "They got themselves into some big trouble or they would be back. They wouldn't still be missing out there."

"Maybe Billy broke his leg, and Martha can't carry him back to the shuttle."

"Then she would have come back alone to get help. Whatever happened, it happened to both of them."

"You know," said Jason 215, "back on *The Home* some people seemed to disappear, but no one ever went looking for them."

"What's that supposed to mean?"

"Well, I had a couple of friends, Thomas and Cynthia, when I was a kid. We got into some trouble in one of the dining halls, and the next day, or maybe a day or two after that, they moved away. Moved into another part of *The Home*."

"Well, there you have it. They moved."

"Yeah," said Jason 215 slowly. "But, I have never seen them again. Not at university. Not at any of the rallies. Not at the Med Center. I haven't seen them, or heard from them. E-mails were never answered. Some even bounced back to me."

"So?"

"I was just thinking that it's strange they disappeared so completely."

"Did you ever try to go to visit them?"

"Once or twice, but I couldn't get permission to use the transports or was denied permission to leave my area. So, I tried but I didn't."

"What are you trying to say?"

Jason 215 stopped walking. "I don't know. I'm only saying that it was weird."

"Now that you mention it, I can think of some people who seem to have disappeared. One man who was bothering my mother, kept calling her at home, following her, then, one day, he simply stopped all that. My mother was happy about it, relieved really. I asked, and she said Security had taken care of it."

"But that man was engaging in criminal activity," said Jason 215.

"Or he was just an overly aggressive suitor. I mean, I could not understand why she was upset by the guy. Just some calls and the like."

"Maybe you don't know the whole story," said Jason 215.

"No, but the guy still vanished. My mother never went to a trial or anything like that."

In front of them, in the distance, was a shadow over the plain. Jason 215 pointed it out, and asked, "What do you think that is?"

Leslie 207 stared and began to hurry toward it.

At the edge of the circle, they stopped. It was clear that Billy 209 and Martha 212 had reached the circle and then walked into it. Their trail ended at the edge of the flattened grass, so it was the only place they could have gone.

In the dim light reflected from the gas giant that now seemed to be sitting on the horizon, they could see something sticking up in the center of the circle. It was getting hard to see as the light faded.

Jason 215 walked forward and stopped near the post. He reached out and touched it, feeling the carvings on it. One more proof that some intelligent creatures lived on the moon.

Leslie 207 said, "They walked into the circle."

"And probably out on the other side. Let's take a look around the perimeter."

They found one spot where the grass was flattened, as if one person had walked out of the circle, but a little beyond that, no more than five or six feet, they found a half dozen other paths. Each one looked like the next.

"Now what?" asked Leslie 207.

Jason 215 crouched and looked at the ground. He didn't know what he was looking for or at. These were trails in the grass, each looking like the others. Nothing to tell him which path had been made by what or whom. Since they had followed Billy 209 and Martha 212 to the circle and they were no longer there, two of the paths were theirs. There was nothing in them that would tell him which ones they had made.

"Do we follow them?"

"Which ones?"

"Well, they all seem to go in the same general direction, so I guess we follow them all."

Jason 215 turned back and looked toward the shuttle. The flare was hanging low. They would certainly be able to find their way back, even in the dark. But they wouldn't be able to follow the trails and might not be able to see any threat that lurked around them. If there was some kind of creature that attacked from ambush, they probably wouldn't be able to spot the danger.

"I guess we go on until we run out of light, then we head back."

They exited the circle. In the distance, it had to be three or four miles, they thought they could see a flickering of light, but they didn't recognize it. Something about it looked familiar, but something also looked strange. It was just a light bobbing in the distance. Jason 215 didn't like it and was frightened by it, but he said nothing to Leslie 207 about it.

And then the trails split, first into two, then into four, and finally into nearly a dozen. Leslie 207 said, "I don't understand why there are so many."

"They were walking one behind the other. Could be ten individuals on each of the trails."

Leslie 207 stopped, and asked, "So we turn back now?"

Jason 215 said, "Which trail do we follow? They're not going in the same direction anymore. We don't even know if any of these trails were made by Billy and Martha."

"Maybe we should head to the light over there," suggested Leslie 207.

"I don't think so."

"Why not?"

"Because whatever happened to Billy and Martha happened in that circle, and all the evidence was carried away. If it could get them, it can get us. We need to go back to the shuttle and report on this."

"But we don't know what happened to Billy and Martha."

"I have a feeling that if we continue, we will find out, but we'll be in no condition to report those findings either."

[9]

JASON 215 AND LESLIE 207 SAT OPPOSITE Ken 197, whose face was now wrapped in bandages in the hope that without further stimulation his eyes would have a chance to recover. Ken 197, injured and blind, was still in command of the mission, and while Sarah 202 sat nearby listening, the final decisions about the mission would be made by Ken 197.

He asked again, somewhat angrily, "You saw no sign of either Billy or Martha?"

"We followed the trail until we reached that circle I told you about, then followed the multiple trails out of there until they all fragmented. We couldn't follow them all."

"So you followed none," said Ken 197, his tone sarcastic.

"What would you have had us do?"

"You could have followed one of the paths."

"Yeah, and we could have split up and followed two of them, but if Billy and Martha have been captured—and no I don't know by what—then you could have been out looking for us tomorrow morning."

Sarah 202 stepped forward, and said, quietly, evenly, "What we must decide, given the information we have, is what we are going to do now."

Jason 215 said, "I don't really want to be the one to say this, but there isn't much we can do with two of the people here badly injured. That leaves three of us, and, as Ken pointed out, Sarah, you have to stay here."

"What are you suggesting?" asked Ken 197.

"I think you know. We have no choice but to take off in the morning as planned. Both Billy and Martha know the schedule. If they could get back here, they would have. That we haven't heard from them tells me that they can't."

"That's pretty fatalistic."

"What's the flaw in my thinking?" asked Jason 215.

"Let me put it to you this way," said Ken 197. "If you were in command, what would you do?"

"Take off. Head for home and try to get some sort of a rescue mission started. Have them take off as soon as possible."

Sarah said, "Why don't we survey the crew?"

"Because, in the end, it's my decision," said Ken 197. "Vote how you like, it's still my decision."

Leslie 207 spoke for the first time. She said, "It's really not a decision. We have to go. Maybe we can do something for Billy and Martha once we get to *The Home,* but we can't do anything for them now."

"That's a long time for them to survive on their own," said Ken 197. "We don't know if the water is drinkable or that they'll be able to find anything to eat. We take off now, we are almost certainly condemning them to death."

They were all silent for a moment. The only sound other than the chirping of the electronic equipment was the quiet moaning of Helen 214 in one of the rear cabins.

Finally, Jason 215 said, "They might already be dead. They ran into something, and they haven't returned from that. I think that should figure into the decision."

Again they fell silent. After several minutes, Ken 197 said, "We need to take off in the morning. Sarah, transmit a message that will tell control what has happened here and that we'll be returning in the morning. We'll repeat it every day until we get an answer."

"Yes, sir," she said.

Leslie 207 said, "I just want to point out that there really was nothing else to be done." Even as she said it, she didn't like it, but she knew that it was true.

[1 0]

THE TAKEOFF, WHEN IT CAME AT FIRST LIGHT, was anticlimactic. No alien or strange creatures attacked, there were no attempts to stop the shuttle, and the plain out in front of the shuttle was long and flat, with no hidden obstacles. It was as good as any paved runway.

They lifted off easily and pointed the nose nearly straight up, climbing as rapidly as they could. In the upper reaches of the atmosphere, where the air was thin, they leveled the wings and continued to accelerate. They fell into an orbit around the planet that continued to expand outward, using the gravity of the gas giant to increase their velocity.

They reached escape velocity, broke orbit from around the moon, and took a dive toward the gas giant to slingshot themselves into a new flight path with more speed. They used that to escape both the gravitational pull of the planet and the system's sun. They soon found themselves exiting the system and flying toward *The Home*.

As soon as they were set on the course, as calculated by Jason 215, Sarah 202 left the flight deck. The automatic systems were on, the sensors were looking for any sort of space debris that could harm their ship, and Leslie 207 was making a sweep to verify what the sensors did much better.

Once the flight path was established, Jason 215 left his position and entered the rear cabin where Helen 214 slept. Her face, which had been a bright red, had faded to a duller pink, but some of the skin was beginning to peel. The swelling on her hand and arm was beginning to shrink, and though she seemed to be in some pain, she was sleeping quietly.

Jason 215 shut the door and returned to the main cabin. He sat down near Ken 197 and noticed that the redness on his face had faded slightly. His skin was also peeling, and the skin underneath, while darker, was closer to the normal color. He didn't know what to make of that.

Sarah 202 dropped into the seat near the other two, and said, "Well, we're on our way home. I haven't received any response from control. Of course, there hasn't been time for a response, so I'm not surprised."

"We'll hear from them when they have something to tell us," said Ken 197.

"I wish this trip didn't take so long. Poor Billy and Martha are going to have a rough time of it."

"If they are still alive," said Jason 215.

"Well, there's always that."

"I guess there isn't much we can do now except wait."

"And go over what we have seen and what we have found," said Leslie 207.

"I wish we would hear from *The Home*."

"So do I. I wonder what is happening there."

What they didn't know was that things were getting worse.

CHAPTER SEVEN

YEAR TWO THREE FIVE

[1]

MICHAEL 177 SAT IN ONE OF THE CHAIRS IN the civilian command center and looked at the screens arrayed in front of him. He wasn't sure about what he was seeing, other than a shuttle launch in progress.

Sitting next to him was the Captain, Christina 160. She looked relaxed, as if she had spent her whole life in the command center and was used to being the one in charge. She sat in the center seat with an array of buttons on the arms that allowed her to change the scene on any of the screens, change the magnification, what sensors were being used, or what segments of *The Home* were on display. She could see everything from her seat, control nearly everything, and even jettison sections of *The Home* if that became necessary for safety of the whole. There was a great deal of power concentrated in those buttons.

"That the last of the shuttles to be launched?" asked Michael 177.

"Last to be used in our survey. Probes and scouts are all out as well. We have quite an armada out in the space around us at the moment."

By reflex, Michael 177 looked at his watch, then asked, "When can we expect the first word?"

"We'll have the beginning of the definitive reports within three weeks. The travel time to some of the targets has set the schedule for us."

"Why nothing earlier? I mean," said Michael 177, "not all the targets are that far away."

"We've staggered the launches so that those with the greatest distance to go were launched first. Everything will get there about the same time, reports will come back, at the speed of light, but will be spread over several days."

Michael 177 looked at the center screen, where a shuttle was beginning a slow spin so that the nose seemed to be pointed down. There was a brightness at the rear, and the shuttle began to accelerate. The camera stayed with it for several seconds.

"Who's that?"

Christina 160 touched a button, and the information was displayed on the screen. She read it, and said, "I don't think they'll have much luck. The system is made up of mostly gas giants, and the moons all seem to be little balls of rock without any redeeming features. Astronomy has found nothing that will be suitable for us."

"Then why waste the time?"

"Because you always have to look. There could be something about the system that we have overlooked on the sensors or that the first robotic probes missed. It's close, and if we find something there, we can get there with *The Home* in a matter of weeks rather than months."

Michael 177 waved a hand as if wiping a slate clean, and said, "I don't understand."

"Well," said Christina 160 patiently, "it is a matter of

acceleration and deceleration, and changing the flight path of *The Home* . . ."

"No," said Michael 177. He glanced over his shoulder, at the empty chairs, at the unmanned stations, at the hatch that led from the flight deck. "I don't understand why someone would sabotage *The Home*."

"What's Security been able to learn."

Now Michael 177 turned his attention to the Captain. He remembered that the last Captain had tried to take total control of *The Home*. That hadn't been a pleasant time. He'd done what he had to do for the protection of the starship. The look on that Captain's face, when the sentence had been pronounced, was one of surprise. George 148 couldn't believe they would do that to him. He couldn't believe they would do it to anyone. He couldn't believe that he was going into the recycling pit before he died.

Michael thought about Christina 160's question. There wasn't much that he was going to tell her, but Security had found some interesting records. Security had made good progress in its investigations.

And he didn't tell her that the situation was getting worse by the hour. Only a handful of people knew how bad it was, or what had actually caused the crisis.

[2]

CHRISTINA 160 WALKED SLOWLY ACROSS THE park, heading for the elevator that would take her up to the flight deck. She nodded at people she didn't know, waved to those she had met, and spoke to those she considered friends. She had to be careful. The internal politics of *The Home* demanded that everyone believe that she was an objective leader whose only concern was what was best for *The Home*.

She knew, however, as had the previous Captain, George 148, that the Captain's responsibilities were such that he, or she, could never be objective. Sometimes the Captain was required to act in his, or her, own self-interest, and, at other times, the welfare of *The Home* was paramount.

She opened the hatch that led to the flight deck, saw that Ryan 171 was sitting in the center seat, the one reserved for the Captain when she was on the flight deck. He hadn't noticed that she had entered. He was lost in thought, studying something on the large, center screen.

She walked up, and said, "What have you got there?"

Ryan 171 looked up annoyed, saw that it was the Captain, and leaped out of the seat. "Sorry, Captain."

Christina 160 took the seat, and said, "Don't worry about it. What's going on?"

"Reports from the shuttles."

"Anything?"

"Nope. We haven't found anything that would be suitable. One world had the proper atmosphere and was about the right size, but it was a cold place. Very cold. No growing season to speak of and quite a bit of radiation from the star. That effectively rules it out."

"The others?"

"Planets outside the biosphere of the star, or atmospheres that are poisonous, or much too hot, or little more than balls of rock and mud. Not even anything that we could terraform in the time we have."

"That's everything?"

"Except for a report from Ken 197. They landed on a planet, moon actually, right atmosphere, warm enough, but they've had some trouble, and they might have evidence of intelligent life."

"What sort of trouble?"

"People injured and two missing. They're off now, on the way back."

"They left people behind?"

"Yeah," said Ryan 171. "I wondered about that, too. I sent a query back, but the distance is such that I won't get an answer for a while."

"Well, if there is any form of intelligent life on the planet, we can't use it."

Ryan 171 nodded, but asked, "Why not?"

"The moon belongs to its inhabitants. They own it by right of occupancy."

"What if they don't use it all? Maybe there would be enough empty area that we could use that, at least temporarily. Get things settled here, then take off again."

Christina 160 wondered what was being taught in the university. Everyone should know that joint occupancy never really worked. The dominant partner always took advantage of the submissive partner. If those with the power needed something, they could take it. Earth's history was filled with examples. All one had to do was look.

And even if the dominant partner worked hard not to force its will on the others, the mere introduction of new technology destroyed civilizations. Even the Plains Indians of the United States came to understand that. The black cooking pots and the muskets the Europeans introduced required a manufacturing base to reproduce. The Indians wanted the black cooking pots and the muskets because they were superior to the things the Indians already owned, but the Indians had no way to make them, repair them, and, in the case of firearms, produce the gun powder necessary to make them work. Even without the conflict, the Indian culture would have been destroyed.

To Ryan 171, she said, "We can't land on that planet if there is another intelligent species there."

"Yeah. Well, we just might have to."

Christina 160 looked at him and asked, "Why?"

"Because things are getting worse, not better."

[3]

DAVID 181 STOOD ON THE CATWALK IN THE hydroponics pod and looked down at a scene of complete and total disaster. The plants in the vats were dead, and those areas that had been replanted failed to spout, or grow, or bloom. They had tried to replace the sand and gravel. They had tried to sterilize it and bring it back to life by adding in the chemicals and bacteria necessary to energize it. They had tried everything, and it was clear that nothing was going to grow in the pod. At least nothing would grow for years to come.

And, to make it worse, they couldn't recycle the material because it began to look as if that act would contaminate other areas. The hydroponics pod had been turned into a barren waste, where nothing could grow and nothing was going to grow.

David 181 turned, walked back to the elevator, and took it down to the main level. He stepped out into what was now operating as an airlock. He waited for the lock to cycle, spraying disinfectant on him and on his shoes. Once that was done, he slipped some blue cloth "booties" over his shoes to protect them and walked out into the pod.

He wandered around, unsure of what to do. He knelt near one of the vats but touched nothing. The water had been drained away, leaving a muddy residue in the bottom that was organic matter, only a little dirt and water. It was the result of more than two hundred years of use.

There wasn't much to see. He stood up and walked among the vats, looking into them. A few still contained water, and fewer still held some of the plants that had been genetically engineered to respond to the aqueous environment.

He came to the dormitory and pulled at the doors. It was vacant, with everything that could be useful removed. He was walking through a ghost town where the ore had run out, or the water was depleted, or the reason for the very existence of the town was gone. It was a depressing place that reeked of death and destruction. He could think of no use for the pod at the moment. They might as well jettison it.

He turned around and walked out of the dormitory. As he crossed the open floor, he was struck by how quiet it was. With no other people around, with nothing growing, with all the other activities shut down, there wasn't anything to make noise. Maybe an almost inaudible sigh from the air-conditioning, and that was it. No servo motors, no voices, absolutely nothing.

He reached the airlock, entered, and took the booties from his feet. He removed the coverall and stood under the light mist of disinfectant, turning slowly to make sure his body was covered. Finished, he left the airlock and pulled a new coverall from a locker. He donned it and left the pod area, taking the resident mover down to *The Home.*

As he exited, Doris 188 approached. "Well?"

"Looks dead. Completely dead. I don't know what we can do. Everything that goes in there seems to die."

"I have found nothing on the macro level to cause this. Whatever it is, it operates on a genetic level."

"Could it be that everything is simply worn-out. We've recycled everything so much that we've reached a point where it can no longer be reused?"

Doris 188 shook her head. "But it's not as if we're using everything the same way. Yeah, there is going to be a diminution of the elements in our society. Even a closed system is going to lose something—"

David 181 interrupted. "But it is a closed system. How do we lose anything?"

"We create an artificial environment that requires heat. We have to produce the heat, and some of that heat is lost into space. That's just one example."

"And we recover that through the engines and the gathering of hydrogen."

"Well, all I can tell you is that I believe we are slowly, have been slowly, losing elements, and we might have reached a point where we can't recover."

David 181 said, "I don't understand this, but we're going to have to report to the Mayor. Maybe we can dismantle the pod and use the materials in some other way."

"Or cross-contaminate everything."

"Maybe."

They walked on quietly for a few moments. Finally, David 181 said, "I just don't understand why that pod failed. I don't understand what is going on in there. It's almost as if there is another agency at work, attempting to destroy all that we do."

"Maybe that's your answer."

"But why? Oh, I know that we've had some vandalism, some of it quite destructive, but this is something else. This is more like committing suicide." It was the same thing that he had said half a dozen times.

"I don't begin to understand how the mind works," said Doris 188. "I just know that some people do get crazy ideas and are willing to sacrifice anything to get their point of view across to everyone else."

"Well, it makes no sense to me."

But it would make sense in the very near future.

[4]

STEPHEN 168 SAT IN THE CENTER SEAT, AT the main security console, flanked by the Mayor, Michael 177, and the Captain, Christina 160. He had only the larger center screen in use, but the images were incriminating. Faces could be seen and actions could be witnessed.

Stephen 168 pointed at the screen, and said, "We have identified a number of people who have spread the disease in the ag pods."

He touched a button, and their pictures displayed in a rapid-fire matter. Not really enough time to get a good look at any one of them, but enough to see that there was a mixture of men and women and a few children. All were in poses that suggested they didn't realize they were being photographed though each had to know that he or she was being monitored. The cascading pictures provided a very good look at what was being done in the ag pods to destroy the crops and the facilities.

"Can we slow this down a little bit?" asked Michael 177. "I can't see anything."

"Certainly. I wanted to give you an overview first. See the number of people who were involved. It was not a random act of violence or vandalism by a couple of angry people. It's much more than that."

Christina 160 leaned forward so that she could look at the Mayor. She said, "I thought we had testing to avoid this sort of thing. I thought we could catch the vandals before they had a chance to do any real damage."

"That is not my responsibility. Medical . . . better yet, Psychological, should have seen this coming and taken steps to prevent it."

"Blame," said Stephen 168, "is not the issue here. It has happened and someone screwed up."

"Speaking of that," said Michael 177 somewhat angrily, "we have Security, which is supposed to catch them in the act if Psychological falls down on its job."

Stephen 168 didn't react with anger. Instead, he said, quite calmly, "I will show you all the surveillance we have on this. You will have to remember that we pieced it together from hundreds of hours of stored video. We could have had someone, meaning a physical presence, witnessing every act, and I don't think he or she would have tumbled to what was going on until there was some evidence of destruction. It was just so subtle that, unless you were watching, or had some warning about it, you weren't going to catch on. Our only clue was when the crops began to die. Then we knew what to look for."

"Show me," ordered the Mayor.

Stephen 168 touched a button, moved the cursor, and let the video stream. He said, by way of narration, "Here is a lab tech working. Notice that she is being supervised during that work and is doing nothing out of the ordinary. She is contaminating culture dishes with various organisms, closing each dish, and entering its number into the computer. But if you watch carefully, you'll see that as she puts her fingers on the keyboard, they don't move. Glancing at the video, everything seems to be in order until it is scrutinized. Then you notice that one minor deviation. She didn't log one of the culture dishes as was required."

The scene shifted, and Stephen 168 said, "Now she carries all the dishes to the incubator and sets them in their racks, everything normal, except there is now one dish too many. She looks around in question, then closes the door, the single dish in her hand. She goes to her supervisor to report the unexpected overage, as is required."

"Good procedure," said the Mayor.

"Yes, but there is no video of her going to the supervisor. The problem is that she has moved from one camera's area of coverage to another, and in that transitional area, the extra dish has disappeared."

"Now wait a minute," said Michael 177. "Are you telling me that these people are so sophisticated that they are aware of the transitional areas and are able to make use of the switching to make things disappear?"

"Yes, Mr. Mayor, that is exactly what I'm saying. We have reviewed every bit of recorded material that we can find of that lab, and that area and the dish simply disappears."

"What does she do with it?"

Stephen 168 backed up the video, slowed it, and showed him. As the tech moved into the "shadow" area between camera coverage, she slipped the dish into her pocket. She then continued on, spoke to her supervisor, and left the lab area altogether.

"We didn't bother to add the rest of the video here because it was routine. We know that she left the lab with the dish and went to her apartment."

"You should have caught this," accused the Mayor.

Stephen 168 shook his head, knowing that he could never convince the Mayor that without some clue as to what was happening, he didn't have the staff to catch such subtle little deceptions. If residents wanted to hide something and were clever about it, Security had no real chance against them.

Instead, he said, "I can show you a hundred different bits of video where someone has slipped something by us. Maybe pocketing an extra bit of food, or hiding something from someone, or exchanging notes . . ."

"What in the hell is going on?"

"It's just residents being residents," said Stephen 168. "Most of the stuff is harmless from a security point of view. A man slips a woman a note and they meet later, out of sight of their respective spouses. We don't care because it does nothing to damage *The Home*."

The Mayor slammed a fist down on the arm of his chair. "No!" he nearly shouted. "It is not harmless. It demonstrates a mind-set of deception that needs to be corrected. There should be no notes and no secret meetings, not to mention the trouble it causes in society."

Keeping his voice even, Stephen 168 said, "My job, as outlined by the original residents, is to make sure that no one is doing harm to *The Home*."

"Well, you've mucked that up, too, haven't you?"

Christina 160 finally spoke. "This is not doing us any good. Show us the rest of the video, Stephen. Maybe we can think of something."

Stephen 168 let the video stream, telling them, "As you can see, we have one of the ag workers smearing something on his clothes though it looks more like he is brushing dust from himself. Then we see him walking among the plants. He's not touching them, only brushing by them and moving on. Later we were able to see the beginnings of the disease, and it was along the path this resident followed, spreading out from there."

Quietly, almost to himself, the Mayor said, "No way to have caught that. No way at all."

"How much more of this is there?" asked Christina 160, turning toward Stephen 168.

"We could go on for another hour or so. I can show you how we put all this together."

"You have the names of all those involved?"

"Well," said Stephen 168, "we have forty-six names now, which I believe to be all the conspirators. But they have been very careful. We need to keep working to make sure that we have identified everyone involved."

"I don't get this," said Michael 177. "What did they hope to accomplish?"

"I don't know," said Stephen 168. "We haven't arrested or interrogated any of them yet."

"Maybe you should do that."

"Yes, sir. We'll get on it."

[5]

MICHAEL 177 WASN'T OVERLY SURPRISED THAT someone had deliberately sabotaged the ag pods since they had discussed that possibility before. He was surprised by the scope of the conspiracy and the fact that Psychological had failed to find so many residents who harbored resentments deep enough to become involved in such a plot. It all seemed counterproductive since it eliminated a source of food. It made no sense.

He returned to his office so that he could be ready for a conference with the people from the Ag Department, and was surprised to find them waiting for him. He hadn't expected a face-to-face meeting. He'd thought they would all just chat through the computer hookup. He said as much to them.

David 181, who had stood up when the Mayor entered his office, said, "I know, but I just didn't want to put this out over the net."

"Why?" asked Michael 177.

David 181 looked at the young woman sitting behind a desk, then into the Mayor's office. The implication was clear. The news was bad, and he didn't want to share it with anyone not authorized to hear it.

Michael 177 shrugged and opened the door, letting David 181 and Doris 188 proceed him. Once inside, he closed the door and pointed to the chairs.

"Please. Be seated."

The Mayor's office was bigger than some of the single resident apartments and bigger than any of the rooms in any of the family dwellings. There was a carpet on the floor, and the walls were not painted the institutional gray that seemed to infect *The Home*. Instead it was a light green. There were curtains along one wall for a window that looked out onto one of the parks. Curtains on another concealed a video display that could be tapped into the cameras outside *The Home*, giving the Mayor a view of space around the ship. Or, if he was in a voyeuristic mood, he could tap into nearly any security camera feed and watch the residents as they moved about *The Home,* or as they engaged in activities in their bedrooms. None of the residents knew that the Mayor could do that.

David 181 dropped into a chair of simulated brown leather. Doris 188 sat in its twin. Both were set in front of Michael 177's desk so that all of them could easily engage in conversation.

Michael 177, still angry about the sabotage, still stunned that residents would work that hard to destroy something so important to *The Home,* sat down behind his desk, and said, "What have you got to tell me?"

David 181 looked first at Doris 188, then at the Mayor. He said, "There is nothing we can do to reintroduce crops into the hydroponics pod. There is something lingering there that kills anything we try to grow."

"This a permanent thing?"

"I believe so. Doris and I wondered if we just hadn't exhausted the area. If we were on a planet, I'd say we have to let the field go fallow for a number of years and let it rebuild itself naturally. Here, we can't do that."

"And you can't do it artificially?"

"I haven't figured out a way. I just walked through the pod, and everything in there is dead."

"This I don't need," said Michael 177. "Not with everything else."

"There's more," said Doris 188.

"Good or bad."

"Very bad, I'm afraid."

"What could be worse than the loss of the ag pod."

"The loss of several more of them," said David 181.

"What?"

Again Doris 188 took over. "We have inspected several of the other pods, and we find similar diseases spreading through them, killing everything."

"Quarantine!" said the Mayor. "No one in or out."

"Too late. Once the disease begins to work its way through a pod, it continues until it has killed everything in that pod. Everything."

"How far has it spread?"

"It's in half the pods now."

Michael 177 sat for a moment, then felt the blood drain from his face as he realized what had been said. He had been aware of infection in another of the pods, but this was the first time he had been told that nearly half were infected. The food supply would be cut in half, at best. And the other benefits from growing plants, such as oxygen production and the elimination of carbon dioxide, would be cut in half. *The Home* was suddenly deeper into a crisis.

"You have to get those pods replanted, and you must stop this disease."

"We don't know how," said David 181. "We don't know much about it."

The Mayor was about to speak, then decided against it. Sometimes it was better to listen than to talk. David 181 and his ag residents might not know anything about the diseases, but he knew who did. Security could round them up in an hour, and, under interrogation, they would tell what they knew. The antidote would be available before the crisis became any worse. Security would make the culprits talk.

David 181 noticed a change in the Mayor's attitude. He didn't seem as worried or distracted as he had upon their entering his office. And the news about the destruction in the ag pods didn't seem to worry him all that much.

David 181 said, "We are going to have a huge reduction in our food supply and no way to replace it. If the blight or disease spreads much farther, we are going to use all our reserves, and there will be no way to replace them."

"I understand that," said the Mayor in a somewhat sarcastic tone.

"Then understand this: Inside of a year, there will be no food left on *The Home*. Every single resident will be dead."

[6]

THE ORDERS FROM THE MAYOR HAD BEEN quite clear, and Stephen 168 knew what had to be done. Those who had been identified from the security videos would be arrested. It was a task a little more complicated than arresting George 148, but only because there were more people to arrest. He wanted to take them all at once so that no one could alert others, who could then do more damage. Once he had them in custody, he would be able to find out why they had done it. The destruction of the food made no logical sense to him. Of course, the first thing he would do is make them tell him how to undo the damage. Once he had that information, he could ask other questions.

Unlike the mass arrest nine years earlier, Stephen 168 could not arrange for everyone to be arrested simultaneously. So this time, rather than participate in one of the arrests, Stephen 168 stayed in the Security control room, where he could watch the progress and react to anything that happened during those arrests. He would be in overall command.

As his teams spread out in *The Home,* Stephen 168 sat with two backup teams watching. The first few arrests happened quickly and quietly because no one was expecting to be arrested at that moment. The men and women surrendered peaceably, leaving their apartments and their families without much in the way of protest. Like most of the guilty, they tried to avoid the looks of their neighbors, turning their heads as if that would somehow prevent them from being recognized.

The word of the arrests somehow leaked. Some of those on the list knew what was coming and tried to run. Of course the cameras followed them, and there really weren't any places to hide on *The Home.*

Stephen 168 watched as a female resident, cornered in the dining area of her apartment, stabbed a security man with a paring knife. He staggered back, more surprised than injured. The other two security agents leaped forward, knocking the resident from her feet. They rolled her to her stomach and pulled her arms behind her so they could restrain her.

Stephen 168 turned his attention to the wounded officer. He sat on the floor, his hand on his side. Periodically he looked at the blood staining his fingers, then cradled his hand to his body. He didn't look badly hurt.

"I think we're beginning to lose it," said Winston 199.

"Someone's running," said Mindy 200.

"Where?"

"There. Monitor four."

Stephen 168 turned his attention to that monitor. A male resident, dressed in a light green coverall, had fled his apartment, run along the alley and out across the park. He stumbled once, then plowed into two other residents, bowling them over. He bounced off, jumped back to his feet, and kept running.

"Where's he going?" asked Mindy 200.

"Not far," said Winston 199.

"The ag pods," said Stephen 168. "He's running toward the ag pods."

"Why? He can't escape in there."

But Stephen 168 knew that escape was not what the resident wanted. He was going to infect the crops that had yet to be contaminated. He was going to finish the job now that it was clear what was happening.

Stephen 168 reached down, touched a button, and used the intrasecurity radio. "Security deploy to all ag pod access hatches. Follow numerical order. Deploy now."

Having given that order, Stephen 168 leaped to his feet, pointed at one of the spare squads, and yelled, "You can come with me. Let's go."

The men and women ran from the Security control room, down a narrow, poorly lighted corridor, and out into the open. They ran across a green belt, between two buildings, and through a park. Residents stopped and stared but didn't move, sometimes pretending they didn't see what was happening. Running security forces meant bad news for someone.

They reached the far side of *The Home,* then turned. Still running, Stephen 168 used the radio. "Have you got him?"

There was a series of responses, all negative.

Stephen 168 didn't slow. He ran past an access hatch to a maintenance pod, and past another that accessed a weapons pod. He ran along, dodging residents and obstacles, leaped a short barrier, and spotted the running resident. Stephen 168 turned, angled toward the resident, and tried to run faster. Just as the resident reached the hatch, Stephen 168 jumped, stretched, and slammed into the runner. Both went down.

Stephen 168 rolled and jumped up. He spun, facing the resident, ready to attack.

The resident lay on his back, breathing hard. Slowly, he rolled to his side and got to his knees. He looked at Stephen 168, made a quick move toward the hatch, then sat back, on his heels, raising his hands. He knew that he was beaten, and all he could do was surrender.

Stephen 168 climbed to his feet slowly, his attention focused on the resident. His breath coming in gasps, he asked, "Just what did you plan?"

The resident shook his head. He wasn't going to answer that question.

As the rest of the security team caught up, Stephen 168 bent forward and put his hands on his knees. He let the others restrain the resident.

Stephen 168 followed them as they walked back, toward the holding cells, close to the Security control room. As they crossed one of the green belts, the resident looked back at him, grinned, and said, "You know you're too late."

[7]

STEPHEN 168 HAD NO STOMACH FOR THE more brutal methods of interrogation. Some of the more subtle methods involved drugs, hypnosis, and appeals to the subconscious. Stephen 168 knew that no one method worked all the time on all the residents.

Rather than be present in the interrogation chamber, a small room hidden inside the Security Building and unknown to most of the residents, Stephen 168, along with the Mayor and the Captain, watched on a closed net.

There was a single resident strapped to a table that, for all the world, looked like an autopsy table. She was alone in the room and wide-awake. There was nothing for her to see and nothing for her to study for distraction. The walls and ceiling were flat black. A single recessed light was overhead, but that was the only break in the otherwise featureless room.

The Mayor turned his attention from the screen and looked at Stephen 168. "Where is your team?" he asked.

"Outside waiting. In this sort of circumstance a resident has no idea how much time has passed, what is going on in *The Home,* what has happened to friends and families and who might have said what by now. We can convince them that an hour passed in five minutes, or that days have passed in a matter of hours. It is quite disorienting."

"I might remind you that we don't have a lot of time. The situation is getting worse."

"Mister Mayor, you'd be surprised at how fast people can break when they are seemingly taken out of the normal time stream. It is quite disturbing."

"Get on with it."

At that moment, the door in the interrogation room opened and four residents, dressed in black without visible insignia, without variation, entered. Two were women and two were men. They surrounded the table, but none of them spoke.

"Building anxiety," said Stephen 168.

A needle appeared though it wasn't clear who held it. The arm of the resident was seized, held tightly, and she was injected. She screamed once, as if she believed she was being killed.

When she didn't lose consciousness, she demanded, "Who are you? What do you want?"

The four left the room and quietly closed the door.

"This is taking too long," said the Mayor.

"Patience."

Minutes later the door opened again, and a single man entered. He was dressed in black without any insignia. His face had been disfigured, giving him a permanent but evil-looking grin. One eye was opaque and the other dark. He had little hair.

"Why?" he asked.

The woman looked at him, but all defiance had drained from her. She was clearly scared. She had become disoriented in just under an hour, thinking that maybe a day had passed, never realizing that the injection had added to her feeling of confusion.

But she said nothing.

The man moved closer, and asked again, "Why?"

She watched him with wide-open eyes. Her respiration increased, and she began to sweat, but still she said nothing.

"Some of your colleagues have already begun to talk. It goes easier for those who are the first to assist us. The rest . . . well, it's their tough luck."

Finally, she said, "Because it is so perverted."

"What's perverted?"

"Everything."

"This isn't going to help you."

"Go to hell. I won't tell you anything."

If the grinning man could have smiled more, he would have done so. The real trick was to begin the dialogue. Get them to talk about anything. Engage in an argument, but get them to talk, then slowly steer the conversation around to where you wanted it to go. It was an old interrogation technique that few outside of Security understood.

"We're all going to hell if we can't find a way to stop this thing," said the grinning man.

"There is no way."

"There is always a way."

She looked away but eventually looked back. She didn't speak.

"Why?"

"Because."

"Why?"

"Don't you get it? We're not free here. Nobody is free here. That's why."

"What did you do?"

"I didn't do anything."

"What did you do?"

"Nothing."

"What did you do?"

"I mixed some chemicals. I made a growth medium. And here I am to prove my point."

"You made a growth medium."

"Yes. So that the bacteria could thrive. I made a compound that they liked."

"What was it?"

"It's too late now."

"Then it won't hurt to tell me."

For an instant she was quiet, then she grinned, as if suddenly proud of herself and her role in the destruction of the crops. She told him all that she knew. She told him the composition of the growth medium and the requirements of the disease. She told him how she had been approached and why she had agreed. She told him everything.

It had taken eighty-two minutes to break her.

The Mayor nodded his approval, and said, "Now what?"

"We get with our lab people and see what they can tell us."

"And then we can stop these diseases and reverse it," said the Mayor. It sounded more like a question than a statement of fact.

Stephen 168 said, "And our interrogations will continue. This was only the first."

"You keep it up," said the Mayor. "We need all the information we can get."

Christina 160 spoke for the first time. She said, "I was surprised at the scope of her hatred. I thought Psychological would have spotted that and stamped it out."

"Clearly there are some things that we must correct," said the Mayor. "Many things that we need to do just as soon as we resolve this crisis."

The Mayor, satisfied, stood up. He walked to the door and left the control room.

When he was gone, Christina 160 said, "We're screwed aren't we?"

[8]

THE IDEA HAD BEEN TO DISCOVER HOW MUCH damage might have been done in the ag pods that had not been attacked and determine the size of the harvest because it would help to create a rationing program. Once they knew how much food there was, including stored food, prepackaged food, and how much artificial food they could produce, they would know the size of the disaster.

Their problem was that they had not caught all the conspirators in the first roundup, and those left had a chance to finish the plan. Because the leaders were at the higher end of the social structure, they had been harder to catch because everything had been so subtle.

Stephen 168 had gone toward one of the ag access pods and was waiting when Warren 199 exited. Unlike most of the residents, Warren 199 was stoop-shouldered, had short legs, and seemed to be a genetic misfit. He didn't look like a resident. He looked like a visitor from another part of Earth.

Warren 199 recognized the uniform worn by Stephen 168 and misinterpreted why he was there. As Stephen 168 approached, Warren 199 called out, "You're too late."

Stephen 168 didn't understand the comment, and asked, "What do you mean I'm too late?"

"I've already been in there. I walked all over. You won't be able to stop the disease now. The harvest is ruined, and the food destroyed."

Stephen 168 could feel the anger build, then burn

white-hot. He stepped in close, his face only inches from Warren 199's. "You infected that pod."

"We've infected them all now. It's too late to stop it. It's all gone."

[9]

THE NEWS WAS ALL BAD, AND THOUGH BOTH Christina 160 and Michael 177 reviewed it again and again, it still came out the same way. In all the closest star systems, those that could be reached before *The Home* ran out of food, even when rationing and other desperate measures were instituted, there was just nowhere to land. The planets were either too large, the atmospheres poisonous, or they were little more than lifeless rocks orbiting too close or too far from the central star, making them too hot or too cold.

And even if they could reach some of them, there was no way to plant crops and wait for them to mature before many thousands of residents starved. The residents who had devised the scheme had managed to come up with the one way that they could destroy *The Home* and its society without blowing up the engines or putting holes in the protective shell surrounding *The Home*.

Stating the obvious, Michael 177 said, "We need a planet close to us and one that already has an abundance of life that we might be able to adapt to feed the residents. We need it now, not two or three months from now."

"And I have said," repeated Christina 160, "that no such planet exists. The solution will have to be found here, on *The Home,* or it won't be found at all."

The astronomer, Allen 197, said, "I have tried to review the preliminary material transmitted by our probes and shuttles and have eliminated all that have a distance that would prevent us from arriving soon enough. There is one planet that is quite promising, but the star system is too far for us to reach with our current speed and our current population."

Michael 177 asked, "Where is this planet?"

Allen 197 touched a button, and a holographic display coalesced above the table at which they sat. A slowly spinning blue ball with splotches of green and brown appeared. "This is nearly perfect," he said. "Liquid water. Some indigenous plant and animal life and no sign of any intelligent species. Inside the star's biosphere though it might be a little warmer than we like it. The problem is that we couldn't reach it for three years, and by that time . . ."

Christina 160 said, "We are thinking too large here. We have shuttles and other smaller craft that can save some of the residents. We can move a great deal of equipment, including the genetic material for the food animals, in the time we have left here, on *The Home*. We can save some but not all."

"Only a thousand, at the most," said Michael 177.

"But our mission," said Christina, "is not to get every one to The New Home, but to establish The New Home. We can do that with a thousand or with the entire population. Or we can do it with a hundred."

Michael 177 didn't respond to that. He sat quietly looking at the planet that was just out of their reach. A perfect solution that would do them no good.

"We can implement some strong measures," suggested Jane 158, the residents' advocate. "The residents will understand the need for greater conservation. We can recycle everything. There is waste in the dining halls. We can eliminate personal meals in apartments."

"I'm afraid we're beyond that," said Michael 177. "It will help, but it will not avert the disaster."

Stephen 168 said, "There is a way of eliminating some of the problem. Execution for those involved. Immediate execution. They stop sucking up our resources."

"That's barbaric," said Jane 158.

"Barbaric?" sneered Stephen 168. "It's barbaric to use biological terrorism against your neighbors. It's barbaric to remove the food supply so that people starve. That's what they've done. They have condemned every resident, every child, to a slow and rather unpleasant death."

"We could begin euthanasia," said Christina 160. "Those residents who no longer contribute to society, or those whose contribution is no longer necessary . . ."

"And who decides that?" asked Jane 158.

"Computer analysis."

"This is wrong," said Jane 158.

"I think we're getting ahead of ourselves here," said Michael 177. "We have other things to discuss first."

"There is a planet within our range," said Allen 197.

"What?"

"There is a planet in our range, but from the preliminary reports, it has an intelligent species on it. I didn't mention it earlier because of that intelligence, but I didn't understand the full magnitude of the disaster."

Michael 177 realized what Allen 197 meant. He knew about the planet, the moon, but had thought of it as inappropriate because of the report of an intelligent indigenous species and hadn't considered it. Now there were no longer any choices except to begin a policy of euthanasia. That was how desperate the situation on *The Home* had become. None of that mattered any longer.

"Could we get there in time?" asked Michael 177.

Linda 168, who was responsible for all flight operations involving *The Home,* as opposed to the shuttle missions, didn't say anything for a moment. Finally, after consulting her Palm Pilot, and running numbers, she just nodded, and said, simply, "Yes, we can."

"Then the problem is solved," said Michael 177.

But, of course, it wasn't.

CHAPTER EIGHT

YEAR TWO THREE FIVE

[1]

JASON 215 SAT IN FRONT OF ONE OF THE monitors, occasionally glancing at it, but he was more interested in the stone arrowhead that he held. Clearly it was something that had been worked by intelligent hands. Probably fairly ignorant hands, but intelligent hands nonetheless.

The stone was a kind of flint with a slightly pinkish color and might have been picked for that reason. It was clear that someone, or something, had worked the stone, taken off large flakes first, then smaller and smaller flakes until he, or it, was left with a sharp point, sharp sides, and short flukes that would prevent the arrowhead from pulling free of the flesh without doing more damage.

The arrowhead was a precision instrument, or as precise as a stone implement could be. It had been crafted by a skilled hand and looked as if it had been used, probably more than once. All of this led to the conclusion that there were intelligent creatures on that moon because people from Earth, or residents of *The Home,* would not have been using stone arrowheads even if they had somehow gotten to the moon before this latest expedition.

Helen 214 dropped into the seat next to him, and said, "What do you have there?"

Jason 215 looked at her. The swelling was long gone, the redness of her face and arms had faded to a pink, and some of the skin had peeled away, leaving her a little darker than she had been.

She still moved with the lack of grace of the recently sick, and she had lost weight. Her eyes were bright but surrounded by darker circles, suggesting that she hadn't completely recovered. But at least she was getting better.

Jason 215 held up the arrowhead so that she could see it. He said, "It's that stone we found."

"And that rules the planet out. I remember."

Jason 215 shrugged, and said, "I didn't know if that poison might not have inhibited your memory."

"No. Just made me sick."

"Well, given that, too, it probably makes the place unsuitable anyway," said Jason 215. "Wasn't really a planet but a moon, and we don't know how all the orbital mechanics would affect it and if the planet, moon, would be inhabitable all the time."

"Still, it's the best thing we found."

Jason 215 shrugged and kept his eyes on the arrowhead. He didn't know if it was the best. It was only the place they had landed, and there might have been another body in the system that would have been better. Ken 197 had the task of locating the planets, in consultation with Billy 209. Now Billy 209 was gone, having been left on the planet, and Ken 197 had been blinded by something and wasn't getting better.

"Have we sent a preliminary report to *The Home*?" asked Helen 214.

"I think Sarah has done that, but it's only a preliminary. We don't know enough. If Martha was here, she might be able to tell them something about the animal life, but . . ."

"Where are the little beasties?"

"Stored away. Refrigerated."

"Won't that kill them?"

Jason 215 smiled, and said, "I was going to say of course, but I really don't know. We don't know anything about them, and the one person qualified to make those sorts of observations isn't here anymore."

Helen 214 lowered her eyes, studied the sensor array in front of her, and asked, "What do you think happened to them?"

"I don't know. If they were able to get back, they would have done so. Maybe they ran into something like you did, only a little worse. Maybe it got both of them, so they couldn't get back."

"Which means they were alive when we left them."

Jason 215 looked at her, and said, "Yeah, it would certainly mean that."

"And if we're not going back, then they'll die."

"I guess so."

"You understand what that means?"

Jason 215 had a flip answer but didn't use it. Instead, he thought about what it meant. There were two of them so that they weren't completely alone. But if one died quickly, then the other was stranded on an unknown world with no hope of going home unless a rescue ship was sent. Jason 215 couldn't believe that would happen simply because the task was too difficult. No one knew where to look or how to look? And not knowing how long Billy 209 and Martha 212 could survive alone on an unknown world argued against any sort of rescue attempt.

Quietly, he said, "Yeah. I know."

"I wish we could help them."

"The only thing we could do is return, now, try to relocate our landing area, and search from orbit. The odds are we would not succeed."

"And we need to get home."

Now he smiled. "Well, a day or so ago, I would have argued that we need to get the injured to *The Home* as quickly as we could, but you seem to have recovered, and Ken 197 isn't in danger of dying from his injury. So that imperative has been removed from the equation."

"So we could go back to look?"

"Except we don't have the resources to do it. We have to go to *The Home* first."

"Will you tell them that we have to go back once we get there?"

Jason 215 thought about that for a moment, and said, "Yeah. I'll tell them that we have to go back for Billy and Martha. I'll tell them that as far as I know, they're still alive and there's no reason for them not to have survived."

Helen 214 reached over and touched Jason 215 on the thigh. She let her hand linger there, and finally said, "I really feel much better."

"I can tell that you do."

"Why don't we go back to the cabin. I think I would like to lie down for a little while, and I don't really want to be alone now."

"I'm right behind you."

[2]

SARAH 202 SAT ON THE FLIGHT DECK WATCHing the sensors, instruments, and monitors, and wishing that something interesting would happen. Contrary to what everyone said, spaceflight was not filled with danger. It was filled with routine. Everything was so far apart that there was little chance of running into anything. All the large objects—stars, planets, asteroids, meteors, rocks, and ice—seemed to be spotted so far away that there was plenty of time to maneuver if necessary. Anything smaller was smashed by the electronic shields around the shuttle. They were nearly as safe as they would be on *The Home*.

Leslie 207 tapped on the side of the hatch to announce herself, then asked, "You need some company?"

Looking around, Sarah 202 grinned, and said, "Sure. Come on up and have a seat."

As soon as she was settled, Leslie asked, "How long until we reach *The Home*?"

"I make it a little over three weeks now if we push it and run into nothing that causes trouble."

"Run into something?"

Sarah 202 laughed. "Sorry. If our engines function properly, our navigation is on, and we don't find ourselves in some kind of ion or hydrogen storm."

"There are those?"

"Well," said Sarah 202, "not really. Not like a hurricane or anything. Mostly it's an area of more dense material that causes us a little trouble with sensors and reduces our ability to see. It's mostly just an annoyance but not much of a real danger to us."

"Then we'll get to *The Home* in three weeks?"

"Give or take a day or two. What's on your mind?"

"Billy and Martha."

"Yeah. Mine, too."

"What can we do for them?"

Sarah 202 was quiet, then said, "I've already sent a report to *The Home*. I told them the situation and that we believed both to have survived."

"What will they do?"

"Probably nothing." Sarah 202 held up a hand to stop the protest. "There's really nothing they can do. Maybe a scout ship to try to find them. At full acceleration, it could be back at that planet in a few weeks, but even that might be too long. We know so little."

"What are the odds for them?"

"Not good. Think about it. They're on a new world, and we know nothing about it. I think they can drink the water and there is some food there if they have the ability to digest it. I don't think we could get back to them in time."

But Leslie had already thought about it, and she knew that both Billy and Martha were probably dead. To Sarah 202 she said, "Do you think they'll try a rescue?"

"Realistically. No."

Of course she was wrong.

[3]

SARAH 202 HAD SPOTTED THE HOME ON THE long-range sensors three days earlier and had been in communication with them on a regular basis longer than that. She had briefed them on the situation, on the injuries to Ken 197 and Helen 214, but told them that Helen 214 had recovered fully. She told them that they had many biological samples with them though all the animals had failed to survive the trip, either because of the duration or because they had been frozen.

On the other hand, *The Home* had told her nothing, and she had expected that. They had provided the routine information that other explorations had failed, meaning they had found no inhabitable planet or moon for the population of *The Home*. She hadn't been surprised by that news. What humans needed to survive ruled out more than 99 percent of the possibilities.

When she was close enough to begin maneuvering for docking, she turned the piloting duties over to the flight computers and sat on the flight deck watching everything carefully. Naturally, if something went wrong, the computer would catch it long before she saw it, but she felt better by being handy, just in case. Nothing went wrong.

They were drawn into the flight pod, on what to her looked to be the top of *The Home,* but that was only the orientation of the shuttle. Had she been watching the docking from the control room in the pod, she would have had a different impression. In fact, she could have called up the video signal and watched on one of the display screens just as if she were in the control room. In the past she had found such a view to be confusing and sickening.

The Home, from the outside, was a gigantic black shape with pods and appendages stuck all over it. Since it did not fly in an atmosphere, it was not required to be aerodynamic, and none of the designers, engineers, or construction workers had worried about it. *The Home* was an elongated football with crap stuck all over it. There were lights on some of the outer surfaces that periodically illuminated portions of *The Home*, then went out. It looked like flashes of lightning striking the surface.

Over the radio, Sarah 202 heard, "I have main docking sequence initiated. Flight control has been activated."

That meant, simply, that *The Home* was now controlling the approach of the shuttle. Sarah 202 had even less to do. She could sit there and enjoy the ride.

The hangar door opened, and there was only a dim red light showing. She could almost see the shape of the door but nothing beyond it. The light was too dim to reveal any features.

With no guidance from her, the shuttle approached the hangar pod, seeming to slow in relation to *The Home*. The nose of the shuttle was centered on the open bay, and the craft moved forward slowly as if drawn in by some unseen hand.

One the shuttle was inside the hangar pod, the door closed, and the lighting slowly changed from red to orange to yellow to white until it was bright inside the pod. The shuttle then touched the deck and settled on the landing gear as the gravity began to pull on it.

Sarah 202 unbuckled her seat belt, threw the harness over her shoulders, and stood up. She opened the door between the flight deck and the rear of the shuttle, and said, "We're home."

Jason 215 got out of his seat and walked over to Ken 197. "You need a hand?"

"Just guide me to the hatch, and I'll be fine."

Sarah 202 opened the hatch and was surprised to find several residents standing there waiting, including two members of the Security Department.

"What's this all about?"

"We're to escort you and your crew to a debriefing with the Mayor and his staff."

"Before we see Medical?"

"Yes."

"We have one injured man and a woman who was injured but seems to have recovered."

"We've been fully briefed on your mission," said one of the security officers. "Please come with us."

Sarah 202 dropped to the hangar deck, then turned and reached back to help Ken 197. He crouched, felt the sides of the hatch, and finally sat down. He pushed himself off and landed on the deck easily.

"What's wrong with him?"

Ken 197 said, "I have trouble with my eyes, not my ears. I can't see at the moment, but I hear just fine. If you have questions, address them to me."

Helen 214 dropped to the deck and waited for Jason 215. He landed next to her, and said, "I don't think I like Security showing up here."

"Well, there's not much you can do about it, so you might as well forget it," said one of the security officers a little nastily.

Leslie 207 joined them, and said, "We've some biological samples on the shuttle that should be collected before we do much of anything else."

"Someone from Biological Sciences will be here for that. Your job, at the moment, is to come with us without a lot of further dialogue."

Leslie 207 looked to Sarah 202 as the shuttle commander and waited for her to make a decision.

"We'll debrief after we meet with the Mayor."

"What's this about the Mayor?" asked Jason 215.

"Security is here to escort us to a meeting with the Mayor," said Sarah 202.

"Shouldn't we get Ken to Medical?"

Ken interrupted. "Look, I've waited this long. Another hour or so isn't going to make any difference. Besides, I think we need to tell the Captain and the Mayor about Billy and Martha. Talk about getting something going to help them."

"I don't like being dragged away like this," said Jason 215. "There's something wrong with it."

"Nothing we can do, and it's not that big a deal," said Sarah 202.

She turned to the security officer. "Take us away."

[4]

ALTHOUGH JASON 215 BELIEVED THAT THE same could have been accomplished by a standard computer hookup with the shuttle crew at Medical while the Mayor and the Captain interviewed them from the municipal building and the flight headquarters, the Mayor had insisted on a face-to-face meeting. Jason 215 didn't know why that was necessary, but the reason was because anyone could access the meeting hookup and watch the debriefing. Neither the Mayor nor the Captain had wanted that to happen. And, had they debriefed on closed circuit, there would be a number of questions about why that had been necessary that neither the Mayor nor the Captain had wanted to answer.

The meeting room looked precisely like a conference room anywhere else in the universe. It was long, somewhat narrow, and had a table in the center, surrounded by chairs. The table was diamond-shaped so that the Mayor, sitting on one side, and the Captain on the other, could see the faces of those arrayed around them. Everything was focused on those two leaders.

Jason 215 and his colleagues, who all felt they could use a real shower, some real sleep, and even a real meal, entered through the single door and were directed to fill in the chairs along one side of the table. No one had planned for water or food. No refreshments were available.

As soon as everyone was seated, the Mayor looked directly at Ken 197, and said, "Can we live on that planet?"

Jason 215 didn't wait for Ken 197 to answer. He said, "Yes, but there is an intelligent species already there."

"Not that I asked you," said the Mayor, "but what is your proof of that? Did you find cities. Did you see an industrial base? Cultivated fields?"

"No, but we didn't look for those sorts of things. Didn't have time." He knew the moment he said it that it sounded lame. The cities, the fields, the industry would have been visible even if they hadn't looked. The evidence of even a primitive organized civilization would have been simple to find.

"Then what is your proof?"

Jason 215 took the arrowhead from his pocket, set it on the table, then pushed it toward Michael 177. It left a long, light scratch on the table.

The Mayor picked up the artifact, turned it over in his hand. "This is it?"

"We found some markings in the grass. A circular area in flattened grass, and at the center some sort of carved pole."

"Did you photograph this?" asked the Mayor.

"Well, no. We were searching for Billy and Martha. They'd gotten lost . . ."

"Maybe," said Christina 160, "it's time for a proper report rather than our jumping all over the place."

The Mayor looked pointedly at Ken 197, and said, "All right. Let's begin at the beginning."

Ken 197 seemed oblivious to the Mayor's stare. He said nothing.

Sarah 202 said, "Ken has been injured, Mister Mayor. He hurt his eyes and can't see very well. I took over command of the mission after we left the planet's, that moon's, surface. I've kept him advised of what we have been doing."

"Then maybe you should tell us what happened," said the Mayor, staring at her.

Sarah 202 then ran through the mission, beginning with the launch, navigation, and entrance into the star system. She mentioned that Billy 209 had discovered a moon that seemed to have favorable conditions. They had orbited and seen nothing from orbit to suggest any kind of civilization, even the most primitive. They had landed to gather some samples and to check the surface conditions. During the thirty-six hours they had been on the ground, Ken 197 and Helen 214 had been injured, and Billy 209 and Martha 212 had disappeared. They had taken off and returned to *The Home*.

"Then you saw no signs of this intelligent life?" said the Mayor.

"Well, we really didn't look," said Sarah 202. "We had other things on our minds. We didn't see much in the way of animal life. Lots of plants and trees and insects but no real animals as we think of them. And we did find a couple of indications of intelligence."

"Will that planet sustain human life?"

Sarah 202 looked at the arrowhead in the Mayor's hands, then at the other members of her team. She said, "None of us have displayed any ill effects, except for Ken, and we don't know what caused that . . . and Helen had an acid burn from tree sap, but she got over that."

"What about the intelligence already there?" asked Jason 215, pointing at the arrowhead.

The Mayor said, "You saw nothing to suggest an active intelligence." He slipped the arrowhead into his pocket.

"But that doesn't mean they weren't there."

"Even if they were, they are so limited that you saw no signs of them. We could land there, and they might never even see us. A full survey might not turn up any sign of this intelligence. For all you know, it might be long gone."

"We don't know that," said Jason 215. "That artifact"—he pointed at the Mayor's pocket—"tells us that there was intelligent life there."

"And I'll bet you left something behind that another explorer might find and interpret as intelligent life. But it was not from that planet."

"It was more than simply trash left behind," said Jason 215. "It was that circle in the grass and the pole. That couldn't have been more than a couple of weeks old."

The Mayor ignored that, and asked, "Does anyone else have any questions for these residents?"

When no one spoke, the Mayor said, "Then let's get them to Medical and after that, give them a chance to relax a little. We can always find them if we need them and we owe them a little free time."

Sarah 202 stood up, and said, "Thank you, Mister Mayor. We are happy to do our duty to *The Home*."

"You have no idea how valuable your service has been. Thank you."

[5]

STANDING IN THE MED CENTER, WAITING FOR his turn with the doctors, Jason 215 couldn't help but think about the irony of the situation. He had left *The Home* for the first time in his life, had actually walked outside with only the atmosphere of a planet to protect him, and now, suddenly, it was as if it had all been a dream. He was right back in the Med Center with no one around him seeming to notice him.

He sat in a chair and watched as other residents came and went. They all seemed to have a mission, as if they had to be somewhere to do something as soon as they finished with their appointments. They had an air of importance about them that he had never noticed before. But they also had a lack of curiosity. That had been demonstrated by the meeting with the Mayor. Jason 215 could think of a dozen, a hundred questions, yet no one had asked much of anything. They weren't excited by the discovery of another intelligence. No one seemed to care about anything, other than the fact they had been outside the shuttle for hours on end without any noticeable side effects.

A door opened, and the doctor looked out. He looked at his palm, holding his small computer, and said, "Jason, we're ready for you now."

Jason 215 stood up and walked into the treatment room. There was nothing different about it except that there were two additional people there. Each seemed to be holding his or her own tiny computer.

The doctor asked, "Any ill effects from being on the planet? Anything that you've noticed?"

"No."

"Sit up here," ordered the doctor, and patted the top of the padded table.

Jason 215 sat down and waited as the doctors poked at him, prodded at him, checked his reflexes, his eyes, ears, heart rate, blood pressure, and a dozen other things. Finished, they drew blood, labeled the vials, and sent them out with the technician who had brought them in.

"Just making sure that there are no new microbes in there," said one of the doctors unnecessarily.

"Maybe we should be quarantined," suggested Jason 215.

"You've been effectively quarantined since you left the planet's surface, and nothing new has appeared. I don't think anything will. Now, how long should we quarantine you here? What would make a difference?"

Jason 215 shrugged but didn't answer.

Finished with all that, the doctor turned to a flat-screen and read the information off it. He nodded, and said, "I see that you've been out of touch for a while here. Need a bit of a booster for your mental health."

"I feel fine," said Jason 215.

"Of course you do, but I'll bet if you think about it, you'll have noticed that some things irritate you more than they did a couple of weeks ago. I'll bet you've had some thoughts about the best way to do things and wonder if the Mayor has it all figured out."

"Nothing unusual about that," said Jason 215. "Sometimes it doesn't seem as if the Mayor, or anyone else, has thought their way through everything. Some things don't seem to make a lot of sense to me. Like this afternoon as we were talking . . ."

The doctor held up a hand, and said, "I'm sure that it is interesting, but I really don't believe you should be telling me about what the Mayor said in a private conversation. There are some rules."

"There was nothing said there about . . ."

"Let's get your treatment out of the way here, then we can talk about some of these other issues."

Jason 215 lay back and closed his eyes against the bright lights in the ceiling. He held out his right arm and felt one of the nurses take him by the elbow. He felt a prick at the inside of his arm, more of a sensation of terrible cold than anything else, then felt relief wash over him. He was more relaxed than he had been in weeks and believed it to be the sudden realization that he was back on *The Home* and not wandering among the stars, where so much could go wrong.

He opened his eyes slowly and sat up. The doctor was smiling at him. "How do you feel?"

"Fine. Better. Relaxed."

"Well, you were a little tense there. I thought this might help."

"You were going to tell me something about the Mayor," said the doctor.

"Yeah, but it's really not all that important now. Sometimes I just let my mind run, and it comes up with all sorts of strange ideas." He laughed. "You know once, when I was young, I wanted to know how we knew the teachers were telling us the right stuff in our lessons."

"Shows a little bit of independent thought. How did you resolve it?"

Now Jáson 215 was a little embarrassed. "I checked what they said against what I could find in the library.

The only thing I learned was that they sometimes simplified concepts for us, especially when we were very young, but they were telling us the truth."

"Well, unless you have something to report, I think that's it."

Jason 215 hopped off the table, and said, "I feel fine. Thanks."

He hadn't noticed how his attitude had changed in the few minutes that he had been under the doctor's care, but then, he wasn't supposed to notice.

[6]

THE MAYOR, MICHAEL 177, LOOKED AT THE others in the room with him. The Captain would agree with him, of course, as would Linda 168, Roger 171, Gary 169, and Stephen 168. The only dissenting voice would be Jane 158, but then, she was always a dissenting voice. Michael 177 often thought that she had been selected for her position because she could be counted on to reject any idea and to be against any proposal. She was there only to create strife and so they could all feel better when they overcame it. She was, to his mind, a necessary evil.

He pointed at Roger 171, who had taken a full report from David 181 and inspected some of the now desolate and desertlike pods. He asked, simply, "How bad is it?"

"We're done," said Roger 171. "David has inspected many of the ag pods, and the destruction in them is complete. We're not going to be able to fix this easily, and not long before we run out of our ability to replace the crops."

"How long until the food supply is exhausted?"

"If any of the ag pods have not been infected, and there are two that have yet to show signs of the disease, then we have eighteen to twenty-one months. If we lose those, cut six, eight weeks off that. I think that is when we would run completely out of food. The most hardy residents could last two or three weeks beyond that, but then this whole thing will turn into a flying coffin. Everyone on it will be dead."

"If we cut the population in half?"

"Well, naturally, that would increase the food supply, but some of the items are perishable. We might have two years, three if you make large enough population cuts, but the only way to do that would be to . . ." He didn't bother to finish the thought.

"There is no way to reverse this . . . plague?"

"We know of nothing now." He looked toward Gary 169 who was the head of genetics.

"Given enough time, we'll be able to find an answer. If we have some luck through Security, some help from those who created the diseases, we could reverse it in a month. It might take two. Of course we could luck out and find a solution tomorrow. It's really a crapshoot."

"But there is no guarantee?" asked Michael 177.

"No."

"Anybody have anything else to say?"

Stephen 168 said, "Under questioning, we have learned a little about the cell that initiated this action . . ."

"Cell?" said the Mayor.

"Meaning a group of residents operating together to accomplish a specific mission to the detriment of society. A secret group that might be related to other organizations or to other groups of like-minded individuals."

"Are there other cells?"

"So far we have not identified any."

"And you believe that you'll be able to obtain the information we need to reverse this plague?"

Stephen 168 shrugged, and said, "We can get information out of anyone given enough time. But we have to have the right residents and we have to ask the right questions. We might not have caught everyone involved in this thing."

The Mayor turned back to Gary 169. "If he gets the proper information?"

"Yes, we can reverse it. But it takes time. Even with

the proper formula, even if we know exactly what has been done and how it was created, it could still take months to get a remedy that will be one hundred percent effective. Or, they might have that information, in which case we could start as soon as we had it in hand."

"You mean that eighteen months isn't necessarily enough time to reverse it."

Gary 169 looked down at the table as if the answer might be written there. "I have no way of knowing, but eighteen months isn't very much time."

"Then we have little in the way of options here," said the Mayor. "We can ship some of the population out in shuttles and scouts, searching for worlds we can inhabit, we can kill half the population . . ." He held up a hand to stave off the protest. "That's the right word here. Kill. Or we can find a world that is within eighteen months of here."

"Less. We're going to have to grow food once we get there, or we'll have just moved the problem."

Michael 177 shook his head and felt the emotions wash over him. A small group of residents, who had never officially complained, had banded together and worked out a way to destroy *The Home*. It was as simple as that. It was as deadly as that.

He took a deep breath, and said, "There has been one success among the scouts and shuttles. One world has been found that is within our range."

He reached into his pocket and felt the arrowhead concealed there. He would ignore it. There was no choice. He had to ignore it because to do otherwise would mean the end of *The Home* and everyone on board.

"There is one world that we can reach, and I propose that we alter our course so that we can reach it."

"How soon can we get there?"

"Inside of a year. We have time."

[7]

STEPHEN 168 COULDN'T HELP SMILING. There was no longer any pressure to learn the secrets because the time frame had been changed. It wasn't a race against time. It wasn't necessary to learn how to reverse the effects of the diseases because there was a planet in their range. Things might be tight, but they were no longer impossible. The residents of *The Home* were not going to be killed, nor were they going to starve.

Stephen 168 walked into the interrogation room where Ruby 200 was strapped to a table. He didn't bother with the needle that held the truth drug because he no longer needed to intimidate her. He held all the cards, knew some of the answers, and didn't really care about the others.

He sat down in the chair barely out of her sight, and said, "You going to answer my questions?"

Ruby 200 was silent. There was nothing she could say or do to change the circumstances, and she believed that silence was her only course.

He asked, "Who has been working with you?"

She said nothing.

"You must know that we have arrested a number of residents who were involved in these acts of terrorism, so that your silence is only going to make things rougher on you."

Ruby 200 tried to twist around to look at Stephen 168. She couldn't see him, but she didn't like the tone of his voice. It contained none of the quiet desperation that she had heard during other interrogations. It sounded as if he already had the answers he needed and that this session was only *pro forma*. That scared her more than anything.

"So, who was working with you?"

"What will you do to those residents?"

"Arrest them. Gather information from them. Eradicate the diseases."

"They won't be harmed?"

Stephen 168 laughed. "You attempt to kill us all with

your plague, and you want me to assure you that your co-conspirators will remain unharmed?"

"Some of them didn't know what we planned."

"I'm not sure that matters since they were in the conspiracy voluntarily. They're as guilty as you are."

"What's going to happen to us?"

"Well, I won't lie to you. It doesn't look good considering the damage you've done and the potential for disaster here. It's not good at all. The only thing you can do is to tell me what you know and answer my questions."

Ruby felt the defiance flow out of her. She simply couldn't resist anymore. Maybe it was the tone of voice Stephen 168 was using, or maybe it was his casual attitude, but she knew that something had changed.

"You know, of course," said Stephen 168, "that the damage you caused could have resulted in the deaths of thousands."

She tried to twist around again because she wanted to protest. She wanted to explain that they meant to harm no one. They had wanted to alter the status quo, to prove a point, to change the system that she believed had become oppressive. They wanted to make a statement, but they wanted no one harmed.

She said, her own voice sounding weak in her ears, "We didn't want to hurt anyone."

"Yeah, well."

"We only wanted to make a statement . . ."

"By destroying the ag pods."

"Not pods. Just one. We wanted to show that we had some power. That someone needed to listen to us. But we also knew that the loss of one ag pod wouldn't really harm anyone."

Stephen 168 pushed for more information, and Ruby 200 gave it all. Drugs had not been needed. She had realized that they would be able to learn anything they wanted, and if not from her, then from one of the others involved. The whole thing had collapsed because none of them realized the level of surveillance used throughout *The Home.* The cameras were everywhere.

When he finished with the interrogation, he simply got up and left. He said nothing to Ruby 200, made no mention about what she could expect in her future, or if she would ever be allowed to rise from that table. He just got out as if she had been a computer he had used, and, now that he was finished with her, it was up to someone else to shut down the system.

[8]

JASON 215 WAS RELIEVED TO BE BACK ON *The Home*. All the open space, whether on a planet's surface or just outside *The Home* was overwhelming to him. It was too much space. He liked having a finite horizon and the ability to walk from one end of *The Home* to the other in a single day, if he walked fast enough and didn't run into any obstacle that he couldn't cross.

But on the planet, he couldn't walk to the end. He couldn't see the other side. It was wide-open, and to him that was a tiny bit frightening, though he couldn't have explained why. Their goal had always been to find a world they could populate. Jason 215 had known that he would never see that world, and then all that had suddenly changed.

Jason 215 was sitting in his tiny apartment, cubicle really, reading the mission report as filed by Sarah 202. He learned from it that Ken 197 had burned out his optic nerve, and they suspected he had looked up, or stared at the star in the center of the system. He learned that Helen 214 had no residual effects from her encounter with the local flora. He learned that the Mayor was interested in a return mission that would include the crew from the first. It meant that someone would be around to tell him that he would have to make another trip.

There was a light tap, and he turned. Helen 214 was standing there. She asked, "You reading the report?"

"Yeah."

"Too bad about Ken."

Jason 215 touched a button and turned to face her. "We should have been warned about the stars."

"Yes, we should have been. But who would have thought?"

"They're going to want us to return."

Helen 214 nodded, and asked, "What do you think about all that?"

"Well, if I'm asked, I'm going to tell them that I won't do it. But I think it's going to be more likely you have to return to that planet than I."

"Moon," said Helen 214 automatically.

"Moon."

"Aren't you interested in finding Billy and Martha? Wouldn't you like to rescue them?"

"I don't know what I know or could do that would help them now. I mean, it's not my field of expertise."

Helen 214 walked over and sat down on the cot near him. She looked at the floor, at the darkened computer screen, then right at Jason 215. She said, "I want to know what happened to them. I want to help them if I can. I believe I owe that to them. And, I want you to go with me."

Jason 215 couldn't look at her. He couldn't tell her how scared he was of the open areas. He couldn't tell her that he preferred *The Home* to any planet and that even if they arrived at a planet, he would stay on *The Home*. Someone had to remain behind and he was going to be one of those.

But, he said, "I'll go if I have to."

She reached out and took his hand. She pulled him close and laid her head on his stomach. She wrapped an arm around him. "Thanks."

"How soon are we going to have to go?"

"I think they're planning the mission right now. There is some reason that they want to get going right now."

"Ag has something to do with that," said Jason 215.

"Won't it be wonderful to walk on that planet again. To see the stars from the surface of a world and not on a flat-screen from *The Home*?"

"Sure," said Jason 215. "Sure."

[9]

THE PREPARATIONS TOOK NEARLY TWO WEEKS
because it wasn't going to be a routine exploration but a
combination rescue mission and reconnaissance. It was to
prepare for the coming of thousands of residents of *The
Home.* It was not supposed to happen because they had
been ordered, many years before, to avoid any planets
where there was intelligent life. But that situation had
changed, and that one, almost inviolate rule was going to
be broken.

As he had done before, Jason 215 arrived at the shuttle bay early so that he could look at the ship. He wanted
to see that it was put together correctly and that the preflight proceeded without a problem. He wouldn't have
noticed if anything was wrong unless a wheel fell off; he
simply felt better about seeing things for himself.

He walked into the control room, where only a couple
of technicians worked. They were checking systems for
the launch and talking quietly to one another. Jason 215
heard enough of the conversation to know that they were
lovers and that they were angry at one another, though he
didn't know why.

He watched as the security force entered the shuttle
bay. Dressed in black, carrying weapons and equipment,
they resembled an army about to go on maneuvers. They
entered in two lines, marched across the hangar deck, and
stopped short of the rear of the shuttle. It was not the
exact craft that Jason 215 had ridden to the planet on the
first trip, but it was similar.

As one, the men and women of the security forced
turned to their right and stood at attention. Their leader,
John 193, stepped to the center of the formation and told
them to stand at ease. This was no paramilitary security
force. This was an armed, reinforced platoon of soldiers,
something that Jason 215 had not known existed on *The
Home.*

John 193 was joined by a subordinate, and together
they inspected the equipment, including the weapons.

Jason 215 couldn't tell what the weapons were. He'd never seen anything like them. He didn't know if they were old chemical reaction rifles or something newer. A laser or beam technology. He wondered if they were designed to produce fatal results or if they had been built to incapacitate the victim.

He asked, "What are they carrying?"

One of the technicians looked out of the control room, then back at Jason 215. "Beats me. I've never seen anything like them."

The hatch cycled, and Jason 215 turned. As before, Helen 214 came early.

"What's going on?" she asked.

Jason 215 hitchhiked a thumb toward the hangar deck. "Looks like an army."

"Well," she said, "you have to remember that last time we did lose two people."

"Or they lost themselves."

"Let's not go through all that again."

Jason 215 glanced at the technicians, and said, "We're invading."

"With what? Fifty. Sixty people?"

Falling back on the old argument, he said, "We are not supposed to be doing this. The planet is inhabited."

"You don't know that," she said, taking up where they had left it the last time. "We didn't see anything to suggest it was inhabited. Besides, the intelligent race, if there is one, is so small that we can all live there."

"That's not the way it's supposed to work."

"Damn, Jason, give it a rest. What would you have us do, given the circumstances?"

And that ended the argument before it could begin again because he had no answer for that. The situation was the result of sabotage, and no one could change that. If they didn't make it to the planet, then thousands would die. It was a temporary haven in a cold, cruel area of space. There really was nothing they could do about it.

The security team finished their inspection, picked up their equipment, and began to board the shuttle. In minutes they were gone, and it was as if they had never been there.

The shuttle commander, Ralph 199, entered, trailed by Sarah 202. She was assigned because, like Jason 215 and Helen 214, she had been to the planet before. It might be said that she knew the way.

Leslie 207 opened the hatch of the control room and poked her head in. She asked, "When are you two going to board?"

"Few minutes," said Jason 215. "I'm trying to wait until the absolute last minute."

"I'll wait with you."

They watched Ralph 199 and Sarah 202 walk their way through the preflight, and then open the hatch for access to the flight deck.

One of the technicians said, "They're getting close to launch. You might want to board."

"Actually, no," said Jason 215. "I don't want to board, but then I have little choice."

Together the three of them, Jason 215, Helen 214 and Leslie 207 left the control room and entered the hangar area. They walked across the deck and climbed the ladder into the main seating area of the shuttle. Many of the seats were taken by the security force, which was spread out, but sitting in groups. There were free seats near the rear bulkhead and near the workstations for crew members.

Not only did the larger shuttle they were on have more cabins, but there was a lower deck that could be used to carry extra equipment or extra passengers. It was configured to provide the security force with a training area and a relaxation area. Each person aboard would be able to find a bed for sleeping, though they would have to run it in shifts.

Jason 215, Helen 214, and Leslie 207 took seats at the crew stations, where they could watch the launch. The seats were larger, more comfortable, and reclined to the point that it was almost like being in bed. These were much better than the seats that had been installed for the security force.

As before, the hangar pod darkened, and there was no real sensation of motion. Jason 215, watching the launch on one of the flat-screens noticed that the craft had moved upward slightly, then begun a slow slide toward the now open hangar pod door.

It slipped across the deck and through the door, out into space. The nose turned slightly, away from *The Home,* and the shuttle began to accelerate.

The view on his screen shifted, and he got a good look at one end of *The Home.* He didn't know that he would never see it again.

CHAPTER NINE

YEAR TWO THREE SIX

[1]

THEY ENTERED THE ORBIT JUST AS THEY HAD the first time, near the equator of the planet, or rather, the moon. Sarah 202 watched for landmarks so that she could put them down close to the original landing site, figuring that it would help in the search for Billy 209 and Martha 212. Jason 215, using the scanners, searched for any evidence that they might have left behind, including a scorching of the ground when they had taken off. It took them a little over four hours to find what they wanted and begin the landing procedures.

As he had with the takeoff, Jason 215 watched the landing on the flat-screen in front of his workstation. Behind him, facing forward, were the men and women of the security force. They were waiting patiently, watching the show on a flat-screen mounted to the forward bulkhead, but showed no real interest in what was happening outside the shuttle.

They came in at a shallow angle, actually using the atmosphere for aerodynamic lift. They flew a large, looping course, mapping the area around the landing site out to nearly a hundred miles. Leslie 207 had designed the landing procedure, set the cameras and the computers to record the topography and terrain.

This time they also searched for signs of industry, or agriculture, for anything that would suggest intelligent life on the planet, but they found nothing. If the intelligent life had developed a society, it was either so primitive that it had produced nothing to provide a clue or so well hidden that the sensor arrays were unable to detect it.

While the computers recorded and generated maps, while the sensors produced analyses of the atmosphere and the terrain, and even the water sources, the shuttle slipped lower, until it was only ten thousand feet above the ground. They flew on, slowing and losing altitude until they were close to the original landing site. At that point they flared out, slowed dramatically, leveled the wings one last time, and touched down. There was a rattling, then rumbling as the wheels touched the ground, and the shuttle settled on its landing gear.

As soon as it stopped rolling, John 193 had thrown off his seat belt and shoulder harness and was on his feet. He pointed toward both the exits, and ordered, "Let's get those covered. Fire teams out now."

Both hatches were opened, and half a dozen men and women leaped out, to the ground. Right behind them, another group stood waiting until they could center themselves on the hatch. Jason 215 turned quickly in his seat and watched the maneuver with quiet fascination.

Others in the security party were gathering their gear, weapons, ammunition, power supplies, and equipment, stacking it so that they could get it out of the shuttle as quickly as possible. They weren't going to wait for some kind of attack before they prepared. They landed waiting for a fight.

And Jason 215 suddenly understood what was wrong with that. It wasn't simply that they were taking precautions, but that someone, back on *The Home,* had determined that they might run into something on the planet that required a security force. The authorities had all, while on *The Home,* claimed that there really was no evidence of intelligence, but suddenly, as the shuttle landed, the armed escorts acted as if they expected an attack.

While Jason 215 and the other civilians on the shuttle waited, the security team finished establishing a perimeter. When the civilians exited, there was a fence made of a single strand of wire. It contained an electrical signal and would set off alarms if touched or broken. It would also direct antipersonnel fire to the spot it was touched.

Perimeter lights had been erected though the central star still shone and the major planet still dominated the sky. It wouldn't be dark for hours, and given the rotation of the moon they stood on, the planet around which they orbited, and the location of the star, it might not get dark for days. They hadn't been there long enough during the first trip to determine any of that, though Billy 209, as the astronomer, probably could have predicted the time of nightfall.

Jason 215 dropped from the shuttle to the soft, grass-covered ground. He stood there for a moment, taking it all in, not believing that he was back. It was almost as if he had never left in the first place.

Sarah 202 approached, and said, "John thinks that our first order of business is to see if we can locate any sign of Billy and Martha. He thought you might want to go with the patrol."

"Leslie saw as much as I did."

"She'll be going along as well."

"I simply don't know what I can do to help out. I don't remember where it was. I mean, where that circle was, or those paths were." He stood there, looked at the shuttle, then toward the distant mountains.

"Say," he said. "The shuttle is not facing exactly the same direction."

"No, we didn't come down exactly the same way. Winds were giving us a little trouble at altitude."

Leslie 207 walked up, looking concerned. She pointed to the open ground, and said, "I'm not sure exactly which direction we went in to find Billy and Martha."

"I think," said Jason 215, "that it was in that direction. The mountains were off our left shoulders."

"I don't suppose we'll be able to find the path now, after all this time."

"I doubt it."

John 193 peeled himself away from the perimeter and walked over. He held a small weapon in his right hand. He also wore a helmet and tinted eye protection. He looked as if he expected trouble at any moment.

"I think we have time to make a preliminary start toward that circle you described."

"This might not be a good idea," said Jason 215. "We don't know what happened to Billy or Martha."

"This time there will be trained security with you. Shouldn't be any trouble."

"Do we need to take anything?" asked Leslie 207.

"Nope. We'll handle that. You're only the scouts for us. We'll cover you, and we'll carry all the food and water you might need."

"What about a weapon?" asked Jason 215.

"You trained in its use? You understand how it functions? You know anything about it?"

"Well, no, but . . ."

"No, buts. If you haven't been trained and don't understand it, you'll get yourself into trouble with it. Better to leave that to security."

"Makes sense to me," said Leslie 207. She turned and looked out, over the plain, in the direction she thought the circle might lie.

John 193 nodded, and said, "If you're ready, we need to get this show on the road."

"I guess," said Jason 215. But he wasn't ready. He had

been sitting in the shuttle for weeks with nothing of importance to do. He had awakened in the morning, as designated by the shuttle's clocks, and done virtually nothing of importance until it was time to go to sleep. Instead of any work, he had socialized, he had reviewed the mission profile, or he had watched the nearly endless supply of entertainment available on the flat-screens. Now he was on the planet's surface and suddenly everyone was ready to begin to work. He wanted some time to himself. He wanted to wait until the next day. The last thing he wanted was to begin a walk into some unknown danger trying to find the two residents they had been forced to leave behind. All this was too quick, and he didn't like it.

"The squad will form over there," said John 193. "We'll meet you there."

As he walked off, Jason 215 said, again, "I don't want to do this."

"Be good for you," said Sarah 202. "Besides, what choice do you have?"

"I could always run away?"

"Where?"

Jason 215 shrugged because he knew that he was caught.

[2]

AS THE SQUAD LEFT THE AREA OF THE SHUTtle, walking off in the general direction Billy 209 and Martha 212 had gone, Sarah 202 returned to the shuttle. She climbed up onto the flight deck where Ralph 199 sat, looking at an array of instruments and sensors.

"What you doing?" she asked.

"You know what I find strange?" he said, "I find it strange that I can't seem to locate much in the way of animal life here. Got all the sensors cranked up, got signals going out in all sorts of frequencies and spectrums, but I don't find too much of anything around here."

"What are you looking for?"

Ralph 199 waved a hand at the windshield. "Something alive and moving out there. I can see the security force surrounding us. I can see the patrol as it heads off together. But I don't see anything else. I don't see anything that we didn't bring with us. It's as if the animal life has vanished."

"Maybe it's just rare?"

"That makes no sense," said Ralph 199. "Any species that has no competition will expand to fill the available space in only a few generations. They'll expand beyond that. They'll keep expanding until they run out of food or water, or they come into contact with a predator."

"So, what are you saying?"

"This is like an unfinished work. They've gotten the landscaping done, but they haven't had the chance to get the animals set."

"We saw animals on the first trip. We collected some samples of them."

"I know," said Ralph 199. "What I am saying"—he grinned broadly—"from my position as an expert on zoology, is that I would think we would see more samples of the animal life. Many more. And not just the little things that you found."

Sarah 202 nodded, but said, "What if the planet has only recently emerged from a mass extinction. That happened on Earth a couple of times. What would the animal population have looked like right after one of those mass extinctions?"

"Don't know. All I'm suggesting is I don't see a single reason for the sparse population of animals."

"We didn't see anything that was too large. Little things. In the grass, hiding. Maybe a bird or two."

Ralph 199 turned his attention away from the instruments. "Well, that's just my observation and my opinion. Probably doesn't mean much."

"Unless the mass extinction isn't quite over," said Sarah 202. "What if the intelligent race ate everything they could catch and all that is left are the little animals, the insects, and a few birds?"

Ralph 199 laughed. "Interesting theory . . . might also explain what happened to Billy and Martha."

Sarah 202 looked at him with a horrified look on her face. "You mean they ate them?"

"Wouldn't be the first time that explorers ended up as the main course."

[3]

INCREDIBLY, THEY FOUND THE LOCATION THAT had been a circle of flattened grass with some kind of symbolic pole stuck into the center. It wasn't the precise design that it had been. The grass was not as flat, the edges not as crisp, and the pole was leaning slightly. But Jason 215 was certain that it was where they had lost Billy and Martha's trail and found all the other trails leading away from the shuttle.

The security force spread out around the circle, searching the ground, but they found nothing of interest. The pole was a little more weathered, something had gnawed at the base of it, and it had tilted slightly. There was no evidence of anyone, or anything with intelligence, having touched it since it was erected.

"Where from here?" asked Nick 202.

Jason 215 walked around the perimeter of the circle but wasn't sure about where the trail had begun again. Finally, he gave up and said, "That way, more or less."

Leslie 207 said, "Yes. I think that's right."

"Why don't you lead us?" asked Nick 202.

Jason 215 looked at him, then at Leslie 207, and said, "Sure. Why not?"

He left the circle, stepped up onto a rotting log he hadn't seen the first time, and began to walk slowly in the general direction of the distant mountains. The security force spread out behind him, trying to make themselves into the smallest targets possible, though they couldn't have defined who or what the enemy might be or why they suddenly felt like targets.

They came to a shallow slope and descended. Jason 215 saw a few boulders sticking up through the grass and avoided those. In the distance was a clump of trees, and he remembered what had happened to Helen 214 when she had brushed by the trunk on the first mission.

They reached the bottom of the hill, and Jason 215 stopped. He turned to the security force leader, Nick 202, and said, "This is as far was we went. The trails all broke up here, and we didn't know which one to follow."

Nick 202 looked at his watch and realized they had been walking for nearly two hours. The only break had been the search of the circle. He turned to the other security troops, and said, "Let's take ten here. I want a circle defense."

"What's that mean?" asked Leslie 207.

"It means that we fan out in a circle with everyone facing out. That way nothing can sneak up on us."

"Not much in the way of relaxation," said Jason 215.

"Better than having someone killed because we didn't keep our eyes open."

Jason 215 couldn't argue with that. He moved to the perimeter, but Nick 202 said, "Why don't you sit in the center there. We'll handle the security."

"Sure."

Jason 215 walked to the center of the security circle, saw a rock, and sat down on it. He looked out, beyond the security, but saw nothing other than a long field of waving grass, a distant clump of trees, and, beyond them, a low ridge of mountains that looked brown and green. There was nothing to suggest an intelligence lived on the surface of the planet. There was nothing to suggest that the animal life had evolved much beyond small creatures that hid in the grass.

They sat quietly for ten minutes. Jason 215 noticed that there was absolutely no sound around them except for the wind rustling through the dried grass. He didn't expect to hear the undercurrent of noise that was natural on *The Home,* but he thought there would be something. The silence was nearly chilling.

Leslie 207 dropped to the ground near him, and said, in a quiet, hushed voice, "What now?"

"Don't know," said Jason 215. "I'm along for the ride here. I wish that I had suggested I would be of no help a little more forcibly. I really have nothing to contribute. I mean, we didn't get much farther than this."

"But we need to try to find Billy and Martha."

"Why us? I have no expertise that would help us find them. I could have drawn all this on a map."

Leslie 207 started to speak, but said nothing. She agreed with Jason 215. They really didn't know anything that would help, especially now that they had moved beyond the circle of flattened grass.

Nick 202 suddenly stood up, raised a hand, and those in the security force climbed to their feet, forming into a column near where he stood. He broke away from them and walked over to Leslie 207 and Jason 215.

"Which way?"

Without thinking about it, Jason 215 pointed, and said, "That direction will take us farthest from the shuttle. I guess that would be the way to go."

"Let's take the point then. See if we can't shake something loose."

As they walked forward, to take their places at the head of the security column, they didn't know how much they were about to "shake loose."

[4]

RALPH 199 AND SARAH 202 LEFT THE FLIGHT deck and made their way outside the shuttle. They heard the quiet rumbling of a generator that was converting some of the wind speed into electrical current and using the sunlight to produce the rest of the power they needed. At the moment, it was recharging the batteries of the shuttle, keeping the electrical fence energized, and powering the equipment that was searching for danger within four hundred yards of the shuttle.

As they walked over to one of the sensor stations, the technician, a young woman who didn't look as if she belonged with the security force, looked up, and said, "I have movement out there to the west."

Ralph 199 grinned broadly, and said, "Define west."

She pointed, indicating that the nose of the shuttle was oriented to the north, or so she had decided and she built the directions off that. There was no reason for it, other than the way the shuttle had come to rest upon landing. It made as much sense as anything else.

"And what do you have to the west?" asked Ralph 199.

"Movement. Close to the ground. Something large, maybe a hundred pounds or so."

"First indication of anything large on the planet," said Sarah 202.

"Maybe someone should take a look," said Ralph 199.

"It's coming this way."

"Who's in charge here?" asked Ralph 199.

"Diana 201 on the perimeter. John 193 in overall command."

"Where is Diana?"

"Somewhere on the perimeter."

Unconcerned about the movement of the large creature, Ralph 199 strolled along the perimeter searching for Diana 201. He found her standing in the shade of the tail, looking out over the meadows toward the mountains.

"We've got something coming in," he said without preamble.

"Yep. Sensors don't tell us too much about it."

Ralph 199 wasn't surprised. Everyone seemed to be linked by radio. Diana 201 knew that the patrol had stopped and had just started again. She knew that the sensors had spotted something moving toward them, and she even knew that some kind of underground beast, about five feet long but only a foot in diameter, was moving under them at the moment. She suspected some kind of snake, but she wasn't sure; nor was she worried about it. They had just spotted the creature and were keeping an eye on its progress.

"Are you going to send anyone out?"

"Nah. I'm going to let it come to us unless it looks as if it's going to park on the path between us and the patrol. Then I'll have to think about taking it out."

There didn't seem to be anything else to say. Ralph 199 turned, walked back to the forward hatch of the shuttle, and sat down. He looked at the ground, at the dirt, and dug at it with his fingers. He let the dirt slip through and found a small insectlike creature. It walked up his hand to his wrist and stopped moving. Then it turned and walked back.

Attention on the perimeter turned toward the approaching creature. Diana 201 moved a half dozen of the security troops to reinforce those on the west side of the shuttle. Ralph 199 finally walked in that direction, hoping to see something interesting because, once they landed, he didn't have many official duties left to perform.

Finally, about a hundred yards out, it became clear that the movement of the grass was more than the wind. Ralph 199 thought about getting back in the shuttle, where he could get some elevation and see into the grass, but he stayed where he was, standing near Diana 201.

She was in communication with the guard on the sensor array. She asked, "What can you tell me?"

"It's close to the ground, crawling, about five feet long, but I have the impression that it walks upright. I have a display suggesting a bipedal animal that is using the available cover to conceal itself."

"Stalking us."

"That's what it looks like."

Diana 201 turned to her left, glanced at Ralph 199, and said, "I want a patrol of four. Go get it."

Three men and a woman stood up and moved forward. They fanned out as they walked into the grass and began to head toward the creature. They tried to move without making a sound, but they had been born and raised in the artificial environment of *The Home*. The tall dry grass defeated them. Their clothes seemed to rustle as they walked. They snapped twigs, scraped their shoes, and one of them fell flat, with a thud.

Those at the sensor array watched as the creature froze, then seemed to look right and left, as if it sensed the approach of the humans. It tried to flatten itself so that it would be more difficult to see.

One of the men, Randy 212, held up a hand to stop the others. He pointed to the right and left of the creature and motioned for his comrades to take positions there. When they were in place, he started forward again, his weapon held out, the barrel pointing in the general direction of the creature.

As he approached, the creature suddenly spun on the ground and leaped to its feet. Although it was running away from Randy 212, he was surprised and frightened by the sudden movement. He whipped around, and jerked at the trigger. The weapon fired, a dim, light red light that reached out and touched the creature in the small of the back. It screamed, its voice like the sound of tires on dry concrete. It reached back, then fell forward, landing on its face and chest.

Randy 212 ran forward. He looked down. The creature was a pale orange, almost a light yellow, with a tinge of red. It had long, thin arms that ended in narrow hands with long, slender fingers that were flexible, reminding Randy 212 of tentacles. The legs were long but thick. The ankles, wrists, and groin were covered with tufts of tan hair almost as if it was clothing of some kind.

The head was a bulb set on the shoulders. There was no hair or ears or anything else that looked to be human. There were two folds on each side of the head that could have been the ears, if the creature even had ears.

Randy 212 stood there, looking at the creature he had killed. He felt no emotion. He felt no guilt. He simply felt relief that it was dead and he was not. He didn't think of it as intelligent. It was only an animal, which might have attacked him had he not shot it as it moved.

"What is that?" asked one of the others.

Over the radio, Diana 201 asked, "What's happening out there? Someone tell me."

Randy 212 cocked his head to the right and touched a

button so that he could transmit. He said, simply, "I killed
some kind of a creature."

"Is it intelligent?"

"No, I think it was an animal."

But even as he said it, one of the others had crouched
down and rolled the beast to its back. Under it was a short
spear with a stone point attached to it. Tied at the waist was
a small leather bag that contained a number of items, including two more stone points and flint for making a fire.

The face was certainly not human, but it wasn't ugly or
misshapen. The eyes were round, nearly circular but small,
probably because of the brightness of the system's star and
the proximity of the moon to the large planet that dominated the sky. There was no real nose, but merely a bump
with two tiny holes. Finally, there was a lipless mouth that
looked enormous given the size of the creature and its
head.

The woman said, "I think it was intelligent."

Randy 212 responded, "Well, now it's just dead."

"Do you think there are more of them?"

That wasn't a thought that had crossed Randy 212's
mind until that minute. Suddenly, he was afraid that thousands of the creatures would be coming to get even.

[5]

THEY DIDN'T SEE THE VILLAGE BECAUSE IT WAS
so well hidden from them. It gave no signs that it was
there. Nothing that could be identified as a structure. No
garbage pile at the edge, no stench from rotting food or animal waste. Nothing to indicate that there were inhabitants
other than two rather large holes set in the shade of a bush.
Had the sun been in a different position or had the overhead planet been in full view, the holes might have been
concealed. Now they stood out in stark contrast to the surrounding terrain.

Jason 215 walked toward the holes but didn't know
what to do. It wasn't that he was afraid to enter them be-

cause they looked like some of the smaller access tubes on *The Home*. The only difference was that these were cut into the ground and were made of dirt. As he approached, he saw light near the bottom of the hole and that it seemed to widen there.

Nick 202 strolled over, casually, and looked down. He said, "Well, there's something in there."

"Do we go look?" asked Jason 215.

Nick 202 crouched so that he could see better. He picked up a stone and dropped it. It disappeared into the light, but he didn't hear it hit bottom.

"I don't know. Our mission is to find the missing residents, not go crawling around in the ground."

Jason 215 said, "But this is something new. We need to explore it. This could be something created by an intelligence rather than something natural. That light seems artificial. There shouldn't be light at the bottom of a hole."

Nick 202 sat down and let his feet dangle in the hole. He felt the sides, but they seemed to have been lined with something hard, like concrete. He couldn't get a scraping from it. He looked down, but the light concealed whatever was at the bottom of the hole.

"We can't just drop in," he said.

By then the rest of the security force had surrounded them and taken up positions to protect the group if something came at them from the outside.

Nick 202 slipped over to his stomach and hung his head in the hole. He tried to shield his eyes from the light but still couldn't see much of anything. He reached out across the hole and noticed a shallow indentation. Below it, eighteen inches down was another. Nick 202 had found the ladder.

He pulled back and stood up. He wasn't sure what to do. This clearly was something created by intelligence. Nature didn't build ladders down into holes, and neither did animals. They built slanted holes.

"We're going to have to check this out. I'll take a small team of three down. The rest will stay here on guard.

Jason, you'll come with the team. Les, you need to stay here, just in case."

Having decided what to do, he radioed his intentions back to the shuttle and let them know he might be out of radio range for as much as an hour. He would check in as soon as possible. His decision was not overridden.

Nick 202 stripped off his gear, keeping only a canteen of water and his weapon. He walked around the hole, sat down, and turned, searching with his toes. Once he felt the first indentation, he slowly put his weight on that foot. It wasn't comfortable, but he could move.

He worked his way down several feet, then called back, "I want Jason next."

Jason 215 entered the hole the same way that Nick 202 had done. He climbed down slowly, feeling his way with his toes. After twelve or fourteen feet, he stepped onto solid ground. He looked and saw another opening, about two feet in diameter, and had the impression of a sloping floor leading deeper into the ground. Around that hole was a series of lights that looked as if they drew their power from the ground. It was a bizarre situation, and Nick 202 didn't understand how the lights functioned.

Nick 202 crouched, and said, "You tell the others to follow. Once you've passed the word, you come along."

"Right behind you."

Nick 202 disappeared into the hole, then suddenly shouted, "Oh my God."

Jason 215 dropped to his knees and stuck his head through the hole. Beyond, it opened up into a huge cavern a half a mile across. There was light everywhere and below them was a village. Nothing fancy, nothing modern, but a village of stone, mud, and thatch. A village that might have been lifted from medieval England except that the creatures moving around it were not human. Even at the distance it was clear they weren't human.

Nick 202 stepped forward, along the path that led down into the village. He stopped near a stalagmite that was nearly as tall as he was. He stood with one hand on it, looking down into the village, watching the creatures there.

"I think our missing residents are down there," said Nick 202, though he had no reason for believing that. It was a gut feeling.

"What are you going to do?"

Nick 202 shrugged. "I don't have a clue. We can't go down to try to rescue them. I don't have the force to do it. Besides, we don't know if they're still alive."

Jason 215 was about to respond when he had another thought. He said, "This is proof that there is intelligent life on this planet. A real civilization."

"Except that it lives underground . . . I wonder why."

Jason 215 felt exposed standing on the path and dropped to one knee. There was a noise behind him, and he saw the others begin to come through the hole. Each stopped and stared, surprised at the magnitude of what lay in front of them. A village of two or three thousand residents.

"Now what?" asked one of them.

Nick 202 said, "I think we make a hasty retreat and let John 193 know what we've found."

"You think we're going to be recalled?"

Nick 202 shook his head, and said, "I think we've come too far, and we have no choice. I think we're here to stay. We need this planet even if there is an intelligence on it."

Jason 215 crouched near the stalagmite, peering around it, almost as if hiding. He watched as two creatures, he had no idea if they were male or female or if those categories applied, walked from one hut, around a stone hearth, and disappeared into another hut.

The creatures seemed to be tall, slender humanoids, covered with hair. They had long arms that hung nearly to the knees, which worked strangely. They had bulbous heads, small, nearly impossible to see eyes, and long, flat faces. Although humanoid, they certainly weren't human, but they were intelligent.

"Let's get out of here," said Nick 202 again.

"Shouldn't we recon looking for the missing residents?" asked one of the security team.

"We'll take care of that later. Right now we've got to report what we've found, and that's all we need to do."

Nick 202 pointed at the hole, and said, "Jason, you first. I'll bring up the rear."

Jason 215 crawled through the hole, climbed the ladder, and rolled out onto the ground. He looked up at the huge, orange planet, then off into the brighter part of the sky, where the sun was hanging. He thought about a society that developed underground and realized there had to be a reason for it. He lived in a long, hollow tube that traveled through space, and there was a reason for that.

But these creatures were primitive, at the beginning of their civilization. For some reason they had chosen to live underground. Maybe they had once been technologically advanced but hadn't had the good sense to avoid an atomic war. Maybe that forced them underground, and now they lived there because of tradition.

Or maybe there was something about the system's star or that huge planet they orbited. Radiation that would affect evolution or cause the deaths of those not protected from it. Or they were avoiding some kind of large predator. The exploration team didn't have the information to make an informed guess.

As he watched the rest of the team come up, he realized that it wasn't his problem. There were social scientists who, once they arrived, could begin to look for the answers to those questions. He wasn't going to figure it out based on his limited observation of the creatures from a distance. They had a reason, and someone else could figure it out.

Once he was out of the hole, Nick 202 used his radio. He said, "Base, we have found a village. We have found a village."

There was a burst of static, then a quiet voice said, "We understand. Return immediately."

Jason 215 was surprised by that. He had expected someone to ask about Billy 209 and Martha 212, but the command seemed to be uninterested.

Nick 202 said, "Let's move out. We've a long way to walk, and I don't know when it's going to get dark."

"Can you find this place again?" asked Jason 215.

"If he can't," said Leslie 207, "I can."

[6]

THE SUN HAD SET BY THE TIME THEY REACHED the shuttle, but it hadn't mattered because the planet still hung in the sky, creating a kind of bright twilight. They walked toward on the shuttle and stopped about fifty yards away because the electronic fence was up and activated. Nick 202 used his radio, told John 193 that they were at the fence line, and waited until he was informed that the fence was deactivated.

Once they crossed the fence line, it was activated again. They walked to the shuttle, where the majority of the patrol dropped to the ground to relax. Nick 202, dragging both Leslie 207 and Jason 215 after him, went in search of John 193.

John 193 was sitting inside the shuttle, studying a screen that showed a strange creature. It was a full color, three-dimensional representation of the creature that had been killed earlier in the day.

Nick 202 glanced down at the display, and asked, "What is that?"

"Creature we killed." He pointed to a couple of stones, and added, "These are the points it was carrying. It's an intelligent creature though I believe the intelligence is rather low."

"Oh, no," said Nick 202. "We saw their village. Found their village, and that isn't what was living there."

"Must have been," said John 193.

"We got a very good look at them. This thing you've got sort of looks like them, but hell, so do we."

"What you're saying isn't that there is one intelligent species here. There are two."

[7]

SARAH 202 LISTENED TO JASON 215 AND Leslie 207 talk about what they had seen underground. She listened to the description of the creatures, of the village, and the level of civilization. She listened as they talked of finding the village by following, more or less, the path that had been laid out when Billy 209 and Martha 212 had disappeared. And she felt her blood begin to boil. She felt the anger burn through her. They'd had the chance to fix the problem from the last mission, and they had retreated the first chance they'd gotten.

With Jason 215 and Leslie 207 trailing along behind her, she went in search of John 193. She found him in the shuttle talking to Nick 202. She pushed forward, stood with her hands on her hips, and demanded, "We have to go get our missing crew."

John 193 looked up, surprised, and said, "I don't believe you have the authority to give me orders."

"I might not have it, but Ralph, as the command pilot, certainly does."

John 193 shook his head, and said, "I'm not sure that's correct now that we're on the ground. Command of the mission might be mine, now that we've landed. In the air, in space, no, but we're in neither now."

"Maybe I should go get Ralph, and you two can argue the finer points of the command structure."

John 193 hesitated, then said, "Maybe you'd better."

Ralph 199 stepped down from the flight deck, and asked, "Just what is going on here?"

Sarah 202 spun, and said, "They've found my missing crew, and they aren't going to do a thing about it."

John 193 held up a hand, and said, "Whoa. That's simply not right."

"Maybe someone had better explain the situation."

Sarah 202 ran through it, and finished by saying, "They had the chance, and they ran."

"Not quite right," said John 193. "We didn't have the force in there to make any sort of successful raid. We need to go in with a larger group prepared to fight, but I don't think we should initiate the hostilities."

Ralph 199 remembered what he had been told before they had left *The Home*. This was a situation that was perfect. They were the injured party. Their crew was missing, and they had some evidence, thin though it was, that the creatures in the village were responsible. If they went in and there was some kind of a fight, that would give them an excuse to attack. If they found the missing crew, they still had justification for an attack. It was a legal point that the Mayor and the others on *The Home* had hoped for. They didn't want to be seen as the aggressors.

Ralph 199 asked, "What do you plan to do?"

"I thought we'd wait until first light tomorrow, when the sun comes up, then make a recon in force. See what we can learn that way."

"Any reason that you can't move tonight? Get into position so that you'll be ready in the morning?"

"I don't like moving through an unknown territory in the dark."

"Well, it's not all that dark, and you do have image enhancers. We have some maps of the area. It's really not all that unknown. There shouldn't be a problem," said Ralph 199.

"Are you making this an order?" asked John 193.

"Interesting legal question," said Ralph 199. "Do I have the authority to make it an order, and who will the Mayor back when we return to *The Home*?"

John 193 understood what was being said. He looked from Ralph 199 to Sarah 202, and said, "There isn't any reason for us not to move out. I didn't want to leave the shuttle undefended during the first night on this world. We've already been approached once."

"We have the automated systems up and running. I don't think anything is going to happen to us."

"If you think this is a wise move, I'll take most of the security force with me now and go see if I can find the missing crew."

"How will you be armed?"

That was the critical question. John 199 had any number of nonlethal weapons. But he also had lethal weapons. Beam and laser rifles and even a couple of old-fashioned, slug-throwing pistols. He could kill at long range if he had to.

To Ralph 199, he said, "Everyone will be armed, but we'll use the stunners first."

"I don't want to lose anyone," said Ralph 199. "You need to be prepared for the worst."

John 193 nodded. "I know my job."

"I wasn't suggesting that you didn't. My overriding concern here is for your security force and not the creatures that inhabit this planet. And by extension, the security of this shuttle and the completion of its mission."

"You've made that clear."

"As soon as you have rescued my crew, or rather the other crew, you'll need to return here."

"Of course."

"And then we can figure out what we are going to do next," said Ralph 199.

[8]

JOHN 193, WHO WAS LEADING THE RECON force, didn't like having only a single line of retreat. He was going into an environment where he would be outnumbered, and if the enemy got behind him, his force could be wiped out. In fact, one guy with a rifle could hold the hole because access was just one at a time. It could become a deadly trap.

He surrounded the hole and crawled forward so that he could look down, into it. There was no evidence that anyone had used it recently, other than the first recon team. Maybe it was a back door, a way for the creatures to escape if someone got behind them or was holding the main entrance. They had a hidden line of retreat.

Leaving two of the force behind, he climbed down the hole, then through the opening into the larger cavern. He stopped there and studied the village, searching for some sign that the missing crew were actually there and being held prisoner. He could see nothing to suggest that any of the small buildings was used as a jail.

As the rest of his force joined him, he motioned for them to spread out, using whatever cover they could find on the path. When everyone was down and in the cavern, he took a couple of steps forward along the narrow path that led deeper into the cavern. The ground was firm, might have been stone, and was rough. He wouldn't slip on it.

They spread out along the path, walking down, to the very edge of the village. No one there seemed to notice the humans as they approached. They reached the edge, then moved forward cautiously, around a stone hut that seemed sturdier than the others, almost as if it was a guard shack.

They stopped there, crouched in the shadows, and watched as the creatures moved around. None of them seemed to notice that their village had been invaded. John 193 didn't know what they were doing. None seemed to have any real task.

Holding his hand up, in greeting, John 193 stepped out of the shadows. At first there was no reaction to him. One of the creatures turned, saw the humans, and froze in place. Then it raised one slender arm, extended one thin finger, and let out a wail that started quietly and built until it echoed from the sides of the cavern and sounded as if thousands were screaming.

One of the men behind John 193, aimed a stunner, pulled the trigger, and the creature fell suddenly silent. But it was too late. The warning had been given. Others took up the shout, while more ran toward their houses.

One of the creatures, somewhat taller and more robust than the others, ran right at John 193. He carried a long wooden spear with a large stone point attached to it. John 193 stood, surprised, then raised his weapon, the old-fashioned pistol. He pulled the trigger, saw the hole appear on the creature's shoulder, but it didn't stop. It ran on, now with its head lowered, growling deep in the throat, intent on attacking the humans. John 193 fired a second, then a third shot.

The creature stumbled when the third shot hit its chest. It righted itself, took two running steps, and fell forward. It tried to throw the spear, but the effort was too late, and the spear fell to the ground.

Now there were other creatures attacking. John 193 fired at another, but missed. The men and women around him used their weapons, the lasers, the stunners, and their pistols. Shots rang out and echoed in the cavern. Red beams flashed, touched creatures, and severed arms, or legs, or punched holes through torsos and heads. Creatures fell screaming, unable to understand what was happening to them or their fellows. The attack broke as the creatures fled in terror.

Now the village seemed deserted. No one moved. The doors were closed and the few windows boarded. Smoke rose from a couple of fires, climbing toward the ceiling of the cavern and the natural sinkholes there that vented to the outside.

John 193 looked at the bodies. These clearly were not like the creature that he had seen near the shuttle. The answer seemed to be that there were two intelligent species on the planet, and, if there were two, might there be a third?

"Let's circulate through the village," he said. "We're looking for signs of a human here. Anything that will tell us if the missing crew is here?"

"Bodies?" asked one.

"Don't know what to expect. We might not even be in the right place."

"They seemed mad about something."

"Maybe our being here violated some taboo," said John 193. "I don't know. Be careful, and let's not break up into groups smaller than four."

John 193, with Candy 202, Robert 202, and Charles 203, split from the group and moved to the edge of the village. John 193 wanted to keep the uninhabited walls of the cavern to his back so that he could concentrate on the search. He didn't want to break into any of the houses unless he had to. He had wanted this to be as peaceful as possible. That was no longer possible.

Keeping their weapons and their eyes moving, they skirted the edge of the village. John 193 saw that the buildings were made of stone and something that looked like adobe. The windows were framed in wood, but there didn't seem to be glass in them. Of course, since they were in an enclosed environment and deep in a cave, there wasn't much need for glass.

The ground was muddy in spots, but mostly it was stone. There were some stalagmites and places where stalagmites were broken off. They passed one shallow pool of water and a couple of places where they could hear running water, but they couldn't see it.

A door opened, and John 193 looked inside. There were four creatures in the house, two standing near the door and two, smaller beings, huddled in a corner. There were chairs, a table, and a fire set in the middle of the room. Neither of the creatures near the door moved to exit, and a moment later one of them closed the door. John 193 didn't want to search the house.

"John, over here."

John 193 saw Robert 202 crouched near the wall of a house. When John 193 approached, Robert 202 pointed to a single word in English. It said, "Martha."

"Guess that confirms they're here," said Robert 202.

"Or were here."

"Now what?"

"I didn't really expect to find anything. I thought the odds that we would find the right place were remote, and even if we did, we'd find no evidence. I hadn't thought this thing through."

"They're probably dead by now," said John 193.

"How do you know?"

"Because if they weren't, they would have made themselves known after that firefight."

"I suppose."

John 193 wanted to get out of the cavern. He wanted to

retreat to the shuttle and let Ralph 199 make the decisions. But he couldn't. He was there, on the scene, and any delay might mean disaster for the two missing crew. They might be alive, and if they were, he had to rescue them immediately.

He touched a button on his belt that activated the short-range radio, and said, "Rally to me. Rally to me."

Over the next few minutes, the security force gathered at the edge of the village. John 193 pointed out the name scratched in the mud and stone, and said, "Our mission is now a little different. We have evidence that the crew members were here and alive. Now we must determine their fate. We begin to search for real, looking everywhere that two humans could be held captive or might be hiding."

"In the houses?"

"Everywhere," said John 193. "We leave no stone unturned, but we also watch our own backs. I don't want to lose anyone to a stupid mistake."

"We stick together?"

"Right. We sweep forward with two or three looking in a house while the rest of us watch. Anything moves at us, we put it down. I don't care if you merely disable it or kill it, but I want it down."

A number of them said, "Yes, sir."

They began with the house that had been marked by Martha. They pushed in the door and two of them entered, weapons at the ready. The creatures, all fairly small, moved back, away from the invaders. They made no move to defend themselves or to hide. They simply moved away.

John 193 watched as the search continued. There wasn't much in the house. It was a single large room. It was obvious that no humans were in it. As soon as they were sure, they backed out and closed the door.

The search continued that way. Each group looking into a house while others guarded them. No resistance by the creatures. No attempts to push the humans out of their village. Just a passive response to the personal invasion.

And then, finally, the last bit of the puzzle. Over the radio came, "John. We've got something."

"I'm on my way."

John 193 separated from his team, ran to his right, and found Nell 204 standing in a doorway waving at him. As he approached, she stepped back, and said, "I think we've solved the mystery."

He stepped through the door and at first didn't understand the excitement. Then, on a shelf set about shoulder high he saw them. Two human skulls. There was no doubt in his mind that they were human, and no doubt that they had been Billy 209 and Martha 212. They had found the missing crew.

CHAPTER TEN

YEAR TWO THREE SIX

[1]

IF THE MOON CIRCLING THE GIANT PLANET IN the not-too-distant star system could be used as The New Home, then the situation on *The Home* was suddenly less dangerous. It was less disastrous. If the moon was suitable for long-term human habitation, then the majority of the population of *The Home* could be saved. There was enough food available to feed everyone for about eighteen months, even if they grew and harvested nothing else. If they went on any sort of rationing plan, they could extend the food supply for two years without hardship. If they were forced to find another planet for The New Home, they were all probably doomed to die in space traveling toward it.

The Mayor, Michael 177, was not worried about any of

the possible outcomes. He had given orders to the head of the security force. They would be able to adapt the planet, moon really, to The New Home.

The only problem was the possibility of an intelligent life on the planet, but Michael 177 had ordered that kept secret. He wanted no dissension until they were near the new world and it was obvious that their survival hinged on landing as quickly as they could. Then any voices raised about an invasion would be quickly shouted down.

That is, of course, if those alien creatures didn't give them an excuse to attack. Everything hinged on the timing. Everything had to be handled exactly right, or they might not get the opportunity to land.

He reached over and touched a button. The flat-screen displayed pictures of the various staff members. Now he touched the pictures of those members he wished to consult. The computer would automatically find them and alert them to the hastily called meeting. Everyone should be available in five minutes.

While he waited for those others to sign on to the system, he reviewed the messages received from the first exploration party sent to The New Home.

[2]

THOMAS 215 HAD GROWN UP IN ISOLATION, or rather in as much isolation as was possible on a generation ship in deep space. He had been separated from his friends after an incident in a dining hall and had been placed in an environment where there were few opportunities to interact with others his own age. Instead, he had been placed in an environment of constant instruction, where he would be monitored more carefully than most. They had once had high hopes for him because of the highly regimented training school, and had carefully watched his intelligence, but they quickly realized that other factors mitigated against any advantage his intelligence gave him. He was watched, medicated, counseled, and evaluated. He had no opportunity for his own thoughts, especially with his mind dulled. He had been removed from the lists that suggested a life of almost unlimited potential to one in which he would not be allowed to think for himself and would be kept working in jobs that didn't require training or thought.

But the situation on *The Home* had changed with the sabotage. Ag pods had been destroyed, the Med Center had been attacked and rebels were trying to disrupt society. All efforts had been turned to survival of the population. Food was the highest priority, with finding a planet suitable for The New Home second. Making sure that Thomas 215 had all his medications and counseling came at the bottom of the list.

So Thomas 215 began to awaken. Not quickly. It was a slow process as the medications were reduced to half, then to a quarter. Counselors whose job it had been to reinforce the medications with hypnosis, deep-breathing exercises, and other such techniques were pulled from those assignments so that they, along with everyone else, could help resolve the crisis facing *The Home*. What had once been important was now trivial. If counseling services were available at all, it was for minutes rather than a half hour or more.

Sitting in front of his flat-screen, reviewing the data that had been brought back by shuttle and later transmitted from The New Home, Thomas 215 suddenly began to feel anger. There was a boiling in his belly and a tightness in his chest. He wanted to strike something, or someone, and he was uncomfortable with these new emotions. After so long, he didn't understand them and didn't know what they meant.

Finally, he turned off the screen, stood, and stepped to the door. He could hear voices outside, and when he opened the door, he saw residents standing around, talking, yelling, gesturing. The crowd seemed to be angry, about to become a mob, and he didn't understand that either. He'd never seen so many angry residents in one place. Usually there was a single angry resident, shouting something no one else understood before he or she was taken away by Security. Now there seemed to be no Security in the area, and, for a moment, he was frightened.

He spotted a young female resident he knew and grabbed her arm. When she turned to face him, he asked, "What's going on out here?"

"You haven't heard? They're going to kill everything on The New Home."

"Kill what?"

"Where do you live? In outer space? The New Home has an intelligent species. We're going to kill it so that we can have their planet."

"No," said Thomas 215. "We aren't going to do that. They wouldn't do that."

She waved a hand to indicate everyone around her. "You think we're out here for fun?"

"Where's Security?"

Now she pulled back, away from him, a look of horror on her face. "Are you from Security?"

"No. I just thought it odd that Security wasn't here since there are so many people out."

"It's beyond Security now. Way beyond Security. There's nothing they can do."

"They can make the residents . . ."

"God, I hate that term. We're not residents. We're people. Residents makes us sound as if we all live in one great community, and someone takes care of us. We're individuals."

Thomas 215 nodded his agreement. That was the thing he had been feeling. Not an anger at the residents . . . people . . . on The New Home, but at being all grouped together under a single term. Sure, they needed to live in harmony, but . . . and then it came to him. He understood exactly what had been done to him, to everyone he knew, maybe to everyone on *The Home*.

But he also realized something that the others did not. The problem was not administration or government but medical. With his medications reduced and with the counseling all but eliminated, he felt alive for the first time

since he was a child. He felt as if he could think and reason and understand the "advanced" concepts that had
been denied to him for so long.

He looked at the residents . . . at the people . . . who
were standing and shouting their anger. They had done
nothing destructive. They had not focused their anger.
They were upset with the coming restrictions on food,
they were angry about the sudden rush toward a planet
that might be inhabited already, and they were uncertain
about their future. That had them worried the most. They
didn't know what would happen, and everything they
were told seemed to be lies compounding lies.

Without thinking about it, Thomas 215 shouted, "To
the Med Center. To the Med Center."

Others picked up the chant, repeating it over and over
until it became the battle cry of the people.

Someone kicked in the door to the dining hall and half
of the mob filtered through the door. They returned carrying parts of tables and chairs they had ripped from the
deck. They had broken up everything they could use to
make weapons. Now they were ready to assault the Med
Center.

They walked across the park, being careful not to harm
the fruit trees or the bushes, stepped over the short fences,
and walked between the benches. They stopped once, as if
organizing, then swarmed forward again. No one had
given any commands. They were moving automatically.

As they approached the Med Center, a small force of
security officers appeared to the right, trotting forward, in
step, their drill batons held in both hands, angled across
their bodies. They slowed, then marched toward the entrance to the Med Center and spread out to protect the
doors.

Slowly the mob advanced, unsure of what to do. Although most had viewed scenes of riots from Earth and
watched videos containing elements of riots, none of them
had ever participated in one. Life on *The Home* was such
that no one was ever angry enough to want to riot, except
once or twice months earlier. Now these residents stood

face-to-face with the security force, and they wanted to get into the Med Center. Security wanted to keep them out of it.

One of the security officers moved forward quickly and centered himself on the mob. He raised his voice, and said, "This has gone far enough. Return to your homes, and there will be no consequences."

There was a moment of hesitation as those in the mob tried to decide what to do. They looked at each other. Some of those in the rear turned as if to return to their apartments. But then, from somewhere, someone threw a wooden table leg at the security officer. He ducked, danced to the right, and whirled so that he was facing the security force.

"All right," he said, angrily. "Let's clear them out of here now."

As one, the security force took a menacing step forward. But the mob reacted. A woman screamed, a man shouted, and they all surged forward, their clubs upraised.

The two forces collided. The security officers were swinging their drill batons carefully, trying, at first, to block blows from the mob and trip them up. The plan was to push through the center, break the crowd into two, then into quarters, until they could force the residents to flee.

But Security had never faced anything like this on *The Home*. The residents had all been well behaved and willing to bow to the orders of any authority. This time they fought back. They didn't run.

Using their clubs, they aimed for the heads of the security force. One man fell and was lost as the mob pushed forward. Another tried to block a blow, had his drill baton ripped from his grasp, and was beaten to his knees. Security began the slow retreat until their backs were against the wall of the Med Center.

It was then that they broke and ran, some forcing their way through the doors, others sliding along the side of the building until they could get away from the mob. In minutes the people stood at the entrance to the Med Center; all control by Security had been lost.

Without a command or an order, the mob pushed through the doors and shattered the glass of the windows. They charged up the stairs and attacked the equipment. One doctor tried to stop them but was beaten until he collapsed.

The mob swarmed down the corridors, smashed open doors, and destroyed anything they found inside. They ripped cabinets from the walls, broke bottles of medicines, tipped over examination tables, and kicked fixtures until they broke. They tore equipment from the walls, smashed it on the floor, and stomped on the debris, trying to crush it.

They worked their way through the whole building, up and down the stairs, wrecking everything they could find. Although no one had said anything about it, and no order had been given, their mission was to make sure that the Med Center would never manipulate the minds and emotions of any of the residents. They all began slowly to understand what had been done to them, and to their parents and grandparents. They saw this as an opportunity for payback, and they weren't to be denied.

The old order was out, and they were in the process of creating the new. The Med Center had become their Bastille. It represented everything that had been wrong on *The Home*. With it ruined, everyone would be able to see that life as they knew it was about to change.

[3]

THE MAYOR, MICHAEL 177, SURROUNDED BY security forces, including the chief of Security, Stephen 168, watched as the riots spread from one section of *The Home* to another. He watched what had begun as a simple protest, with a few angry residents, turn into a riot that had attacked the Med Center. He sat there, shaking his head.

Stephen 168 said, "We can switch to another camera, or to another area, but you're going to find the same thing.

The residents are angry. They feel betrayed, and they are attacking the symbols of our society here."

"But it's not going to do them any good."

"No, but it'll make them feel better."

Michael 177 couldn't help smiling at the irony of the statement.

"We have noticed that when they finish in the Med Centers, they tend to return to their apartments."

"We can identify them, can't we?" asked the Mayor.

"Certainly, but you have two or three thousand people involved in this. We could not possibly arrest them all."

"What about the leaders?"

Stephen 168 shrugged. "Who's to say who are the leaders. No one really leads here, so we have the same problem."

Michael 177 looked to Roger 171, head of the Ag Department. "This affect the food supply?"

"No. They've carefully avoided destroying that. They know that the food is not irreplaceable. They're not going to destroy it."

"Captain," said Michael 177, "this is getting bad. Can we reach The New Home?"

"Yes, we'll reach it, but I don't know what is going to be left. I have increased our speed as much as I can, but that is going to increase our braking problems. There will be noticeable ramifications if we brake too abruptly."

"How much time do we cut off?"

"Six weeks."

Michael 177 looked at the calendar. "It would save a great deal of food and give them more time for planting and growing crops on The New Home."

"What if we dispatch a shuttle filled with farmers and seed?" asked Roger 171. "They plant when they arrive, and by the time we can get there, a crop should be ready for harvest."

Michael 177 waved a hand. "I'm not sure that we need to worry about that now." He pointed at the flat-screens. "We've got residents rioting in the street."

Christine 160 said, "There is a shuttle ready to launch

now. We certainly could evacuate some of the critical staff on it so that when the rest arrive, everything will be up and running smoothly."

Michael 177 grinned, and said, "It would have to be senior staff because we would have to make critical decisions. Middle level could manage here because everything is in place. Just follow the procedures."

Roger 171 said, "Might I suggest that we launch the ag residents first. They have the critical job of establishing the food supply. It won't take any high-level management for those tasks. The Ag Department is filled with residents who would be competent there."

"A second shuttle could launch inside of twenty-four hours," said Christine 160. "We've been planning this for more than a month now."

Michael 177 turned his attention to the flat-screens. He could see the destruction at the Med Centers. Smoke poured from one building, but firefighters had already contained the fire. He didn't know how much damage that might have done to the air supply and hoped the scrubbers could remove the particulate matter without reducing the oxygen content. It was simply one more problem to compound all the others. It reminded him of the trouble from several weeks earlier.

Turning to Roger 171, the Mayor asked, "How would you alert the farmers?"

"Closed network . . ."

"Which can be hacked by anyone who understands the system," interrupted Stephen 168.

"Or, on a personal and individual basis. I tell two people, who each tell two. We could have everyone alerted in half an hour and have them moving toward the shuttle for boarding an hour after that."

"Equipment loading?"

Roger 171 grinned. "Everything is in transportation pods that we can move to the shuttle bay. Load the pods, and we're ready to go. Pods even have a computerized weather station that should be able to determine the weather patterns after only a few days. Yes, the information will be preliminary and subject to modification, but we'll have an idea of what to expect in the way of weather. Other equipment can test the soil and determine which crops will do best. It's foolproof."

"Then let's get that mission under way immediately," said Michael 177.

Stephen 168 said, "One of the causes of these riots was our incursion on this planet. Residents were upset that we would be displacing an intelligence."

"That can't be helped. These . . . residents . . . are the cause of the trouble. If not for them, we could have by-passed that moon and found something else. We no longer have that luxury."

"Then what are we going to do?"

"Simple," said the Mayor. "We are going to send a farming team in to begin the process of establishing our colony. We are going to send in an administrative team to begin to prepare for the arrival of the residents, and we are going to augment security so that we do not have to worry about the local population attacking and destroying our colony."

"And when is all this going to begin?"

"Just as soon as we finish here."

[4]

ROGER 171 LEFT THE MEETING AND WALKED over to visit with David 181. David 181 would lead the farming expedition, if it came to that.

Roger 171 was surprised to see litter on the ground. Normally it was picked up as quickly as it fell. But not that day. The workers who had the responsibility were running with the mob, breaking into the Med Centers and creating destruction there. The well-kept, well-manicured lawns were strewn with broken tables, chairs, crockery from the dining halls, paper, and trash, and even parts of computers.

Now the parks were cleared of residents, but not because Security had clamped down. The residents were gone because they had finished. They had vented their rage and it had burned out, at least for the moment.

He came to a residential area and saw that there was minor destruction there. One apartment had a broken window. Another had a hole in the door, as if someone had punched it. Some trash littered the walkway, but nothing like the mess in the park.

He found David 181 standing outside his apartment, surveying the limited damage that had been done to the residential area. Roger 171 raised a hand, and called out, "What do you think?"

"Can't believe it."

"Let's go inside," said Roger 171.

Once in the small living room, which looked precisely like everyone else's living room, Roger 171 said, "This is strictly on the QT. We have, of course, been worried about our food supply and it strikes us that an ag group, sent in early, could plant some crops and prepare for harvest about the time *The Home* arrives on the scene."

David 181 nodded slowly, and said, "Makes some sense."

"We can't afford to wait until the last minute on this. If there is an ag problem, we've got to know about it as soon as possible so that we can fix it. A fully equipped ag exploration is necessary."

"I suppose it would be good to know if we can't farm The New Home before we get there and are stuck."

"Right," said Roger 171. "We need someone to lead that exploration."

"I can think of a number of residents who . . ."

Now Roger 171 grinned. "I don't think you understand. That selection has been made. You'll lead the expedition."

David 181 was quiet for a moment, staring down at the deck. He wasn't sure that he liked the idea. He wasn't sure that he wanted to travel that way to The New Home. Finally, he said, "Whatever you believe to be best."

"Listen, you know the ag pods are now sterile. It'll be

months before we could do anything to reverse that, if we can. You have experience and have been a leader in the farming community. Seems to me that you are the perfect choice."

David 181 couldn't help grinning. He said, "Or, it's the best way to get rid of me without having to go through the formal process."

"I suppose you could look at it that way."

David 181 held up a hand. "No. I understand the rationale here. It makes sense to me."

"Good. Then I don't have to sell this to you."

"How long before we would launch?"

"From the discussions I have had with the Mayor and the Captain, I think they are thinking in terms of twenty-four to forty-eight hours."

"Who's on the team?"

"Well, I'm thinking of a variety of people from different ag pods. And there will be some security personnel, but the plan there is to fill the roster with those who have spent time in the ag pods. In other words, we're stacking the deck here."

"This is awfully quick." He looked around the little apartment and realized that nothing in it was really his. The furnishings came with the place. The computers were already installed and were upgraded by technicians. If something critical broke, they replaced the unit. The coveralls and other clothes were the same as those worn by everyone. There was nothing that he needed to pack, and no preparations he needed to make. If he walked out the door in ten minutes, he would be as ready as if he prepared for a day or a week.

"What do you need?" asked Roger 171.

"I suppose someone else is making all the preparations, like deciding what equipment I'll need."

"Shuttle is being prepared. Lists of the residents who will accompany you are being prepared. Supplies are being loaded, along with the seeds and tools. Everything is manifested through computer lists that were prepared before the launch of *The Home* based on the projections of those who built it originally. We've updated those listings as the situation has changed, and now we plug in the names."

David 181 rubbed his face, looking as if he had just awakened. Finally, he said, "Well, then, I guess I'm ready."

Roger 171 grinned. "I knew that we could count on you. Why don't you stay here and relax? You'll be alerted when you need to report to the shuttle."

"Maybe I should review the list of those coming with me. I might have some insight into who would be most valuable."

Roger 171 was going to protest, then thought better of it. He said, "We can always use a little expert review. I'll have the list sent to you in a few minutes."

Roger 171 stood up. "I envy you this. I wish I could go with you, but my duties require that I stay here."

"I'll try to live up to your expectations."

[5]

AS SOON AS ROGER 171 HAD LEFT HIS apartment, David 181 walked to the computer. He touched the keys, found that Kim 185 was in her apartment, but didn't try to communicate with her. Instead, he left, closed the door, and hurried along the alleyway, past a number of people who were discussing the days events, one or two of whom were still angry, then around a corner. The alley was a little narrower, the apartments a little older and smaller than the one he occupied. But then, Kim 185 was a little younger than he and hadn't had the chance to work her way up the ladder into a better neighborhood.

As he approached her front door, he realized that no matter how hard they had tried to remove status from society, there were always little things that indicated who was on the success track and who had been relegated to manual labor. It might be nothing more than the cut of the coveralls, the size of the apartments, which were based solely, he believed, on longevity, and the overall location in The Home where a resident lived.

He stepped to the door and tapped on it. A moment later Kim 185 answered. She was of a size and shape that matched nearly everyone else on *The Home*. She had let her hair grow a little longer, and David 181 suspected that she dyed it because it was blacker than almost anyone else's. But her eyes matched his, and she was only an inch or two shorter.

"Can I come in?" he asked.

She stepped back, out of the way, and waved him into the tiny living room.

She said, "I didn't expect you."

He looked around, as if he expected spies, then lowered his voice. "I'm being sent to The New Home."

The color drained from her face, and she reached out to take his hand. "When?"

"A day. Two days."

"Am I going, too?"

David 181 shrugged helplessly, and said, "I have a list coming to me, but I didn't wait for it."

She pointed to her flat-screen. "You can access it from right here."

David 181 walked over to the computer, sat down, typed in his private access code and scrolled through his most recent mail. The list was the third item. He opened it, looked down, then shook his head. "Nope. You're not on the list."

"Why?"

"I don't know. I didn't prepare it. I can put in a request to have you added, suggesting that your expertise in soil composition would be valuable to us."

Kim 185 walked over to the couch and dropped onto it. "I'm not sure that I want to go."

"Why wouldn't you?"

"Comfort? How comfortable can you get on a shuttle? And how long does the flight last? I mean, we'd be living in each other's pockets for weeks, months, on end. That could be more than a little annoying."

David 181 laughed. "You live on a spaceship. You've always lived on a spaceship."

"Yes, but I have this nice little apartment to myself. I have some privacy. Not much, but some. On the shuttle, even that would be gone."

David logged off and walked over to the couch. He sat down next to Kim 185 and took her hand. He pulled her around so that she was facing him and touched the Velcro at the throat of her coverall. He ran his finger down to her waist with the sound of ripping cloth, opening the front. She sat still, quiet, not moving and not objecting.

"We'd be together," he said.

"We'll be together when the rest of us arrive on *The Home,* all without that annoying shuttle ride."

"It would be months, maybe more before *The Home* is going to arrive at the system." He fell silent, wondering about the physics of turning *The Home* and decelerating into a star system. To him it seemed an impossible task, but the Captain should have been trained to handle all the forces that would come into play. Planetary bodies, all the moons, the debris of comets and asteroids, and finally the star. It was a problem that overwhelmed his mind, but then, it wasn't his responsibility.

Kim 185 shrugged her shoulders, and her coverall fell to her waist. She grinned at him as he tried not to look at her body. He was trying to have a serious discussion, even though he had opened her clothes. Now he didn't want to be distracted.

"I can wait," she said. "Can you?"

He reached up and put a hand on her bare shoulder, letting it slide down, feeling the soft, smooth skin under his fingers. He shook his head. "I don't want to wait. I want you to go with me."

"No."

He faced her, let his eyes dip once, then looked at her face. "But why?"

She sighed. "You aren't listening to me. I don't want to be trapped on the shuttle for weeks and weeks. I can't do that."

Daniel 181 said, "There are drugs that could fix that. And other treatments that don't involve drugs."

"And I would do that, but I only have forty-eight hours. That's what you said."

"You'd take the treatment?"

"Of course. Why wouldn't I? But there's simply no time. They couldn't do anything in so short a time, especially after the attacks on the Med Center."

"I'd forgotten about that."

"So, there really is no way."

David 181 moved his hand from her arm to her stomach. As he tried to slip it lower, she drew in her stomach to make it easier for him. He hadn't even left, didn't have to leave for hours, and already he missed her. He wished there was something he could do, but couldn't think of a thing. They were stuck with the situation as it developed, and it meant that they would be separated for months once the shuttle was launched. Longer if the situation didn't develop properly or if there were added complications, and David 181 knew there were always added complications.

[6]

IT WAS AN HOUR BEFORE HIS ALARM WAS SET to go off, but a pounding on the front door awakened David 181. He had been ordered to be ready to move to the shuttle, so he had left Kim 185 and returned to his own apartment. Now, suddenly, someone was at the door, trying to get to him.

As he swung his legs out of bed, the lights came on. Standing in the door were two security men dressed all in black, including black helmets with dark visors. All he could see was their mouths. Every other inch of skin was covered in black.

"We have been sent to escort you to the shuttle bay," said one of them.

"I'm not scheduled to be there for another hour or so."

"It's been changed. You are to come with us."

David 181 held up a hand to block the light and blinked. "I'm not ready . . ."

"You need nothing from here. Everything you will need has been stored on the shuttle."

"I have friends . . ."

"You can communicate with them from the shuttle. You must get dressed and come with us now."

David 181 was going to protest that he needed more time, but as had happened when he was told of the assignment, he realized that he could leave at any time. There was nothing to hold him in the tiny apartment.

"Let me brush my teeth, comb my hair, and I'll be right with you."

"Mind if we sit in the living room?"

"No. Go ahead. Make yourselves comfortable. Look at the newspaper. It should be up on the flat-screen now."

David 181 went to his sink, brushed his teeth, combed his hair, and put on a clean coverall. Once he got his boots on his feet, he walked out into the living room. Both guards stood up.

"If you're ready."

David 181 nodded but took one last look around the room. He had lived there for more than a decade. It had been his home. His sanctuary. He had spent time there with Kim 185. Suddenly he knew that he was going to miss it and wondered if he would ever see it again.

One of the guards said, "We've had a little trouble this evening. Some of the residents believe that the shuttle flight is the beginning of an evacuation of the hierarchy here, and they want to stop it. There has been some rioting."

"I haven't heard anything."

"This section has been quiet. There are some others where the residents simply wouldn't go home."

They left the apartment, one of the security officers first, followed by David 181 and the other officer. David 181 felt a little strange. He wouldn't be coming back, at least not for a long time, but he carried nothing with him. He felt like he was abandoning the place, though that wasn't the case. He wondered if someone else would move in when he was gone. Only a little step up in the social order.

They walked along a somewhat darkened alley. Lights had been cut as a way of forcing the residents back to their apartments. It hadn't been entirely successful, yet the lights remained dimmed.

As they approached one of the shuttle pods, they heard the sound of angry voices. Although the lights had been turned out, the residents had found, or made, makeshift flashlights. The beams could be seen bobbing along various vertical surfaces.

The security officers halted and surveyed the situation. One of them said, "They're not going to be happy to see two more representatives of Security. Maybe it's best that they go ahead without us. Crowd won't attack one of their own."

David 181 wasn't sure that he liked the idea. Mob psychology wasn't an exact science. They could turn on anyone they saw as a representative of the establishment. They might not realize it until he was past them. He didn't know, and he was enjoying the protection of the two bodyguards.

He said, "Are you sure that's wise?"

"I don't know. It just seems to me that the mob will direct its anger at us, and by extension, you. So we'll create a diversion as you slip past them."

Without any real warning, both the security officers ran toward the rear of the mob shouting. As attention was drawn to them, and as the mob began to move in their direction, David 181 slipped around the side, sliding along the facade of an apartment complex.

He reached the access tunnel that led up to the shuttle pod. He couldn't get the hatch opened from the outside, but someone on the other side turned the wheel and pulled. The hatch opened.

"You the ag guy?"

"Yeah."

"Get in here and let me lock this hatch."

David 181 did as told.

With the hatch locked, they began a rapid climb toward the shuttle pod. Behind them, someone was banging on the hatch, trying to force it, but without the correct tools, all they could do was make some noise.

They reached the hangar deck, and David 181 hurried toward the shuttle. Light wisps of smoke, or gas, were coming from the rear. Crewmen were moving packages, boxes, crates, and equipment into the cargo bays.

There was a line of residents and technicians waiting to board the shuttle. They were moving forward slowly, and each was being checked by security to make a positive identification. One woman was pulled from the line, escorted toward the control room, and taken inside. David 181 didn't know what happened to her.

Finally, he was checked by Security, who made sure he was the right man, checked for contraband items, though no one explained what those might have been, and passed forward, to the ladder leading up into the shuttle.

He gripped the thin rail, climbed through the hatch, and saw rows of seats, most of them filled. He moved quickly to an empty seat, then saw Judy 199 sitting nearby. He moved closer to her so that he would have someone to talk to.

She said, "Hectic morning."

"Though not unexpected."

"You bring anything?"

David 181 shook his head. "Only the clothes I'm wearing. The Mayor said that everything we need had already been decided. I would have liked to check the inventory, but they followed the standard listings, so I guess it will be fine." He realized that he was talking faster than he needed. He was nervous.

Looking out the tiny porthole, he saw the line seem to break down and someone scramble to move a crate away from the shuttle. The hatch closed, and the engines began to fire.

Over the intercom he heard, "All passengers prepare for takeoff."

"That's fast," said Judy 199.

Through the window, David 181 saw a new group of residents pour from the access tunnel. They raced forward, but were met by Security. The leader of the residents tried to dodge around, but a security officer grabbed him and threw him to the deck. Someone raised a club and swung. As he twisted around, another security officer punched him in the kidney, knocking him to the deck.

And then the shuttle began to move. It slid forward, the sound of its engines growing. In front of it, the hangar door slipped open, the weak force field holding the air in place.

Then, suddenly, the shuttle lurched forward, seemed to drop as it broke free of the artificial gravity of *The Home*. David 181 twisted in his seat but could see little, other than the exterior of *The Home,* and a square of light marking the shuttle pod. It winked out as he watched.

"We're free," said Judy 199.

"Yeah. But at what cost?"

[7]

BOTH THE MAYOR AND THE CAPTAIN HAD EX-pected some sort of trouble. They had seen the disintegration of order as the Med Centers were attacked by the angry residents. They had taken a chance, ordering a reduction in the various medications that were injected into the residents and slipped into their food. The calming psychotropic drugs had been used for so long, and the populace had been so socialized, that both the Mayor and the Captain had believed that the patterns of behavior induced by the drugs would remain consistent.

So, sitting together, on the flight deck, watching the various monitors and flat-screens, they were surprised by the new riots. They were surprised when they spread throughout *The Home,* but then, as the hours passed, they knew that the riots would not end quickly.

The Captain, Christina 160, looked right at the Mayor, Michael 177, and said, "Maybe it's time for us to leave."

"Desert *The Home*?"

"I'm just thinking that we don't want to lose our chance to immigrate to The New Home."

"We have a responsibility here," said Michael 177.

"We have a larger responsibility, and that is to ensure the survival of our colony."

Michael 177 was going to protest, but then realized the Captain was right. The whole point of *The Home* was to move them or their descendants from Earth to another world for them to colonize. That mission was winding down and was being threatened with destruction. His job was to make sure that The New Home had the best chance for survival.

Christina 160 continued. "We have done everything we can here. We have located a world where we can live. I think it's time for us to go."

"But we could take *The Home* closer so that we could use its resources when we got there."

Christina 160 pointed at the monitors and flat-screens. "I don't think *The Home* is going to survive much longer. There is too much pent-up rage, and we're not going to be able to stop it. We don't have enough Security."

"If we can get the Med Centers repaired . . ."

"No," said Christina 160. "No one is going to voluntarily return to the Med Centers, and even if some of them did and we could force the others, they would remember this. We can't wipe out the memories of so many residents. We've lost here."

Just as Michael 177 was going to respond, his eyes were drawn to a flash on one of the monitors. He saw the explosion, saw the ruins of another of the Med Centers, and saw the bodies scattered along the path and into the park. He didn't know how any of the residents had gotten explosives, but then thought that there were so many chemists and so many available chemicals that someone with the proper training had simply mixed up the explosives and used them. These were the same thoughts he'd had earlier, when the riots had been fewer and the number of residents participating had been smaller.

He stood up, and said, "Let's get up to one of the shuttle pods and get out now."

Christina 160 jumped to her feet. "Now you're talking."

They left the flight deck and were escorted by a group from Security, including their chief, Stephen 168. Even though he had watched some of the destruction and rioting from the flight deck, he wasn't ready for the extent of devastation he saw. The residents had taken out their anger on the government buildings, breaking windows, kicking in doors, and smashing computers. They ruined everything they could, stealing some of the equipment. Michael 177 didn't understand the stealing. That equipment could all be recovered later.

They hurried along a pathway that led through a green belt. The fruit trees had all been stripped, but little of the fruit had been eaten. Instead, it had been used as ammunition. Residents threw it at the security forces, at the buildings, and sometimes at one another.

They crossed into a residential area, where nearly every building showed signs of damage. The residents were not only ruining the food supply, but attacking their own homes. It suggested a level of rage that surpassed anything that Michael 177 could have imagined even hours earlier.

They rounded one corner, moving toward the resident mover, but there were a hundred residents in the way. They were an angry crowd armed with makeshift clubs, knives, and a few spears made from broom handles, with knives taped to them. When they saw the security forces, they screamed with a single voice and began to rush forward.

Michael 177, along with the Captain and other officials, were shoved roughly to the rear of the Security formation. The guards lifted their weapons and opened fire. These were not the nonlethal weapons used earlier. The beams reached out, touched the residents, and severed arms, legs, or punched through bodies, killing several.

The crowd, aware that residents were dying, broke apart. In seconds the only residents left were either dead or wounded. They made no attempt to stop Security or the officials.

As they passed the scene, Michael 177, looking into the face of a badly wounded female resident, demanded, "Who authorized the use of deadly force?"

Stephen 168, overhearing the question, said, "Computer analysis suggested that the only way to stop the riots now is with a show of deadly force."

"The consequences of that act alone could be catastrophic later."

"Computer estimated that it would cause the residents to return to their apartments in fear, and that they would be hesitant to return to the rioting environment."

Michael 177 stopped walking and looked directly into the face of Stephen 168, and said, "And you believed that analysis? Where in the hell did you study human psychology?"

"I was reacting to an unstable situation with the best analysis I had."

Michael 177 began to walk again, toward the resident mover. He didn't know what to say but thought that a line had been crossed. The residents had been killed and injured by Security, and they wouldn't forget that. Security had erected a wall and destroyed any trust there might have been. The situation was only going to get worse.

And then he noticed smoke hanging in the air. Something was burning with an intensity that defied the scrubbers. It was producing so much smoke that, for the first time, the Mayor saw a haze hanging over part of *The Home*. Too much smoke . . . he began to worry about people dying from it. They didn't have an endless supply of oxygen, and some of it was being consumed in the fires. The situation was getting out of hand.

"Maybe we had better hurry," said Michael 177.

They began to trot along the resident mover, using its

speed to increase theirs. Around them, noise grew. Residents shouting. There was an unidentified noise that sounded like someone banging on a huge drum. There were screams, then another explosion. A radio was blaring, but they couldn't understand the words.

Around them chaos swirled. Residents ran toward them, then retreated. The ground, the resident mover, everything was littered with bits of paper, debris, broken glass, wood, metal, and the remains of computers that had been demolished.

Stephen 168 slipped closer to the Mayor, and said, quietly, "It's beginning to come apart."

Michael 177 nodded. He couldn't believe how quickly it had all fallen to pieces. Not that long ago there had been an orderly population that could be described as docile. Now, every resident seemed to be angry, every resident had found some kind of weapon, and every resident was bent on destroying what was left of *The Home*.

They all began to run faster, toward the access tunnel that led to one of the larger shuttles. They left one resident mover, ran down the next, then cut at an angle across a park that no longer held any trees. All had been cut down and destroyed, the leaves, wood and fruit scattered, leaving a thick, carpet of rotting plant matter.

They reached the access tunnel. Michael 177 was relieved that no one was around it, but behind them they heard shouting. He turned to see residents, armed as the others had been, running forward, screaming.

Michael 177 shouted, trying to give orders to the security force, "Don't kill them. Don't shoot them."

But the security force didn't listen. They opened fire. Residents fell. They scattered, and for a moment, the threat of attack was gone.

The access hatch was opened, and Michael 177 was the first one through. He was followed by other members of his staff and the civilian officials of *The Home*. Christina 160 and some of the senior members of the Flight Crew followed.

Michael 177 reached the hangar deck first, opened the

hatch, and tumbled out. He climbed to his feet and saw technicians scurrying all around the shuttle, trying to get it ready to launch.

Michael 177 was pushed from behind and got out of the way as others spilled out onto the hangar deck. Christina 160, in a breathless voice, said, "They're right behind us."

Michael 177 stepped forward, as if unsure what to do. A female technician, sweat staining her coverall, ran forward. She bowed slightly, and said, "Mister Mayor. Please come with me."

Together, they crossed the hangar deck. The tech stopped short of the ladder, and said, "You go on up. We'll get ready to launch in short order."

Michael 177 felt as if he was deserting his sinking ship. He felt that he should remain behind to help Security reestablish control. He should be there so that as many residents as possible could get from *The Home* to The New Home. That was his job, yet he was boarding a shuttle as the order, discipline, and civilization collapsed all around him.

Christina 160 appeared near him. She said, "Security holds the access tunnel, but I don't know how long they'll be able to stay there. A lot of residents are getting killed, and they don't seem to care."

Michael 177 turned and looked back at the access hatch, but only his own staff and the Flight Crew were near it. He ducked his head and stepped into the shuttle.

A technician, this one male, said, "Welcome, Mister Mayor. Please take a seat. We're going to launch in only a few more minutes."

Michael 177 took one of the plush seats that faced a flat-screen showing the hangar deck. From a vantage point that was somewhere near the main hangar doors, and about twenty feet above the floor, the camera relayed everything that was happening on the deck and behind the glass of the control room. At the moment, there was organized confusion as crews worked to load equipment and get people onto the shuttle.

The Captain entered, looked around, and sat down by Michael 177. She said, "This is getting scary."

Michael 177 ignored that, and asked, "Aren't you going to fly this?"

"I'm not qualified as a shuttle pilot any longer. Took the training once, but that was years ago. I haven't bothered with keeping up. There are pilots better qualified than I."

Michael 177 just shook his head. The Captain, the ultimate authority on all aspects of spaceflight was now telling him she didn't feel competent for the simple task of flying the shuttle. He wasn't sure that he liked the sound of that, and, had things been different, he might have suggested that she stay current in all the assets available on *The Home*. But now was not the time to make such a suggestion.

A warning horn sounded, and Michael 177 turned his attention back to the flat-screen. Near the hatch, he could see residents flooding the hangar deck. Security turned to meet them, but the security officers needed the advantage of distance. They needed space to bring their weapons to bear. Somehow the residents had made it into the access tunnel and forced the hatch without alerting Security. In moments the black-uniformed forms were lying on the deck, and the residents were running toward the shuttle.

Technicians moved to intercept them. Someone sprinted from the control room and ran up the ladder into the shuttle. She kicked it away and pulled down the hatch.

She turned, and shouted, "Get ready for takeoff."

"We don't have everyone."

"There's no time."

Michael 177 tore his eyes away from the scene on the flat-screen. He said, "We're not ready."

"You better get ready. There is no time." She moved toward the cockpit.

"Will you need assistance?" asked Christina 160.

"Yes. Any help I can get."

"Have all access doors been closed?"

"We initiated the sequence from the control room."

"There are still others outside," said Michael 177.

"We've lost them," said Christina 160 as she headed for the cockpit.

There was a sudden banging on the side of the shuttle. It was more felt than heard. Residents had reached it and were trying to destroy it.

From the cockpit, Christina 160 shouted, "Get your seat belts buckled. We're going."

There was a deep rumbling as the engines were started. The crowd retreated, unsure of what the shuttle was going to do. They turned and rushed the control room, hammering at the blast-resistant glass. Others attacked the door at the side, hammering at it. As the shuttle began to move, the mob grew more frenzied.

But it was too late. The shuttle reached the open hangar doors. There was a moment's hesitation, then the engines roared as the shuttle shot out into space.

Behind them the lights flickered and went out as the fragile screen that held in the oxygen collapsed, and those on the hangar deck died in the hard vacuum of space.

[8]

DAVID 181 WAS PERCEIVED TO BE THE MAN IN charge of the flight. Or rather, the man who would be in charge once they reached The New Home. He was the highest-ranking official on the shuttle, so the shuttle commander left the flight deck and went in search of him.

The shuttle commander, Lisa 202, leaned over him, and said, in a quiet voice, "I need to talk to you in private."

David 181 raised his eyebrows in inquiry but said nothing. He unbuckled himself and followed Lisa 202 into one of the private cabins in the rear of the shuttle.

As soon as they were inside, he asked, "What is it?"

She held up a hand, and a moment later they were joined by the chief of the security team. He didn't look happy about the secret meeting.

Lisa 202 said, "We need to keep this quiet, but we've lost contact with *The Home*."

"What do you mean?"

"I mean that I have lost their signal, and we have been unable to reacquire it."

"What's that mean?" asked David 181.

"It means," said the security officer, "that we are now on our own."

CHAPTER ELEVEN

YEAR TWO THREE SEVEN

[1]

JASON STOOD ON THE PLAIN AT DUSK, SCAN-
ning the horizon for some sign of the local, intelligent life.
They had seen no sign of the alien creatures since they returned from the underground village. There had been no
reconnaissance by the aliens, no attempts to approach
them, and no attempts at contact. Jason 215 thought that
curiosity would have driven the creatures up and toward
the shuttle, but maybe the display of power had scared
them. The humans had invaded their village, recovered the
skeletal remains of their fellows, and retreated. The creatures had been powerless to stop them.

Each night the electric fence was activated, but nothing
ever approached it other than human patrols. Using both
radio and normal voice, they requested that the power be

turned off until they could cross into the perimeter. Once inside, the power was turned on again.

Sensor sweeps, radars, instruments, and every other detection device they had failed to find anything moving across the plain near them. Once in a while something seemed to be digging nearby, but when security approached, the digging stopped, and the creature, whatever it might have been, fled. They didn't try to capture it.

Jason found that he was more comfortable sleeping on the shuttle and took one of the small cabins in the rear as his own. No one objected, and many of the others preferred the outside, where they could look up into the night sky where thousands of stars appeared when the planet and the sun were below the horizon.

Sitting in the shuttle one afternoon, Helen entered and dropped into the seat next to him. She looked at him, smiled, and finally asked, "You planning to stay in here forever?"

"Well, I hadn't really thought about it."

"The outside is so beautiful," she said.

"Yes, it is. But I like having these walls around me. I like having a roof."

"We're got nice shelters out there. We've expanded the perimeter, and we're building the first of the permanent structures. Someday this shuttle will be nothing more than a hollowed-out ruin."

Jason turned and looked into her eyes. He asked, "Can I tell you something?"

"Sure. Anything."

"I don't like being outside. I want to stay in here. I like it in here. When *The Home* arrives, I want to be one of those who stays up there on it and takes care of it."

"But, Jason, the whole point of the trip, the whole point of everything, was to move us to a new world. We need to expand down here."

"Yes, but they're going to need residents on *The Home*. We can't simply abandon it. Think about the resources available on it that we'll need to tap. I'd be perfect for a job on *The Home,* helping keep everything running and available."

Helen sighed, and said, "Then I can't see a future for us. I want to stay here. I love the freedom here."

Jason shrugged. "I would think that *The Home* will be put into orbit. I wouldn't think that commuting between here and there would be all that difficult."

"But we shouldn't have to do it."

"Then I don't know what to say," said Jason.

Helen leaned forward as if she was going to kiss him, then straightened up again. She said, "I suppose we don't have to make any sort of decision now."

"No."

"How about coming out tonight, and we'll sleep under the stars. You'll see the beauty of the night sky."

Jason looked around, at the protection offered by the shuttle, and knew, deep in his heart, that his feelings of safety were illusions. And, even if he agreed and decided that he needed some time inside, it wouldn't be all that far away.

"Sure," he said. "Outside tonight."

John, followed by Ralph, entered the shuttle, glanced at Jason and Helen, and then moved forward to the flight deck. Jason, surprised by their attitude, followed them, and stood by the open hatch, listening.

He lowered his voice, and said to Helen, "They've lost contact with *The Home.*"

Helen frowned. "That's serious."

Jason shrugged and listened some more. He told Helen, "They don't seem worried. They think there is something wrong with their equipment. They've just put out a general message asking for a response as soon as possible."

Helen looked at a chronometer set into the console in reflex. Jason laughed, and said, "Even at light-speed, it's going to take a while to hear back."

Ralph stepped down from the flight deck, glanced at Helen, then looked at Jason. "What'd you hear?"

"We're out of contact with *The Home.*"

"Well, it's no big thing given the distances, our sitting

here, in a system with a huge star and a planet in our way. We've got to expect some communications problems."

Jason thought about what Ralph had said, but he had nothing to say about it. He believed that they would hear from *The Home* sometime in the near future; but, of course, he was wrong.

[2]

LIKE MOST OF THE OTHERS ON THE SHUTTLE, David 181 was watching their approach to The New Home on the flat-screen. They had followed the signal beamed by the first shuttle, detected once they had entered the star system. They fell toward the orange gas giant and began serious braking, dropping into orbit around the largest of the moons. Now, with their cameras on and set at full magnification, they were looking for the first shuttle and its landing site. They would touch down near it.

The shuttle commander ordered them all back into their seats and put the nose camera feed up on the main flat-screen set against the bulkhead. That allowed the passengers to watch the approach as if they were sitting on the flight deck with the pilots.

David 181 watched as they circled the landing area, dropping lower and lower, as if they were an airplane coming in for a landing. Finally, they broke out of the circle, flew off, away from the landing site, turned, and came back, losing more altitude. As they neared the ground, the nose came up, but the camera compensated so that those in the rear could still watch the approach.

About a mile in the distance was the first shuttle. David 181 was studying it, looking for signs of life. He had expected to see the crew and passengers standing near it, cheering as they came in for a landing, but it looked as if no one cared. He couldn't see any sign of life.

There was a sudden bump, then a second, and finally a rumbling as the shuttle touched down. He heard a roar as the power to the engines increased, but this time to slow

them. He felt pressure on his seat belt and shoulder harness
that slowly dissipated.

Finally, they stopped, about a thousand yards from the
first shuttle. Now, on the flat-screen, David 181 could see
people, some of them standing near the electric fence,
some of them in the shade of that first shuttle, and a few of
them walking slowly toward them, as if they didn't know
what to expect.

Over the intercom, the shuttle pilot said, "We're down
and stopped. Once we get the hatch opened, you can get
out. Remember, this is a new world. Be alert."

David 181 unbuckled himself and stood up. He moved
toward the hatch just as it was opened and the bright light
and clean atmosphere of the planet filtered through. He
waited his turn, then dropped to the ground.

As he moved away from the shuttle, he looked at the
vegetation. He stooped, pulled at the grass, and felt it come
free easily. The root system wasn't very extensive which
could mean that the plain got plenty of water so the roots
didn't have to expand much, or it could mean this was all
new growth, the result of a fire that burned everything off,
or these were annuals that died off in cold or dry weather.

The soil itself was dark and moist. It clumped nicely,
suggesting it would be a good growth medium for their
plants. He'd need a little better analysis than his eyes and
nose, but he hoped it was rich soil full of nutrients that
would promote the growth of the Earth-based crops.

He stood as the residents from the first shuttle approached, looking like the welcoming committee from
some long-lost tribe. It'd only been a few months.

He heard someone say, "Glad you could make it. What
all have you brought?"

David 181 pushed through the crowd and held out his
hand. He saw the dirt on it, wiped it against his chest, leaving a dirty smudge there. He said, "I'm David 181, with an
agricultural team and equipment."

"Ralph," said one of the men. "We've dropped the numbers after the name. With so few of us here, doesn't seem
all that necessary now."

David nodded, and said, "I need to make a general survey to see where to put the fields. Want them close to our landing site." He looked over Ralph's shoulder and saw the rough houses constructed from local materials. They looked like solidified mud with windows that weren't quite square and doors that weren't exactly rectangular. It gave everything an abstract appearance, as if the builders had poor vision or a poor sense of architecture. But the houses were lined up in three neat rows, with plenty of space between.

"Is there someplace to store the equipment?"

Ralph laughed, and said, "No, we haven't built any storage sheds. Everything has been kept in the shuttle when we're not using it, and I didn't know where the fields would be. Thought we'd let you decide that and so we could erect the structures close to the fields."

"Then we have no trouble with vandalism . . ."

"Why should we?"

David didn't know what to say to that. He looked around, at the way the settlement was developing, and thought about the most convenient location for the fields. He hated to go to all the work of planting for a full harvest, but there wasn't time to do much experimentation. Maybe just some germination tests as they prepared the fields before a full planting.

"I said we've got a bit of a welcome planned. You don't need to jump into anything right this second."

David looked back, first at his shuttle, and then out, into the open plains around him. He tried to remember if the soil on Earth in a similar circumstance had been fertile. He thought it had been very good soil and that it was quite thin in a rain forest or a jungle, almost useless for farming. It wore out in a year or two.

Ralph said, "We haven't had any trouble from the local fauna, other than a couple of insectlike bites. No large predators around to worry about. If you have any cattle, sheep, goats, you should have no trouble getting them established."

Idly, David said, "Got the frozen embryos, of course."

"Well, there you have it."

There was a shout from behind him, then their pilot dropped onto The New Home.

"Made it," he shouted. "Made it in great shape."

[3]

MICHAEL 177 WAS WORRIED ABOUT THE LACK of communication with *The Home,* and he was worried about the number of other shuttles that seemed to have been launched within hours and days of his. It seemed that every shuttle, scout ship, and probe was launched, not unlike the lifeboats from a sinking ship. There seemed to have been a panic that swept *The Home* with the launch of a couple of shuttles, and suddenly everyone decided that it was time to get out, or they were not going to make it.

He sat back in one of the cabins at the rear of the shuttle, taken over by him as his office, bedroom, and apartment. As the Mayor, he deserved some privacy and a little extra consideration. Without his expertise, the society on *The Home* would have collapsed and those on the shuttle would have died. That was how he saw the situation and why he had taken over the cabin.

There was a tap at the door, and Christina 160 entered without being invited. She said, "Still nothing from *The Home.*"

"The pilot know why?"

"He said that our signal is going out. He said that we should be able to hear them for quite a long way. Time delay factors in as we move farther away, but, of course, that means nothing to us. We should be able to communicate."

Michael 177 touched a button, and the flat-screen in front of him darkened. "I suspect those idiots did something. Either they sabotaged the communications center or wrecked the power center."

"Taking out the power would kill them in a couple of days," said Christina 160.

Michael 177 took a deep breath. "In those last days we were there, I saw something in the eyes of the residents. We were forced by circumstances to alter our . . . control. The residents began to think more deeply and understand what had been done. They didn't understand that we needed that control because there were so many of them and spaceflight is so dangerous. Individualism could not be allowed. And once our control slipped, they reacted."

"What did you expect?"

Michael 177 grinned, and said, "I expected the residents to understand the situation. We'd been telling them all their lives about *The Home* and the new society developed to allow us all to live and work together in this closed environment. I expected them to understand that any society, no matter how carefully planned, would produce a criminal element, yet we didn't have that on *The Home*. Why not? Yet all they saw were Med Centers that suppressed these baser impulses, and they believed that wrong. They didn't like computer choice for the top jobs, yet it ended the competition that often created bad situations. They didn't understand the necessity for what we were doing, and now, here we are, in this tiny little ship, hoping that when we arrive at The New Home, there will be something there. If there isn't, then we're dead."

Christina 160 shook her head, and said, "I don't need a lecture on this."

"I know. I'm sorry. I just don't like not knowing what happened on *The Home*. Maybe we should have stayed."

"No. We would have died. The residents had changed into a mob. They were going to kill and destroy."

"How many have survived?" asked Michael 177.

"If they filled the shuttles and everything else, maybe a thousand, fifteen hundred. If they haven't ruined *The Home*, then most of them."

Michael 177 shook his head. "I'm always amazed at how dumb some of the residents could be. Unable to connect the dots and running off about conspiracies and hidden leaders."

"But smart enough to wreck our agricultural production and threaten us all."

"That wasn't smart," said Michael 177. "That was stupid."

[4]

NORMAN 200 STOOD ALONE AT THE HATCH that led up to the main engine pod. He was there as a guard, to warn the others if any security forces showed up. Since the rush to the last shuttles, there hadn't been many security officers around. They'd either escaped *The Home,* or been killed in the rioting.

He stood shivering. It had never been this cold on *The Home.* There had been frost in some areas, and the lights were dimmer than he remembered them. Power flickered off periodically. At first it stayed off for only a second or two, but the last time it had been nearly a minute before it came back. Things were beginning to fall apart.

Now he wished that he had pushed forward, into the access tunnels to the shuttle pods. He wished that he had fought for a space on one of the shuttles, but at the time, he had thought they would be better off without the administration and Security residents who were getting out.

A voice came from behind him. "You see anything?"

Norman 200, his arms wrapped around his body trying to keep warm, and his breath hanging in the air, said, "No. Nobody around at all."

"We're almost done up here."

"It going to be any warmer then?"

"More heat than you'll need. Just don't let anyone into the tunnel until we've cleared it."

"They know what they're doing up there?" asked Norman 200.

"We got maintenance crews from long before you were born working. They know what they're doing."

Norman 200 nodded and said nothing else. Instead he concentrated on the last time he had felt warm, about two weeks earlier, as the last of the shuttles left. Residents fighting with one another. He'd never seen someone with a compound fracture in real life. He'd read about them in first-aid class and seen drawings and pictures, but somehow those didn't convey the reality of a bone sticking up through the skin.

He saw a woman lying on the deck, near the hatch, blood on her face and staining her coverall. She wasn't moving, and her skin looked gray, sick, and her eyes were staring at one of the lights. Norman 200 was sure that she had died in the fight to board the shuttle.

Near the control room another fight was going on. Residents armed with drill batons, clubs, and tasers, were trying to breach the control room. Norman 200 didn't understand the defense because it was clear to him that the shuttle would launch before anyone in control could get to it. They were defending their turf simply because it was theirs.

He backed away until he bumped into the bulkhead. He moved along it and reached the hatch where the woman lay. He glanced back, down the access tunnel, and was surprised that it was empty. No, that wasn't quite right. He could see bodies scattered along, some of them moving slowly toward the hangar deck as the resident mover continued to operate.

There was a sharp scream, and another resident fell to the deck. A man in the black of Security stood over him, a laser pistol in his hand. He was yelling at the resident, "I told you to leave me alone. I told you."

There was a quiet bong, and then an announcement over the public address system. "Shuttle engines starting. Shuttle engines starting. All on the hangar deck are requested to leave now or injury may occur."

Some of the residents ran toward the shuttle, but the security officer with the laser began to shoot them as quickly as he could. Two, three, four fell, one screaming.

Others tried to smash their way into the control room but failed.

One of the engines fired and half a dozen residents behind it were caught by the flame. They fell, their clothes, their shoes, their hair smoking.

Without another thought, Norman 200 retreated. He jumped through the hatch, leaped over the bodies, and ran down the resident mover.

Someone emerged from the hatch he was guarding. He said, "That's it. We're done."

"Doesn't feel any warmer in here," said Norman 200.

"Going to take a while to warm up."

Norman looked back, up the access tunnel, and asked, "Where are the others?"

"Be along in a minute. You can go."

Norman 200 hesitated. There was something about the resident's manner that he didn't like. But he didn't know what to say, so he started off toward his own apartment.

The Home was different now. The lights were always set at twilight and it was cold. Not cool, not comfortable, but cold. Residents had burned nearly everything they could to stay warm, and that had created a haze that hung over everything. The air was filled with the taste of soot. Sometimes it was difficult to breathe, and some residents had suffocated. No one wanted to admit that, but Norman 200 was sure.

He crossed into the park. The fruit trees had been stripped of their fruit, their leaves had fallen in the cold, and many of them had been chopped up for firewood. He shook his head at that. Residents thought of the cold and did what they needed to so they would feel warm. But once warm, they'd want food, and they had destroyed one of the few ways left to grow it. In time.

Norman 200 reached his apartment and found the door standing open. That had never happened before, and it frightened him. He stepped inside carefully and saw that the computer flat-screen had been smashed, there was debris on the floor, and the furniture, what little he had, was wrecked, the components that would burn stolen.

"Janice? You in here, Janice?"

He couldn't see her in the tiny living room, but when he looked in the kitchen, she was on the floor. She was curled into a ball, and wrapped in a thin blanket. Her face was blue.

Norman 200 crouched near her and felt for a pulse at her neck, but when he touched her skin, he knew she was dead. The skin was cold. Much too cold.

He sat back, leaning against the bulkhead and stared at the body. He didn't know if the cold had killed her, or if she hadn't been able to breathe. She'd always had trouble with her lungs. Maybe she was another who had suffocated. Not that it mattered.

So, this is the end, he thought. Not with a bang but a whimper. No great explosion as *The Home* smashed into an asteroid or planet, or was torn apart by some great, internal cataclysm. Only the residents slowly freezing or suffocating. No way to escape. Now. Nothing to do but wait for the end, whatever it might be.

Norman 200 slid forward and took his dead wife's hand in his.

EPILOGUE

YEAR ONE

DAVID STOOD ON TOP OF THE SHUTTLE, WHERE he had the best vantage point. He looked out over the fields they had planted weeks ago, and saw an abundance of crops about ready for harvest. In meadows a little farther away, he saw the cattle grazing, growing into animals that would supply more food. Everything was growing and prospering in the warm, moist climate of The New Home. There was virtually no competition from the local plants and animals. Humans had won the race.

He climbed down from the shuttle and found Ralph waiting. Ralph asked, "When do we harvest?"

"I'd give it another three days, then we can begin."

"Beef," said Ralph. "I'm looking forward to some beef."

David laughed. "Well, we could slaughter a couple of the cows now, but they're young. About three-quarters grown. We wait, we'll get a good meal from one or two and can have the others producing milk for us, not to mention having their own offspring which increases the supply."

"Sometimes I just don't want to wait," said Ralph.

"I hear that," said David.

Jason strolled up, hand in hand with Helen. He grinned broadly, and said, "I think we're done for the day."

"You make any progress?"

"Well, the locals are still standing off in the distance, but they've come a little closer every day. They're getting used to us. I think we'll make contact in the next few days. Then we can begin trying to build a language."

"How many are there?" asked David.

Jason shrugged. "Not all that many. On the whole planet, I don't think there's a million of them."

"We're going to ruin their society," said Helen.

Ralph nodded, but said, "When we landed, even if we had done nothing else, we would have changed their society. Couldn't be helped then. Can't be helped now."

The former Mayor, Michael 177, who insisted on the numbers after his name because it forged a tie with his old life, appeared, and asked, "What's going on?"

"Nothing, Michael. Just relaxing at the end of the day. That's all."

Ralph said, "I was just talking about having some beef in the next few days."

"I think we should wait on that," said Michael 177.

"You're not the Mayor here," said Ralph.

Now Michael grinned broadly, and said, "No, I'm not. But I can offer an opinion, and I think we should wait for the beef. We have plenty of food."

"We'll soon have an abundance," said David. "Everything grows so well here."

They fell silent, no one mentioning *The Home* or what might have happened to it. All they knew was that it had stopped responding to messages, and there could be a number of reasons for that, most of them bad. There had been talk of sending one of the shuttles back to *The Home* to answer the questions, but there was little enthusiasm for it. Most were happier not knowing for sure. It provided a hope for them if something went wrong on The New Home. It was a sanctuary.

Ralph asked, "You think there will be any more shuttles?"

Michael 177 said, "There are two unaccounted for. They should have been here by now. They could show up, but I think they have been lost."

"A shame," said Helen.

"Yes," said Michael 177. "A real shame."

The sun was slipping toward the horizon, but the planet hung high in the sky, glowing brightly. It would be a short night and a not very dark one.

"What's on the agenda for tomorrow?" asked David.

"Work on structures, I think," said Michael 177. "We have to finish the living quarters."

Jason was going to ask why. He had gotten used to sleeping under the stars and was not anxious to move inside of anything, though completion of the living complex would not require a move inside. Instead, he stood quietly, holding on to Helen's hand and wondering why he had ever disliked being on a planet. Living on a real world was so much better than living in the artificial environment of *The Home*.

"I think we need to hold a town meeting," said Ralph. He waited for comment, and, when there was none, he added, "Talk about a feast maybe. Roast one of the cattle."

David laughed, and said, "You have a one-track mind, and there's a cow standing on the track."

"True," said Ralph.

"Well, I don't suppose it would set back our plans if we did have something of a celebration," said David. "The cattle are doing very well."

"Now you're talking."

Jason said, "I think we'll wander over to the community center and see what's happening there. I think they plan to show a video tonight."

"Could be interesting. I need to use the computer," said David.

"Well," said Michael 177, almost as if he were moving back into his old role of Mayor, "we're not getting anything done standing around here talking about it."

David grinned, and said, "Who cares?"

"Not me," said Michael 177, "but I do want to see the movie."

Kevin D. Randle is a captain in the U.S. Army, an authority on alien abduction, and the author of numerous works of fiction and nonfiction. He has appeared as a guest on many television programs focusing on extraterrestrial activity, including *Unsolved Mysteries, Larry King Live, Good Morning America, Alien Autopsy,* and *Maury Povich.* He also coauthored the bestselling *UFO: Crash at Roswell,* which later became a popular Showtime movie, and *The Abduction Enigma.*